Jaina had breez warming the pockets of cold loneliness with nothing more than her concern for his nephew.

If she could love the boy that deeply after just one day with him, how much more would she love him in a month? A year? A lifetime?

Connor had a feeling that Jaina had a great capacity for love, caring and nurturing—like no one he'd ever known. Though she was petite, he could tell by the way she walked and talked that her strength of spirit more than compensated for whatever limitations God had placed upon her. She'd probably be the kind of woman who kept an orderly house and cooked rib-sticking meals and made her husband believe he hung the moon. He'd spent a total of perhaps forty minutes in her presence; how could he be so certain, after such a short time, that she'd be good for him, good for his life?

You're losing your mind, that's why, Buchanan, he thought, shaking his head. *Snap out of it!*

LOREE LOUGH

A full-time writer for more than a dozen years, Loree Lough has produced more than two thousand articles, dozens of short stories and novels for the young (and young at heart), and all have been published here and abroad. The award-winning author of more than thirty-five romances, Loree also writes as Cara McCormack and Aleesha Carter.

A comedic teacher and conference speaker, Loree loves sharing in classrooms what she's learned the hard way. The mother of two grown daughters, she lives in Maryland with her husband and an old-as-dirt cat named Mouser (who, until this year—when she caught and killed her first mouse—had no idea what a rodent was).

Mother's Day

A COLLECTION

LOREE LOUGH

Suddenly Mommy

Love Inspired

Published by Steeple Hill Books™

STEEPLE HILL BOOKS

Steeple
Hill®

ISBN 0-373-51295-3

SUDDENLY MOMMY

www.SteepleHill.com

Printed in U.S.A.

To the members of
my First-Monday-of-the-Month Writers' Group
for their never-ending support
and encouragement,
and to Anne Canadeo, for her never-ending
willingness to share her editorial expertise.

Dear Reader,

Years ago I read a newspaper article about a young woman who had abandoned her baby. She'd wrapped him in a receiving blanket, the report said, tucked him into a cardboard box and left him at the emergency-room doors of a local hospital.

On that same day, at that very hospital, I gave birth to my first child. I couldn't stand to be apart from her, not even for the few minutes it took me to bathe! Needless to say, I had a lot of trouble identifying with that young woman....

TV newscasts kept audiences updated on the baby's condition. And oh, what a beautiful little being he was! I came up with a dozen scenarios about why this could have happened. Had his mother been too young? Too poor to take care of a helpless infant? What dreadful trauma had driven her to such desperate measures?

The answer, two decades later: *Suddenly Mommy.*

All my best,

Loree Lough

P.S. They never found that baby's mother. He was placed in foster care until a loving couple made him part of their family. But now and then, as my own children grew and thrived, I wondered whatever became of his birth mother. And when I do wonder, I say a prayer for her, because surely, wherever she is, her heart aches every time she thinks of that day....

Chapter One

⟋⟍

Jaina read the anguished expression on her mother's face and held the baby boy tighter. "What do you mean," she whispered, "his mother is gone?"

Rita ran a trembling hand through graying hair. "I mean, she *isn't here*."

Seemingly oblivious to his mother's absence, the baby filled his hands with Jaina's long dark curls.

"Did you look out back?" Jaina's father wanted to know. "In the parking lot?"

"Yes, Ray," Rita sighed, "I've looked everywhere."

Blowing spit bubbles, the child wrapped Jaina's gold chain around a stubby forefinger and cooed. "Well, I'm sure she'll be right back," Jaina said. "She couldn't have left without this precious little—"

"I found this in the ladies' room." Rita slid a note from her apron pocket. "She isn't coming back."

"What!" Ray thundered. "You mean she walked off and left this boy with total strangers? How does she know we're not murderers or…"

He stomped toward the counter. "Well," he growled, "how far could she have gone?" He pressed the receiver to his ear. "I'm callin' the cops, and I hope they throw the book at her. People like that don't deserve to have kids."

Jaina's dark eyes filled with tears and her heart ached for this abandoned child who clung almost greedily to her. She would likely never have a child of her own, but if God saw fit to reverse her physical condition and bless her with a baby, she couldn't think of any reason sufficient to walk away from him...to leave him with strangers.

"Ray, sweetie," Rita said softly, a hand on his forearm, "calm down. You'll frighten the boy. Besides, I promise you'll feel differently once you've learned what's in this note."

Their eyes met, then held for a moment on a look of understanding that linked them heart to heart.

He hung up the phone. "Okay, Rita. What's in it, anyway?"

She stood on tiptoe to kiss his chin. "There's just one way to find out, isn't there?" Turning to Jaina, she held out her arms and smiled lovingly. "Now, give me that doll-baby."

Jaina traded the baby for the slip of paper and took a seat at the counter, swiveling her red-cushioned stool until she faced the diner's parking lot. "It's so dark out there," she said, more to herself than to her parents. And staring through the mirrorlike black window, she added, "The weather reports are predicting a terrible thunderstorm. Where could she have gone, all alone on a night like this?"

"Where was that last bus headed?" Ray asked.

"I think the driver said he was headed for Chicago," Rita answered.

Jaina crossed the room and peered through the screen door. "There's lightning off to the north. I hope she's all right...."

Ray slipped his arms around his wife, hugged her and the baby she held. "C'mon back and sit down, sweetie," Rita said, "and read the note."

Silently, Jaina returned to the stool and took a deep breath. "'Dear Jaina,'" she began, "'I came to Ellicott City to meet my uncle for the first time. He's a lawyer on Main Street. I was planning to ask him if he'd take care of Liam for me. But I overheard him on the telephone, yelling at the top of his lungs. Something about a baby being an albatross around his client's neck. I couldn't leave my boy with a man like that!

"'I had thought he was my last chance at finding a good home for Liam. He's my only living relative. If I couldn't leave Liam with him, I didn't know what I was going to do!

"'And then God reminded me how kind you were yesterday when the bus stopped at your diner…the free meal, the way you played with Liam, the cheese and crackers you packed up for us to take with us when we left.…'"

Jaina met her mother's damp brown eyes, her father's misting gray ones, and swallowed hard. It wasn't difficult, remembering the sad-eyed girl whose pride made her pretend she'd lost her wallet rather than admit she had no money for food.

"You okay, honey?" Ray asked, handing her a glass of water.

Jaina nodded, thanked her father and, after a quick sip, continued reading. "'I prayed harder than I did when I found out I was dying of leukemia.'"

Gasping, Jaina pressed a palm to her chest. "Dying?" she repeated. "But she couldn't be a day over eighteen!" Tears burned behind her eyelids as she looked into the baby's innocent, unsuspecting face. She took another drink.

"'The doctors say I only have a few months to live at best. Seems I spent my whole life trying to act grown-up, and here I am, talking like one. I think I would have been a good mom, if only…well, anyway, none of that matters now. The important thing is that the Good Lord led me to you. I've had to travel light, coming all this way on a bus.

You'll find a couple of outfits in Liam's bag, some of his favorite toys and his birth certificate. Now that I know he'll be taken care of, I can go to the Lord in peace.'"

With her free hand, Jaina covered her eyes.

"You want me to finish it, honey?" Ray offered.

She met his loving eyes and smiled slightly. "No. It's okay, Dad. I can do it." She focused on the young woman's round-lettered script and began again.

"'My picture is in the side pocket of the diaper bag. When he's old enough, please tell Liam that I never would have left him if things had been different. You're probably thinking that I'm a terrible mother, that there must have been something I could have done besides leave Liam with strangers. You'll just have to trust me, the way I'm trusting the Lord.

"'When my own mother died, I learned firsthand all the terrible things that can happen to a kid who doesn't have a family. I don't want that kind of a life for Liam. You told me you don't have any children and that it wasn't likely you ever would. I could see in your eyes how much you want a baby and I could tell by the way you held Liam and talked to him what a good mother you'll be.

"'You're probably a little afraid right now, finding out that you're suddenly a mommy. I remember how it felt the first time I held Liam in my arms. I was barely seventeen and was I ever scared! But then he looked at me with those big blue eyes of his, and I fell in love.

"'Everything that's happened these past few days is proof to me that God wants you to be Liam's mommy. For one thing, the bus shouldn't have broken down. The driver said it had just been overhauled before we left Chicago. For another, he promised we'd be back on the road in no time, but we were stranded for hours while the mechanic worked on the engine. See? God put me in your diner long enough to get to know you. How does it feel to be part of God's plan? Don't worry, Jaina, you'll be a wonderful mommy. If I wasn't sure of that, I wouldn't be leaving Liam with you.

"'Thank you, Jaina, for what you're about to do for me…and for Liam. I know you're going to do it because, well, you just have to! Sincerely, Kirstie Buchanan. P.S. He hates strained peas, loud music and thunderstorms, and he loves to watch cartoons on TV.'"

The hand that held the note dropped limply into her lap. "I feel like I've just run a four-minute mile," Jaina said, sniffing.

The adults slumped, sad and emotionally spent, into the nearest booth. For several moments, no one made a sound save Liam, who sat in the middle of the table, babbling contentedly as he tried to depress the buttons on the table-top jukebox.

Jaina broke the silence. Patting her father's hand, she said, "I think you're right. We should call the police, report this, get them to start looking for Kirstie. Only after they find her," she said, squeezing his hand, "we'll keep her right here with us so she won't have to spend her last days alone."

Liam popped the salt shaker into his mouth, shook his head and grimaced at it.

"We're duty bound to try and find her," Rita agreed, gently prying it from his fingers, "but Kirstie doesn't want to be found."

Ray heaved a deep sigh. "Where I come from, this wouldn't be a problem. Folks don't need cops and judges and lawyers to tell 'em what's the right thing to do."

"Then I wish we were in Abilene, Dad."

Ray dumped the contents of the baby's bag on the table. A blue flop-eared bunny, a red squeeze toy shaped like a fire engine, a brown teddy bear, a plain white envelope. Squealing with glee, Liam grabbed the truck and bit down hard on it, snickering when it squeaked. "A picture and a birth certificate,'' Ray said, shaking his head at the envelope.

Jaina picked up the birth certificate. "Liam Connor Buchanan," she said aloud, "born November 2 to one Kirstie Ann Buchanan." She patted the baby's hand. "Seven months old."

"Big for your age, aren't you?" Rita observed, running her fingers through his hair.

"What's that his mama wrote on the back of the birth certificate?" Ray wanted to know.

Jaina turned it over, found that Liam's immunizations were up-to-date. "'Nine pounds twelve ounces, twenty-one inches long,'" Jaina said, reading the youthful script, "'forty-two hours of hard labor.'"

"She would have been a good mother," Rita observed as Jaina slid the girl's wallet-size color photo from the envelope.

"Such a beautiful thing, and so *young*," Jaina whispered, running a thumb over Kirstie's image. "I wonder how long she's been an orphan," she asked no one in particular, "and how she came to be alone in the world?"

Rita smiled. "Reminds me of your publicity photo, Jaina." Sighing, she added, "Seems like only yesterday that you sang for your supper."

Traveling from city to city, singing for a living had been fun and exciting, until…. "Let's not talk about that part of my life. Why don't we dwell on positive things, like the way Uncle Jesse's gift was a blessing in disguise…."

Her father shook his head. "Blessing indeed. This diner is more work than it's worth. I don't know if he did you any favors, leaving you this place in his will."

Liam grabbed for Kirstie's picture, effectively changing the subject. Jaina held it out for him to see. "Yes, that's your mommy," she told him. "Isn't Mommy pretty?"

"Mmumm-mmumm?" he repeated, touching a fingertip to his mother's image. Jamming the finger into his mouth, he grinned flirtatiously at Jaina and, crawling across the tabletop, snuggled into her arms. ''Mmumm-mmumm,'' he said, a dimpled hand on each side of her face.

Her heart lurched as she looked into his wide, trusting eyes. *Sweet Jesus,* she prayed, *is he calling me Mommy?*

As if he'd read her mind, the baby rested his head on her shoulder. ''Mmumm-mmumm,'' he muttered with a satisfied, sleepy sigh. ''Mmumm-mmumm.''

Jaina closed her eyes and thought of the morning after the accident, when the somber-faced doctor told her that to save her life, they'd been required to perform emergency surgery…. Liam might well be her only chance at motherhood. But she couldn't keep him.

Could she?

''It's an awfully big responsibility,'' Ray responded, ''and you already have your hands full, what with running the diner and all. We could help some, but with your mother's heart condition…''

Jaina hadn't realized she'd spoken her thoughts aloud.

Rita's gaze met her daughter's, held it for a long, silent moment. Then, head on her husband's shoulder, she said softly, ''But, honey, she's had so many disappointments. If she wants to do this—if the courts will even *let* her do it— we ought to help her.'' She grabbed her husband's arm. ''I'll be careful, I promise.''

''Mother,'' Ray warned lovingly, shaking a beefy finger under her nose, ''don't start with me.''

''It's a moot point,'' Jaina inserted, ''because I can't keep him.''

Liam's lower lip poked out. Ray's broad shoulders sagged. ''Aw, would you look at that? It's like he understands.'' He ran a hand through thick hair that was going gray at the temples. ''Well, folks, I don't know *what's* best here.'' And looking from his wife to his daughter, he said, ''Let's pray on it.''

With Liam sitting on the table in the circle of their arms,

the adults joined hands, bowed their heads and closed their eyes.

"Lord Jesus," Ray's deep, resonant voice beseeched, "open our hearts and minds so we'll know what You have in mind for this young'un. Give us the wisdom to recognize Your will...and the strength to do it."

A moment or two passed before he added, "Call Skip, Jaina. He'll know what to do."

Rita's dark eyes widened. "But...but Skip works for Social Services. He'll—"

"Exactly. More'n likely he's come nose-to-nose with a problem like this before. He'll know what to do." Big callused fingers tenderly tucked a shimmering blond curl behind Liam's ear. "Besides, Skip's our girl's best friend. He wouldn't steer her wrong."

Rita stroked the baby's silky cheek. "So precious, so perfect." Then, in a lighter, brighter voice, she ventured, "Maybe they'll let us be his foster family. It's the least we can do since we're going to deny Kirstie her last wish."

"We're *not* denying it, Mom. She asked me to take care of Liam, and that's exactly what I intend to do. I only want what's best for him."

"Kirstie was right, you know," Rita observed, raising one dark eyebrow. "You're a natural-born mother. *You're* what's best for him, if you want my opinion."

"Now, Mother, is that a tear I see?" Jaina asked.

Rita swiped at her eyes. "Of course it isn't." She held up a finger to silence her daughter's objection. "Don't tell me you can't keep him because you haven't the time. You made time to feed those baby robins every hour on the hour this spring. And what about that little squirrel you rescued last fall?" Rita laughed softly. "Why, it seems ever since you were old enough to walk, you've been bringing home stray critters." She began counting on her fingers. "Let's see...there was the sparrow that fell from its nest, and the bunny whose mama was hit by a car, and the kitten someone had thrown by the side of the road. And remember the time you brought home a skunk? You couldn't have been more than six. You said it was lost in the woods. Oh my, I thought we'd never get the stink out of your hair!''

Jaina sat back in the booth and smiled. "I'd been nagging you that whole summer to camp out in the backyard. That night, *you* suggested it!''

The threesome laughed softly at the fond memory.

"Why the sudden change of heart, Mom?''

Rita's cheeks flushed and she folded her hands on the table. Jaina had seen the pose before, many times. Her father often said her mother was "just a little slip of a thing." But when she set her jaw and squared her shoulders that way, she seemed as strong and immovable as a man twice her size. She had no intention of responding to the question, Rita's tight-lipped, closed expression told Jaina.

"Liam isn't a puppy or a kitten," Jaina persisted. "I can't keep him like some stray animal. There are laws, and he has family right here in Ellicott City. We have an obligation to—''

"Our only obligation is to Liam and Kirstie. She didn't want her uncle to have him.''

If Jaina had married, if she could have had children, would her mother still be so intent upon keeping the abandoned child with them? "You're afraid Liam might be your only chance at being a grandmother, aren't you?''

Rita blanched. "I, uh, well, of all the ridiculous…'' she sputtered.

Jaina's heart ached when she read her mother's face. Rita detested dishonesty, even tiny white lies told to protect others. The fact that she was avoiding giving Jaina a straight answer was proof enough that Jaina had uncovered a well-hidden truth…a truth that made Jaina painfully aware that her own sad and sorry past had affected her parents, too.

"…it's just that the longer I look at him, the more I like him,'' Rita was saying, "and the more I like him…'' She heaved a deep sigh, shrugging. "We'd be better for him than strangers."

"But Mother," Ray pointed out, "as far as this young'un is concerned, *we're* strangers."

Rita's brow furrowed and she stared down her husband and daughter. "I suppose *someone* has to be the voice of reason." She shook her head. "How can you two be so hard-hearted at a time like this?"

Jaina and her father exchanged exasperated glances before Ray said, "Rita, honey, I'm sorry as sorry can be that we never had that house full of kids we talked so much about before we got married. But the doctor made it clear that your poor li'l heart couldn't take the stress of another pregnancy. Why, I nearly lost you when Jaina was born. Much as I wanted those young'uns, I wanted you more."

Rita crossed both arms over her chest and sent him a loving smile. "I love you, too." Then on a more serious note, she questioned, "But what does any of that have to do with Liam Buchanan?"

Ray shook his head. "I think our girl here is right—partly anyway. You want Jaina to keep him so you can get a whack at raisin' another little one." He slid an arm around her shoulders.

Rita pursed her lips and tapped a forefinger against her chin, squinting her long-lashed eyes. "Why does the name Buchanan sound so familiar?"

"It's not that uncommon a name, but I've been wondering the same thing," Jaina admitted. "But you haven't said anything about Dad's comment, Mom."

Rita propped her chin on her fist, smiling at the baby. Suddenly, she sandwiched Jaina's hands between her own. "It's that nonsense the doctor spouted all those years ago, isn't it?"

Jaina raised a dark brow in warning. "Please, Mom, don't." Not once in twenty-eight years had she spoken to her mother with anything but respect, but this subject was off-limits, and her mother knew it.

"What happened was *not* your fault, Jaina. How many years are you going to punish yourself for it?"

She hung her head. "If I live to be a hundred," she said, her voice barely audible, "I'll never atone for it."

"But, sweetie, you were…" She bit her lip. "That awful man. What he did to you…" Rita scowled and shook her head.

Her father grated out an opinion of his own. "He's a butcher, and if I ever get my hands on him, I'll—"

"Mom, Dad, please…"

But Rita pressed on. "You were barely twenty at the time. That doctor wasn't God. He said—"

"I'll never forget what he said." Jaina's voice sounded cold and distant even to her own ears. "'There's less than a ten percent chance you'll ever have children.'" Despite her bravado, the word "children" stuck in her throat. Jaina took another sip of water.

Rita ran a hand through her gray-brown curls and tried again. "There's still a chance you *will* have children."

"He said it'd take a miracle for me to have a baby. You heard it yourself."

"You'll never convince *me* of that." Rita scowled. "What that man did to you is unpardonable. You should have sued his socks off. You should—"

"Mom, please." Jaina wearily shook her head. "We've been through all this hundreds of times. I didn't take Dr. Stewart to court because I had no proof that he botched the surgery. It would have cost a lot of time and money and heartache, and for what? A few measly dollars? Money wouldn't repair me. Money wouldn't give me the baby I've always wanted."

For a long moment, the only sound in the diner was the steady *drip-drip-drip* of the leaky faucet behind the counter. Then her father began to drum his fingers on the tabletop.

Rita arranged and rearranged the salt and pepper shakers like squat glass pawns on a Formica chessboard. Liam yawned.

And Jaina breathed an exasperated sigh. "It's getting late."

Rita leaned across the table and pressed a palm to her daughter's cheek. "Jaina, sweetie, everything you do has gentleness and sweetness written on it. That's why you're still bringing home bugs and birds and turtles and..." She looked toward the ceiling as if the help she sought was to be found up there. "You were born with a mother's heart because you were *born* to be a mother. God wouldn't have given you a heart like that if He didn't plan for it to happen someday. Don't you see?"

"What I see," Jaina said, acknowledging that if she'd made the right decision that fateful night, her mother would have had the grandchildren she so richly deserved, "is that you're disappointed in me."

"That isn't true and you know it!"

But it was true, and she did know it. "Then let's drop the subject, okay? Let's bury it and never dig it up again. Because, even if I *could* have a baby after what Dr. Stewart did to me, what man is going to want a woman with a limp, a woman who's all scarred and twisted and—"

Gently, Ray cupped her chin in his big hand, compelling her to look into his eyes. "Sure you have a scar or two, but I look at 'em as pockets."

"Pockets?"

"You need extra pockets to fit all the love you have inside you. If a man don't see that, well, he's plumb blind." He smiled tenderly. "I told you when you woke up from the operation and saw all those scars—" he swallowed hard "—I told you that one day the right man would come along, and when he does, he won't care one bit if you have a few scars because he's gonna love *you*, the girl with a heart as big as all outdoors."

Jaina sent him a trembly smile. That's what he'd said all right, and she'd known even in the thick of pain and agony that he'd meant every word. If only she could believe him, maybe her future wouldn't seem so empty, so bleak. If only she could find a man like *him*. But what were the chances of that in this world where beauty and perfection were second only to wealth and social position?

She looked at Rita, whose eyes had always lit up at the sight of a baby, a toddler, a small child. It had been a mistake, a cruel joke to play on her mother…behaving for even those few moments as though they might be able to keep Liam. Because if she'd been meant to be blessed with motherhood, would God have let the accident that rendered her barren happen in the first place?

Ray broke the silence. "Jaina's right. It's getting late. Let's hit the road, Mother. We'll pray on it tonight, figure out what the Good Lord wants us to do next. His answer will be there, I believe, after a good night's sleep."

Cooing and smiling, Liam hugged Jaina tighter. It dawned on her, as her arms instinctively wrapped protectively around him, that she'd be changing his diapers, feeding him a bottle, tucking him in…at least for tonight. First thing in the morning, though, there'd be other kinds of duties: a trip to the doctor to confirm his apparent good health, a call to Skip, another to the police.…

Somewhere deep in her soul, Jaina felt the stirrings of long-forgotten yearnings. For as long as she could remember, she'd wanted a house full of children. It was hard, very hard, convincing herself that she might well be holding in her arms the only chance she'd have at motherhood.

"Oh, just look at them, Ray," Rita whispered, lower lip trembling. "She *wants* to be a mommy to this little guy, and he's crazy about her, too." In a louder voice, she said to Jaina, "God is at work here, sweetie. Can't you *feel* it?"

God indeed, Jaina thought bitterly. *Where was God's work when I needed it?* Jaina leaped to her feet, and with

Liam firmly attached to her hip, she grabbed a cleaning rag and began polishing already gleaming tabletops. "What I feel has nothing to do with it. His mother will be back. Of course she will. She'll get a few miles up the road and start missing him—how could she *not?*—and by morning, she'll be—"

"But, sweetie, she's dying."

As painful a burden as her infertility was, it paled before the thought of giving birth, only to know you're going to die and leave a precious baby behind. "Maybe the doctors made a mistake. Maybe Kirstie misunderstood the diagnosis. Maybe—"

"Maybe you're grasping at straws. Remember my friend, Mary?" Rita asked. "The doctors said she had some rare strain of leukemia. One day she seemed healthy as a horse, the next she was gone."

Ray stood, then held out a hand to his wife. "Come on, Mother. Let's go home. Jaina can close up shop."

"I'd take him in myself—"

"Let's not even discuss it, Mother. You know you're not able to care for an infant." Jaina moved Liam to her other hip, then ran a hand through her hair. "Honestly, Dad…what are we going to do with her?"

Smiling halfheartedly, he shrugged. "I've been lookin' for the answer to that one for thirty-one years."

Jaina's lips formed a taut line. "Liam has an uncle right here in town. When he hears what's happened, I'm sure he'll—"

"If his mother felt she had to leave him with a total stranger rather than his only living relative…" Rita extended her hands palms up and gave her daughter a look that said, "What does *that* tell you?" Frustration made her shake her head. "I wish I knew why Buchanan is so familiar. Something in the news, seems to me.…"

Her mother was right. A headline story, if Jaina recalled

correctly. "I'll call Skip soon as I tuck Liam in. He'll know what to do."

Her mother was out of the booth and at Jaina's side in an instant. "You'll be sorry if you do that. Before you know it, you'll be all wrapped up in legal red tape, and court proceedings, and official documents, and a judge will..."

The mention of court papers and judges jogged Jaina's memory. She'd read an article a week or so ago about an attorney who'd defended a well-known surgeon for malpractice. Thanks to a series of legal loopholes and expert-witness testimony, the jury could not convict, and the doctor who'd bungled a patient's surgery got off without so much as a slap on the wrist. She'd have to check a few back issues of the *Howard County Times,* but Jaina felt sure the lawyer's name had been Buchanan....

"You aren't listening to a word I'm saying, are you?"

Jaina was so deep in thought that she never heard the question. Her heart went out to the injured woman who had taken that doctor to court...and her anger grew as she recalled the lawyer who had used the "system" to injure the poor woman further by getting the surgeon off the hook. "Sorry, Mom."

"As I was saying...things like trust and faith aren't born into a person. Those traits aren't passed down from generation to generation like the color of your eyes and hair. Frankly, I wish they *were* inheritable because maybe then you wouldn't be such a pessimist!"

Liam rested his head on Jaina's shoulder, and she automatically began swaying to and fro as if she'd been rocking him that way his entire life. Her mother's accusation hung in the air like a dusty cobweb. Jaina hadn't always been a pessimist. She'd had faith once, plenty of it, before that dreadful night. Right up to the moment of impact, she had prayed for Divine intervention. But her prayers had not been answered. Perhaps it was the Lord's way of telling her He did not approve of the way she'd conducted herself. How else was she to explain that God seemed to have turned His face from her at a time like that?

"I'm sorry if my feet-on-the-ground attitude is such a disappointment to you," she said, meaning it, "but I prefer to put my trust in things I can count on, like working hard and keeping my head out of the clouds." Her normally soft, warm voice tightened with weary resignation. "I'll keep Kirstie's baby, but only until she comes back."

"She isn't coming back and you know it."

Jaina shrugged. Much as she hated to admit it—for Kirstie's sake as well as Liam's—something told her that her mother was right.

Mother and daughter had apparently reached a stalemate and stood facing one another in stony silence. Jaina's father broke the quiet with a blustery announcement.

"Seems our boy here is about to fall asleep."

Jaina chose to ignore his "our boy" reference. Despite his earlier protestations, her father seemed as enamored of the baby as her mother. She was about to warn her parents not to get any more emotionally involved when her mother said, "On our way back to the diner in the morning, we'll stop off at the grocery store, buy Liam more disposable diapers, some baby food, cereal—"

"Well, don't buy too much," Jaina cautioned, "because this is a very temporary arrangement at best." She rubbed noses with Liam. "Isn't that right, cutie?"

"Mmumm," Liam said with an emphatic nod of his head.

The tiny bell above the door tinkled as Ray pulled it open. "G'night, honey. See you bright and early."

"Bright and early," she returned, locking the door behind them, and then to Liam, "with fifteen grocery bags full of stuff and all for you, whaddaya bet?"

Grinning, he grabbed her ears. "Buffoo," he said, "buffoo!"

Jaina blew kisses against his cheek. "Buffoo yourself," she said, laughing as she turned out the lights.

But the playful behavior did nothing to block the warning that echoed in her head. *This baby is not yours, Jaina. This is a temporary arrangement at best. Temporary...*

The contents of her bottom dresser drawer lay in a heap at the foot of her bed, and Liam lay snoozing contentedly on the downy quilt she'd lined it with. Jaina had tried to sleep in the bed with the baby in the drawer on the floor beside her. But it had seemed so far away that she'd tossed down her comforter and cozied up beside his makeshift crib to watch him sleep.

It had been a mistake because, just as his young mother had predicted, Jaina fell feet over forehead in love with Liam Connor Buchanan.

She'd had every intention of calling Skip the moment she closed the door to her apartment. But there had been a myriad of excuses. It was after ten. The baby needed a bath. She had a load of laundry to do. She hadn't eaten since lunch. Telling herself she'd phone her pal first thing in the morning, she'd snuggled up beside Liam, fully intent upon sleeping there all night long.

But she hadn't slept a wink. Instead, she'd watched his every move.

She looked at him now as gentle breaths sighed from him with barely a sound, the corner of his mouth lifting occasionally in the beginnings of a soft smile. *What are you dreaming about, little one?* she wondered. *What sweet pictures do you see?*

Dozens of times during the night, she'd reached out to tuck a wayward blond curl behind his ear, to pull the clean white T-shirt down to cover his fat little tummy, to marvel at the long, lush lashes that dusted his pink cheeks. *Do you miss your mommy?* she'd asked silently when he'd wrapped his hand around her finger. *Of course you do.* She could only hope the Almighty would see fit to give Liam a short memory so the pain of separation would quickly fade away. Still, Jaina knew this much: if by some miracle, she *was* allowed to keep him, she would abide by her unspoken promise to Kirstie Buchanan. She would show Liam his mother's photograph often and tell him about the loving young woman whose last thoughts had been of him and him alone.

Jaina pictured Kirstie, tall and lithe, with gleaming waist-length blond hair, huge blue eyes and a quick, easy smile made all the more remarkable by the reasons that had brought her to The Chili Pot in the first place. With a child to worry about, she didn't belong here, and she certainly didn't look as if she belonged in a cancer-treatment program.

Jaina could imagine Kirstie on a high school stage, doing a top-notch performance of Juliet, or Bianca, or Lysistrata. She'd be a marvelous actress, Jaina thought, because she'd certainly succeeded in hiding the sadness that must have prompted her trip from Chicago in search of the uncle she'd never met.

Had she been married and quickly widowed, or had Liam been born out of wedlock? How had Kirstie supported Liam all these months? And who had minded him while she worked to keep a roof over his head and food in his belly? Kirstie had done a fine job caring for him, and the proof was in the baby's rosy, dimpled cheeks, his sweet and calm disposition, his clean-as-new clothing.

"You were taking a terrible chance, Kirstie," Jaina said, tucking the sheet under his chins for the hundredth time, letting her knuckles gently graze the boy's cheek. She'd caught herself doing that a lot. It was becoming a habit, this stroking and tickling and kissing, a habit that would be hard to break. "You were taking a chance, leaving this precious gift with me. How did you know I'd do right by him?"

Something Rita had said time and again as Jaina was growing up echoed in her mind now. She'd been burning with fever, and on one of Rita's many trips to her bedside, Jaina had asked, "Mom, how do you know what to do for me?" Her mother had perched lightly on the edge of her bed and smoothed back Jaina's bangs. "A mother knows instinctively what's best for her child." She'd said it so matter-of-factly, Jaina believed it. And she believed it to this day. Whether a big-toe blister, a broken wrist or a bout with the flu, her mother had always known exactly what to say and do to comfort her daughter. "How do you know *I'm* capable of love like that?" Jaina asked Liam's missing mommy.

Kirstie had known, Jaina realized, because like Rita, the girl operated from a base of deep and abiding faith. Could this stranger have more in common with her mother than Jaina did? Could she have shared something with Rita... something that was only a dim memory to Jaina?

Maybe Mom's right. Maybe God is giving you a chance at motherhood through Liam....

Jaina blinked and shook her head. "Don't be ridiculous," she chided herself. Still, she wouldn't complain too terribly hard if Skip's advice was that she should keep the baby...at least until a suitable foster family could be located. It made perfect sense, really, since the boy had already been abandoned once.

Jaina sighed, thinking of the recurring dream she had at least once a week since the accident. It had been a mistake to get into Bill's car, and she'd recognized that right from the start. The error in judgment was something she'd have to live with for the rest of her life, and the dream was her mind's way of dealing with the ugly fact that if she'd listened to the silent warning that had gonged in her head that night...

But she hadn't listened.

Jaina glanced at the calendar page.

June 22.

Her heart thundered and her pulse pounded. What could it mean that Liam had come into her life eight years to the day since the accident?

She eased away from his side and tiptoed into the kitchen. Five thirty-five, if the glowing green numerals on the microwave clock were correct. She'd preset the coffee-maker for five-thirty and now inhaled the pleasurable aroma that filled the air. A cup of steaming hot coffee would be the perfect distraction.

Curiosity more than anything else prompted her to slide the phone book from the shelf under the kitchen counter. Plopping it onto the faux chopping-block surface, she opened it to the yellow pages and turned to the Lawyers listing.

Her forefinger passed quickly down the column. "'Baker, Beckley, Bloom, Brown,'" she read softly. The voice froze in her throat as her finger came to a halt beneath one name. "'Connor L. Buchanan, Specializing in Criminal and Divorce Law,'" she whispered, "'371 Court House Drive, Ellicott City.'"

The baby's full name is Liam Connor *Buchanan....*

Her heart clenched with dread. She'd been hoping this search wouldn't turn up anything but more questions, and that those questions would require further research, which would take time. Although she'd tried to rationalize it as attending to small details, it was a stalling tactic, she knew, nothing more—a stratagem that would buy her a few more precious hours with Liam.

"Well, that was smart, Jaina," she muttered. "Now that you've found him, you don't have any choice but to call him."

Or did she?

Buchanan had no idea his niece had been to see him or that she'd decided against leaving her baby in his care. *And what he doesn't know won't hurt me.*

Jaina glanced at the clock. Five forty-three. Ordinarily, she'd be at work, preparing for the breakfast rush. It was really too early to phone most places of business. On the other hand, if she called now and he wasn't in, she could leave a message. And of course he wouldn't be in. *Then the ball is in his court. If he doesn't call me back, I'm off the hook.*

Jaina grabbed the phone and quickly dialed Buchanan's number.

She'd expected a secretary's recorded voice to recite a series of instructions for leaving a message. Instead, a vibrant baritone answered, "Connor Buchanan here."

Jaina wished she'd given at least a moment's thought to what she'd say if a human being answered. But who'd have thought a lawyer would be in his office at this hour? "Um, uh, Mr. Buchanan?"

"Yeah."

Jaina blamed the early hour for his abrupt tone of voice. She cleared her throat. "This is, uh, my name is, um, I'm Jaina Chandelle, and I, uh…"

A brief pause, then, "And you *what*, Miss Chandelle?"

He'd all but barked the question. If he talked that way when Kirstie stopped by, no wonder she was afraid to leave Liam with him!

"I have to be in court by nine," he continued, his low-pitched voice harsher still, "and I'm in the middle of preparing a brief."

Jaina didn't know what had caused his attitude, but she'd had about enough of it. "Then let *me* be brief," she snapped. "I have something important to discuss with you concerning a relative of yours."

She heard a frustrated, exhausted sigh. "For your edification, I have no living relatives, Miss Chandelle—*if* that's your name—so save the con job."

"Con job? This isn't—"

"Look, I've had it with these nuisance calls. Thanks to

caller ID, I've got your number...in more ways than one. I wasn't born yesterday, Miss Chandelle. Either you're casing the joint, or—"

"Casing the joint? You think I want to *rob* you?"

"Either that, or this is a clear-cut case of telephone harassment. Now I'm gonna give you some free advice. I've earned my reputation as a hardnose. You want to find out why, just bug me again."

"Bug you? *Bug you!* I didn't call you to—"

He chuckled quietly.

"I was only trying—"

The chuckle became a full-fledged laugh.

"You're *laughing* at me? When the only reason I was calling was—"

"Wait a minute," he interrupted, his voice softer now. "I wasn't trying to ridicule you—"

But Jaina never heard Buchanan's apology because she'd hung up the phone. She hurried over to the infant seat set up on the countertop to scoop a now wide-awake baby into her arms. "Guess it's time we called my old buddy Skip," she said, blowing a raspberry onto Liam's cheek.

And her heart soared at the sound of his merry giggle. Quite a contrast to his uncle's rasping complaints...

"What's the big frown about?" Pearl McKenzie asked in her motherly fashion. "You haven't even had my coffee yet this morning."

Connor shrugged one shoulder. "I got a strange call this morning."

She rolled her eyes. "Well, unpleasant as they are, you ought to be used to things like that now. Don't these pesty people have anything better to do with their time?"

Connor leaned back in his chair and met the older woman's eyes. "Wasn't like the usual ones, and despite being a pest," he said, grinning slightly, "*she* had a very pleasant voice."

The white-haired woman raised a brow. "You don't say?"

Connor held up his hands in mock surrender. "Now don't get any ideas. I can assure you I have no designs on a stranger who calls me at five-thirty in the morning."

"Five-thirty! What did she want at that hour?"

He shrugged the other shoulder. "Something about a relative."

Pearl dropped her considerable bulk into one of the chairs across from his desk. "Of *yours?*"

He nodded.

"Hmm…"

He met her eyes, narrowed his own. "Hmmm *what?*"

"Well," Pearl began, tapping a pencil against the file folder in her lap, "I was just wondering…" She dipped her head lower, looked at him over the rim of her purple-framed reading glasses. "Do you suppose this woman has anything to do with the girl who was in the office yesterday?"

"The rude little brat who ran out of here without rescheduling, you mean?"

"The one who ran out of here as if she had a pit bull snapping at her heels, I mean…thanks to the way you were going at it on the phone with the district attorney."

He recalled the argument he'd had with Andy Nelson. He had really lost it, he recalled. Connor sat forward, clasping his hands on the desktop. "What did you say the girl's name was?"

Pearl stepped into the outer office, then returned with an appointment book. "Kirstie Buchanan. I remember because she spelled her last name exactly the way you do. Yes, yes, here it is." She removed her glasses and used the earpiece as a pointer. "Says here she wanted to talk to you about a custody matter." Sliding the spectacles back into place, she cooed, "Oh, and you should have seen that little fella. Cute as a bug's ear, and my oh my, what a flirt! You want me to call this woman? Ask her to come in?'' Pearl added.

Connor winced, remembering the way he'd spoken to her on the phone. Somehow she'd gotten the impression he was poking fun at her, when in reality, he'd been laughing at *himself* for being so all-fired certain she'd been another one of the prank callers.

If Kirstie Buchanan was indeed related to him in some way, and the caller had some information about her, it could only involve Susan. He hadn't heard a word from or about his missing sister in nineteen years. The girl Pearl had described was the right age to be Susan's daughter.... He'd had a private detective on the case for such a long time that he'd forged a strong friendship with the man. But two years ago, he'd called off the search. Connor preferred not to think about the reasons why Susan couldn't be found.

''No, I'd better schedule this one myself.''

''Better make it snappy, then,'' Pearl suggested with a nod toward the clock. ''You only have half an hour to get your ornery self down to the courthouse.'' Standing, she placed the message on his desk, then headed unceremoniously toward the door. ''So,'' she began, one hand on the doorknob, ''you think she sounded cute, eh?''

''Cute? Nobody is cute at 5:30 a.m. Now do me a favor and get me the Chandelle...I mean the Adams file, will ya?''

''Sure thing, Mr. B.''

He heard her snickering as she closed the door. Shaking his head, Connor picked up the phone and dialed. He counted five rings and was about to hang up when a woman answered.

''Good morning. The Chili Pot.''

He'd only heard it once, but he'd have recognized that lovely voice anywhere. ''Miss Chandelle?''

A slight pause, then, ''What do *you* want?''

He'd cross-examined plenty of witnesses who'd pulled

this kind of stunt; it was apparent to Connor's practiced ear that Miss Jaina Chandelle was putting on a hard-gal act for him. But even her best efforts at toughness hadn't dulled the music in her voice.

"First of all," he began, "I'd like to apologize for being so abrupt with you earlier—"

"Po-ta-to, po-tah-to," she snapped. "You say 'abrupt,' I say rude."

She was quick-witted and feisty. He liked that. Smiling, he said, "Touché. Not that it's any excuse, but I get a lot of prank phone calls, some of them rather nasty. Unfortunately, I assumed yours was another one of them." He hesitated. "And, in all fairness, you have to admit it was a bit early for a business call...."

Connor tensed as he listened to the moment of silence. Had she hung up? He hoped not because... He relaxed some when she said, "I suppose you're right. Sorry."

"You haven't done anything to apologize for," he admitted. "But let me get to the point. I have to be in court—"

"At nine. So you said during our last conversation," she finished for him.

Chuckling despite himself, he continued, "I'd like to schedule a meeting with you, to discuss this, er, this relative of mine."

"When?"

"Any time after one."

"Today?"

"Yes...if that's convenient for you—"

"Hold on, will you?"

He listened to the sounds of muffled whispering—a man's voice, another woman's...a baby? Connor dismissed the disappointment simmering in his gut. *Too bad, fella,* he told himself. *The lady's married...and she has a kid.*

"I can be there at one-thirty."

At her request, he gave her directions to his office. And

though he'd done it hundreds of times for hundreds of clients, it seemed to take longer to explain the route to Jaina Chandelle than it had ever taken before.

It wasn't until Connor had hung up that he understood why. For a reason he couldn't explain, he hadn't wanted to end the conversation. When he returned the receiver to its cradle, he frowned at the feelings bubbling inside him. *How can you miss someone you don't even know?*

Chapter Two

His secretary's voice crackled through the intercom. "Oh, Mr. Buchanan…Miss Chandelle is here."

He didn't have to see Pearl's face to know what that singsongy voice was all about. She was likely wearing her matchmaker grin again. Sometimes, Connor wished he'd remarried for no other reason than to quell her desire to find his Miss Right. Pearl's heart was in the right place—he had to give her that—but she'd never even come close to introducing him to the woman of his dreams. If she thought Jaina Chandelle was that woman, well, this time his secretary had *really* missed the mark.

He wondered if she'd look anything like she sounded. He hoped not, because if she did, he was a goner for sure. Connor stood, stuck out his chin and straightened the knot of his silk tie. After the way he'd spoken to this…to Miss Chandelle earlier, he was determined to show her he could behave like a civilized gentleman. He strode purposefully toward the door and flung it wide open. Smiling as she breezed toward him, he extended a hand. "Connor Buchanan, Miss Chandelle. Can I get you a soda? Some coffee?"

"No thanks," she said, matching his firm handshake, "I'm fine."

You most certainly are, he thought, eyes following the long, slender fingers all but hidden by his own beefy ones, to the gentle curve of her shoulder, to the graceful slope of her neck. "Please, make yourself comfortable," he said, meeting her gaze as one hand indicated the chairs facing his desk and the other closed the door. He noticed as she passed that she was limping. Had she sprained her ankle? he wondered.

"So, you can be charming, I see...when you have a mind to."

Connor supposed he had that coming but chose not to respond to it. "It's a real sizzler out there today, isn't it?" he asked as she sat in the wing chair nearest the door. *Afraid you might need to make a quick getaway?* he asked her silently, his grin a bit wider.

"Ninety-eight *is* unseasonably hot for June, but you know what they say about the weather in Maryland. Wait five minutes and it'll change."

Connor chuckled and settled into his tufted leather chair. "They say the same thing about Ireland."

"Oh, and do they now?" she asked in a lilting brogue.

Ordinarily, first meetings, whether personal or professional, made him restless and uncomfortable, so Connor didn't understand how she'd managed to make him feel so quickly at ease...and on his own turf yet. "When I phoned this morning, you answered, 'The Chili Pot.' I'm curious. What sort of establishment is that?"

She laughed softly, and he found himself unconsciously leaning forward to put himself nearer the delightful sound.

"My parents and I like to say we're in the restaurant business," she said lightly, "but The Chili Pot is a diner, plain and simple. Like the one in that movie, you know? It belonged to my father's brother. Uncle Will never married. He always said I was like the daughter he'd never had, so he left it to me in his will.'' She tilted her head to add, ''I'm surprised you haven't heard of it. It's been written up dozens of times over the years, and it's been right there on Route 40 since the late fifties.''

He'd been dying to know if she was married. Thank you, he said silently as he saw his opening. ''It's just you and your parents who run the place? What does your husband do for a living? He's not involved in the business?''

Her cheeks reddened and she stared at her hands. ''I'm not...I don't have a husband.''

She couldn't be more than twenty-five, he thought, so why does she seem ashamed to be single?

''You'll have to stop by some time...''

His question had unnerved her—though he didn't know why—but she'd pulled herself together quickly. He liked that, too, because he'd had enough of women who needed to be the center of attention, who felt sorry for themselves, who said they wanted men to treat them like equals...until a tire needed changing or a bill needed paying. ''Maybe I'll just do that,'' he agreed. Nothin' could be finer than to be in Jaina's diner, he hummed to himself.

''...to try my chili,'' she finished. ''The *Baltimore Sun* food critic called it 'awesomely hot.''' She gave a proud little nod of her head as if to emphasize the point, her eyes widening.

Those eyes—now that's what I'd call awesome, he decided, a smile growing on his face. Wa-a-y too much for a first meeting... Folding his hands on the desktop, Connor cleared his throat and reminded himself why he'd set up this meeting. ''I don't mean to be rude, but...''

She cocked a finely arched brow as if to say, ''Again?''

''...but about this relative of mine?''

She sat up straighter and unzipped her purse. ''Yes. Of course. I'm sorry. I certainly had no intention of wasting your time.'' She bristled slightly, as if she, too, had forgotten for a moment why she'd come here. ''You'll find I have a tendency to ramble, but I'm not easily offended,'' she said, breaking into a nervous smile. "If you catch me at it, feel free to nudge me back on track.''

What made her think they'd be together often enough for him to notice such a thing? he wondered.

She took a deep breath and plunged in. "It's like this. A young girl came into the diner yesterday. Turns out she's your niece. She brought her little boy with her. I thought at first he was twelve, thirteen months old, but he's only seven months. He's quite big for his age.''

His niece? Was that even a possibility? "Must run in the family. I'm big for my age, too.'' He smiled.

And so did she. "I'm afraid we're not talking egos, Mr. Buchanan.''

Connor laughed.

"As you'll see when you read this—'' she slipped a sheet of folded paper from her purse ''—your niece was in my diner the day before yesterday, as well.'' She bit her lower lip and sighed before continuing, "Since I don't know how to preface or explain the rest, I'll just let the note speak for itself.''

He reached across the desk to accept it, mindful of the worry lines that now creased her brow. Heart pounding, Connor slowly unfolded it. What made her so certain the girl was his niece? "You're behaving as if this is a matter of life or death, Miss Chandelle,'' he said, fighting the urge to frown. "I'm sure once we get to the bottom of this, we'll find it isn't all *that* serious.''

"Please, call me Jaina. You make me feel like a prissy etiquette teacher with your 'Miss' this and your 'Miss' that.'' She took a long, slow breath before adding, "Besides, I have a feeling we're going to be seeing a lot of one another.''

One corner of his mouth lifted as he made mental note of this second reference to their future together. His pulse also quickened in response. He'd always been drawn to tall and willowy women, with long blond hair, fair skin, pale eyes. They'd been glamour personified with their painted fingernails, made-up faces, designer suits. The reaction he seemed to be having to this petite brunette surprised him, since she was everything they weren't and nothing like the types he thought he was attracted to.

"I don't mean to sound melodramatic, but this *is* a life-and-death matter—" she nodded at the note "—as you'll soon see."

Because she didn't seem the type for histrionics, he decided to take her at her word. Smoothing the note on his desktop, he began to read it aloud. "'Dear Jaina,'" he read, "'I came to Ellicott City to meet—'"

She held a finger in the air to silence him. "Would you mind very much reading it to yourself?" Jaina smiled sheepishly. "I'm a big believer in first impressions, you see, and I don't want you to get the idea I'm a crybaby."

"A crybaby?" he echoed. "Why would you…?"

Heaving another deep breath, she pointed at the note and gave him a look that said, "You'll see."

Simultaneously, they both sat back—Buchanan to read, Jaina to watch him.

From his gruff telephone manner, she'd expected him to be much older, her parents' age at least. Technically, Connor was Liam's great uncle, since he was Kirstie's mother's brother. It was impossible however to think of this man as elderly or doddering in any way. Jaina guessed him to be in his early to mid-thirties. She hadn't pictured him as tall or broad-shouldered, certainly not good-looking. If there had been any doubt in her mind that Connor Buchanan, Esq., was Liam's uncle, his appearance cast it aside, for the lawyer's eyes were the same deep shade of blue, fringed by long, dark lashes. Liam's blond hair was several shades lighter than Buchanan's. She didn't know if Liam would develop an adorable cleft in his chin to match his uncle's, but something told her that when the baby matured, a smile would produce a dimple in the very same spot on Liam's right cheek, too.

She noticed the thick golden mustache above Buchanan's lip quaver slightly as a deep furrow creased the space between his well-arched brows. Had he gotten to the part where Kirstie said she didn't want a man like him raising her son? To the passage that explained *why* she was trying to find a home for her son in the first place? Or had the overall mood of the note caused his mouth to turn down at the corners?

She watched him run long, thick fingers through gleaming, wavy hair, listened to the frustrated sigh that rasped from his lungs. If she'd known him better, Jaina might have been able to determine whether he had angled a hand over his eyes to cut the glare from the window or to hide the threat of tears.

Her heart ached for him. The note had made *her* cry, and she hadn't been related to Kirstie. The girl might have been a virtual stranger to Buchanan, but she was blood kin to him nonetheless. He must have just learned that her short time to live had convinced her to believe she must leave her helpless baby boy behind. The effect of the news was apparent on his somber face, in the slight quaking of his big hands. She resisted the urge to reach out and comfort him, say something to soothe his obvious distress. *Don't forget…this guy isn't your friend,* Jaina reminded herself. *He's the enemy, the man who's probably going to fight to keep you from adopting Liam.*

Adopting Liam?

Jaina felt a bit fickle even considering such a thing. Skip had warned her about getting emotionally involved. In all likelihood, he'd said, in a few weeks, when the paperwork had been filed and processed, she'd be forced to give him up. She couldn't have admitted it to her best buddy because he'd diagnose her certifiable if he knew she'd fallen this much in love with the child after just one night.

Buchanan's yellow pages ad said he specialized in criminal and divorce law. Did he know enough about adoption to represent himself? Or would he hire a colleague who specialized in that area?

She'd made the decision earlier to keep Liam—at least, she'd decided to *try*—despite her conversation with Skip. "Babies of this age require special care," he'd said. "The couple I'd normally place him with already has more than enough to handle." Somewhere across town, Skip was pushing through the paperwork that would allow Jaina to keep Liam until a more permanent arrangement could be made.

Preferably with a relative.

Handsome as he was, the man on the other side of the massive mahogany desk must have a dark and devious side. How else could he have decided to help that conscienceless doctor who'd made all the newspapers? "Birds of a feather," said the sages. Should a man like Buchanan be allowed to adopt a defenseless seven-month-old baby, just because he was blood kin? You'll learn soon enough, little Liam, she thought, that you can choose your friends but you can't choose your relatives.

She hadn't realized how intently she'd been studying him until he looked up from the note. He'd been visibly moved by the news, as evidenced by his inability to focus, the slight quaver of his lower lip and hard set of his jaw. But then, lawyers had to be good actors to convince juries to cast their votes in favor of their clients, didn't they?

Buchanan cleared his throat. "It appears the two of us are facing a quandary," he said, his voice fraught with emotion.

"Quandary?" She uncrossed her legs and planted both feet flat on the floor. "I'm afraid I don't—"

"Says here that Kirstie…that my niece provided you with her son's birth certificate."

He seemed disturbed by his reaction to the letter and

compensated for it by jutting out his chin and adjusting the knot of his already straight tie. He swallowed—to hide the tremor in his voice?—and held up both hands as if surrendering, then closed his eyes.

Well, he's not praying, she told herself, *not a man like him.* Jaina chalked up his behavior to some caveman-type attempt at regaining control of the situation.

"I don't suppose you brought it with you?" he asked, looking directly at her.

A second ago, he looked for all the world like a little boy lost. Yet, with nothing more than a minor adjustment of his posture, he'd assumed a composed and professional demeanor. "The birth certificate, you mean? As a matter of fact, I did," she said, a bit taken aback by his chameleonlike behavior. Jaina withdrew the envelope from her purse and handed it to him. "I haven't had a chance to photocopy it, so I'd appreciate it if you'd..."

He emptied the contents onto his desktop, the little-boy-lost expression returning to his face as he studied the photograph of his niece. Drawing his generous mouth into a thin, taut line, Buchanan abruptly stood. There was nothing to do but....

She watched him turn next to the birth certificate and holding it, he strode from the office. She wondered where he'd taken the official document...and why.

Glancing around the room, Jaina found herself strangely comforted by the bloodred hues of the Persian rug, the deep greens and pale creams in the plaid draperies, the masculine scent of a caramel-colored leather couch and matching wing chairs, the burnished gleam of mahogany.

It was a gray day, the kind that promised refreshing showers, but so far, nature had not delivered any such respite from the early-summer heat. The afternoon's bleakness filtered through the many-paned window behind Buchanan's desk, shrouding the room with a dreary light. Jaina took the liberty of turning on the green-globed floor lamp behind his high-backed armchair. Immediately, the room glowed with diffused iridescence. The heavy bronze figurines on the mantel, the legal volumes that filled the ceiling-to-floor bookshelves, even the bust of Julius Caesar on the credenza, took on a faint and pleasant verdant hue.

The light also gleamed from a brass picture frame on his desk. Jaina crept closer to get a better look. "Kirstie's mother," she whispered, heart beating in time to the mechanical *tick-tock* of the carriage clock. If not for the hairstyle and vibrantly colored shirt reminiscent of the late seventies, the young woman could have been Kirstie herself.

"Entertaining yourself?"

The sudden sound of his baritone startled her so badly that Jaina dropped the picture. Its heavy frame chipped the credenza on its way to the carpet, where it landed amid the tinkling of breaking glass. Jaina was on her knees in an instant, picking up glittering crystal-like fragments and tucking them into an upturned palm. "I'm so sorry. I never meant to... I saw the picture, and it looked so much like Kirstie that I wanted a better look. I'll replace the frame—"

"Don't worry. I have others," he said, smiling gently.

She knew she was rambling but seemed powerless to stanch the flow of words. This man had the power to take Liam from her. "I'm sorry," she said again, noticing for the first time a small dent in the mahogany. "Oh my," she fretted, "would you look at this? I can't believe I...that I..." She ran her fingertips over it. "I've refinished several antiques. And I'm pretty good at it, if I do say so myself. If you'd like, I could bring my woodworking kit over some day when you're not busy or when you're in court and repair the—"

Buchanan got down on one knee beside her and gently wrapped his large hands around her wrists, effectively silencing her. "Miss Chandelle...Jaina," he said softly, calmly, "it's all right. It's more my fault than yours. You wouldn't have dropped the picture if I hadn't scared you half to death.''

His gaze fused with hers, and she thought for a moment that he intended to kiss her. Her heart pounded with fear and dread as every muscle and joint stiffened. When his head lowered and his eyes narrowed slightly, she followed his stare to the palm of her hand.

''You've cut yourself,'' he said quietly. Slowly, their faces lifted, their eyes met. They knelt on the fringed carpet trim for a long moment, not moving, not saying a word. Buchanan stood, helped her to her feet and led her to the window. Cradling her hand in his, he turned it up to the light. ''Doesn't look too serious. Hold still now, while I...''

She watched his brow furrow with concentration and concern as he leaned in for a closer look. She hadn't been this near a man since that horrible night. *Strange,* she thought, *that I can hear my heart pounding in my ears, but I can't make out a word he's saying.* Was it because she hadn't slept last night that her head was spinning? Or because she hadn't eaten in nearly twenty-four hours? Had the tension of this meeting caused her dizziness? Might it be the sight of her own blood, gathering in a tiny puddle in the palm of her hand, or the nearness of him that made her knees go weak and wobbly?

She inhaled the crisp, masculine scent of his aftershave, felt the dry heat of his warm hands wrapped around hers. Part of her knew he meant her no harm; part of her could think of nothing except the last time a man had gripped her wrists, had held her hands, had breathed minty breath into her nostrils....

Jaina closed her eyes and tried to focus on the here and now. *He isn't Bill,* she chanted mentally. *He won't hurt you. He isn't...*

The pounding in her ears turned to ringing, then to gurgling, as if she'd been suddenly submerged in a pool of water. Buchanan seemed to be moving in slow motion...plucking a tiny shard of glass from her palm... dropping it into the brass wastebasket beside his desk...taking a white handkerchief from his back pants pocket... pressing ing it gently, gently against her wound.

"Just a little cut," she heard him say, his voice taking on the grinding, guttural quality of an old record being played backward. "Barely a scratch. A little scrape that won't even need iodine."

If it wasn't any more serious than that, why did she feel hot and cold at the same time? Why was she breathing as if she'd just run a five-minute mile? Why had her hands begun to sweat? And why was she powerless to still their trembling?

If she could find her voice, she'd tell him to let go, take a step back, give her space to breathe. *He's not Bill,* she told herself. *He won't hurt you. He...*

"Jaina..."

Connor Buchanan's voice, not Bill's. *He's close, so close. So why does he sound so far away?*

By now, the room was spinning, and she reached out for something, anything, to steady herself. It was his hard, muscular forearm she grabbed onto. Should she hold on and endure his nearness, or let go and fall down?

"Ah, Jaina, you're looking a little pale."

The worry in his voice penetrated her frenzied fog. Was his concern genuine? She didn't know because she couldn't see his face, couldn't focus on anything in the spinning, reeling room.

Then, strong hands gripped her waist, eased her into a softly cushioned chair. One of those hands, cool and smooth and steady, cupped the back of her neck, forcing her to rest her face between her knees.

"Deep breaths, Jaina," he instructed, repeatedly stroking her back. "Get some oxygen into your lungs, some blood to your brain."

Mechanically, she did as she was told.

"That's the way. Nice, steady breaths. You're gonna be fine, just fine...."

The dizziness was passing, the trembling easing, and she was able to think a bit more clearly at last. *So why can't I sit up?*

Because Buchanan's hand, pressed against her back, prevented it.

"Easy now," he coached. "Atta girl."

"You can let go now," Jaina said, words muffled by her denim skirt.

"Oh. Sorry." He let go and, with a hand on each of her shoulders, helped her sit up.

Their faces were no more than six inches apart, he facing the window and she facing him. Even in the cloudy light that eked through the glass, his eyes seemed so big and bright. A shudder passed through her when he blinked and she made note of long, dark blond lashes and clear blue irises.

She almost said aloud, "No, don't," when he narrowed his eyes and muttered, "Remind me never to sneak up on you again. You put the fear of..." He hesitated, frowned, then licked his lips. "You really had me going there for a minute."

Funny thing was, she believed him. Who'd have thought a lawyer, who defended society's worst, could be so kind?

"You okay?" he asked, strong fingers combing her damp bangs back into place.

Jaina nodded. "I feel like a little fool, damaging your whatchamacallit, your...thingamajig, swooning like some kind of—"

"I'd like a copy of your thesaurus," he interrupted, chuckling, "'cause it's gotta be more interesting than the one I've been using."

Jaina smiled shakily, ran a hand through her hair and, wincing, looked at her still-bleeding palm.

"I'll buzz Pearl." Buchanan reached for his phone.

"That woman is prepared for any emergency. She'll have a bandage and some—"

She grabbed his forearm. "No. Please, don't. I'm embarrassed enough. One witness to my display of weakness is one too many."

He perched on the edge of his desk and regarded her carefully. "The color is coming back into your cheeks. I think you'll live." The words were no sooner out of his mouth than he seemed to realize the inappropriateness of them, considering the content of Kirstie's note. Beneath the ruddy complexion, his cheeks reddened slightly.

"I've wasted far too much of your time already," Jaina said, changing the subject. "Besides, I told my folks I'd be away an hour or so. It's been a long time since they've been alone with—"

"A baby?"

Jaina nodded. "Yeah," she said dully, reminded of the reason for her visit, "a baby." She shook her head and sighed. "I know it's ridiculous after just twenty-four hours, but I really miss the little guy."

He went on as if he hadn't heard her. He handed her photocopies of the note and the birth certificate. "I feel like a first-class heel for scaring Kirstie off yesterday. She overheard one humdinger of an argument, and I'm afraid she got the idea it's my normal personality." One side of his mouth lifted in a wry grin and he spread his arms wide. "I'm not so terrible, am I?"

On the one hand, she felt she had good reason to believe he was so terrible, when she considered the malpractice suit he'd won and that was just *one* case! On the other, he'd been so gentle with her, so kind and sweet and...

But she couldn't admit either of those things straight out, not to the man who stood between her and Liam. Jaina chose her words carefully. "I don't suppose 'fee, fi, fo, fum' is a regular part of your vocabulary."

His smile softened. "I have a friend who's a private investigator. If he can find Kirstie, will you vouch for me?"

Would Jaina tell the girl it had all been a terrible misunderstanding, that her uncle was goodness personified? She honestly didn't know. "When we realized that she'd left, I told my parents we should try to find her so she wouldn't have to spend her last months..." The next word froze in her throat.

"Alone?"

Jaina nodded.

His expression warmed. "You mean...you'd have taken her in? Just like that? You would've cared for a total stranger until...?"

"Well, of course I would!" she said, rescuing him from having to finish the dreadful sentence.

The blue eyes darkened as his brow furrowed. "How very kind of you."

What was going on in that handsome head of his? What had changed his mood *this* time?

"There isn't much I can do to alter the outlook for Kirstie, but my nephew's future has yet to be decided."

His nephew.

So, Buchanan was drawing boundary lines, was he, and daring her to cross them? Would he have issued the same cold challenge if he'd known Jaina had never run away from one in her life? "Kirstie made it perfectly clear that—"

"She's barely eighteen—*dying*—and completely alone in the world." On his feet now, he began to pace back and forth behind his desk. Then he stopped abruptly, pressing both palms on his desktop and leaning over it. "Nothing she said under the duress of these conditions can be taken seriously."

Oh, you're good, Buchanan. I'll give you that. I'll bet juries just love you. She matched his tone decibel for decibel. "I hope you aren't saying Kirstie wasn't of sound mind when she wrote that note, because she looked sane and reasonable to me." She hesitated, then lifted her chin and boldly added, "And I'm *perfectly* willing to testify to that fact."

He straightened, crossed both arms over his chest. "You must be *perfectly* healthy, too, because you sure did make a fast recovery."

If you weren't so perfectly *arrogant, you might be* perfectly *gorgeous!* Jaina thought. Was he accusing her of faking the fainting spell? What sort of woman did he think she was? "What?" she protested.

Either he hadn't heard her or had chosen to ignore the question. "I wasn't aware you had a degree in psychology, Miss…er…Jaina."

She didn't like the way he stood there, towering over her. Fighting the last of her wooziness, Jaina got to her feet. "I don't need a degree in psychology to know an unbalanced person when I see one. Kirstie was as…" She narrowed her eyes. "I was about to say she was as rational as you, but you're obviously not rational, or you wouldn't be—"

"*I'll* determine her health, mental and physical," he asserted, all but ignoring her, "if and when I find her."

Perhaps if she appealed to his sensitive side… *Please, God, let him* have *a sensitive side.*

"Mr. Buchanan, you haven't had much time to absorb all this information. Why don't you give yourself a day or two, let it sink in while your friend looks for Kirstie. And while you're waiting, maybe you'll give a thought or two to what Kirstie is going through. I mean, it couldn't have been easy, physically or emotionally, to make that long trip from Illinois to Maryland with a baby, especially on a crowded bus. But she did it because she was desperate to find a good home for Liam before…"

Before she dies.

Try as she might, Jaina couldn't make herself complete the sentence.

"I'm thinking of nothing *but* what she's going through…what she's *been* going through. Which is why I want to find her. I want to make sure she'll get the best of—" he spread his arms wide "—the best of *everything*. We're minutes from Johns Hopkins after all, where the country's top doc—"

Jaina held up a hand to silence him. "I haven't lived my life on another planet, Mr. Buchanan. I've heard a thing or two about the great work they do at Johns Hopkins." She clasped her hands to her waist. "I hope you find Kirstie, because I have a feeling she'll need all the help the hospital's specialists can give her." She returned to her seat, took a calming breath. "Until then, may I make a suggestion…in the best interests of Kirstie *and* her son?"

Buchanan headed back to his own side of the desk. "I'm all ears."

"Won't you let Liam stay with me, for now at least? He's been through so much in such a short time. It would only confuse him to move again so soon." She smiled nervously. "He's happy with me…you're more than welcome to come see for yourself."

A thumbnail between his teeth, Buchanan regarded Jaina through hooded eyes as he contemplated her suggestion. After a while, he buzzed his secretary. "Pearl? What's my schedule like for the rest of this week?"

Her voice crackled through the speakerphone. "Have you forgotten? You leave this evening for that conference in New York."

Buchanan exhaled an exasperated sigh. "That's right," he said, more to himself than to Pearl. "I *did* forget, what with all this baby stuff and—"

"Your speech is typed up and ready to go," Pearl continued, "and I've booked you on a flight leaving BWI at eight o'clock. All you have to do is go home and throw a few things in a suitcase.''

''You're the best, Pearl.''

The secretary chuckled. ''Sure thing, Mr. B.''

Hanging up, he swiveled his chair until he faced Jaina. ''You've been in touch with the authorities, I presume?''

''Yes. I called Social Services and—''

''Good.'' He nodded somberly. ''They have no problem with your keeping the boy?''

The boy? Jaina swallowed her disapproval. *''The boy'' has a name.* ''They're fine with it,'' she said emphatically.

He studied her face for what seemed an eternity. ''I suppose you're right. If I interfere at this juncture, it might possibly traumatize him.'' Buchanan steepled his hands beneath his chin. ''All right, Jaina, I'll take you up on your generous offer. For the time being at least, Liam can stay with you.'' He shoved his chair back and stood. ''I'll be back in Baltimore on Friday. We'll start the preliminaries first thing the Monday morning after that.

''Meanwhile,'' he continued, walking toward the door, ''I'll get my investigator started on the search for Kirstie. I'll make him photocopies of her note and the baby's birth certificate, too. That ought to help with his search.''

''Speaking of which,'' Jaina said coolly, ''if I'm going to take care of Liam, I need the original birth certificate…just in case anything should happen.''

He winced. ''You're right. I never thought of that.'' He traded the copies for the originals.

Right now, Jaina wished with all her heart that she hadn't called him. There didn't seem to be room in his schedule *or* his heart for a baby boy. Liam needed a full-time parent, not a man whose career obligations came ahead of ''baby stuff.'' And there was that matter of the caliber of people he defended….

''Well,'' she said, forcing a smile, ''let's not forget that you're big for your age.''

Chuckling, he nodded and opened the door. "I'll call you from New York so you can introduce me to Liam via the telephone."

She stepped into the outer office. He needed to understand that she intended to take her mothering job seriously for as long as it lasted. "Keep in mind he's only seven months old. Call before eight o'clock or he'll be fast asleep."

Buchanan raised a brow. "What a fortunate boy to have such a fastidious guardian in his corner."

Despite her better instincts, Jaina felt warmed by his compliment. She did her best to hide her reaction and offered only a small smile in response.

"You sure you're okay to drive?" he asked. "You're not still dizzy or anything, are you, because I'd be happy to—"

"I'm fine, thank you." She headed for the exit. "And Liam will be, too," she flung over her shoulder.

"I never said he wouldn't be."

That stopped her dead in her tracks. "So you'll be calling tonight?"

He nodded.

And so did she. Aiming for the elevators, she added, "Talk to you later, then, Mr. Buchanan."

"Jaina?"

She turned. "Yes?"

"Call me Connor. Makes me feel like a prissy etiquette teacher, what with all your 'Mr.' this and your 'Mr.' that."

She smiled and pressed the down button.

"Did the picture frame land on your foot?"

Jaina sighed inwardly. Hard as she had tried to hide it, he'd seen her limp anyway. How else was she to explain the pitying expression on his handsome face?

She'd always been one to confront things head-on, and saw no reason to hide from his concern. "Thanks for asking, *Connor,*" she said, deliberately emphasizing his name, "but no, the frame didn't cause my limp."

There seemed to be nothing left to say, so she pressed the first floor button.

"I'm sorry for asking," he apologized in a gentle tone. "That was stupid of me," he added, though his concern had been genuine. "Maybe someday you'll tell me how...."

The elevator doors hissed shut, closing off the end of his sentence.

Connor cleared the remainder of broken glass from the carpet, then carried Susan's picture to his desk. He couldn't stop thinking about the wide-eyed fright that had registered on Jaina's face when he barged into the office earlier. Since she didn't look like the type who'd be bowled over by a little blood, he assumed something from her past, something horrible and terrifying, must have been responsible for her behavior.

"He's not Bill. He won't hurt you." She'd chanted the words under her breath, saying them out loud without realizing it. Who's this Bill guy? Connor wondered, and what did he do to make her so afraid of being near a man?

He leaned back in the chair, one hand tucked behind his head as he stared at the camera-frozen image of his older sister, his only sibling. He knew by what Kirstie *hadn't* said that Susan was dead and buried. How long ago she'd died and of what, he didn't know. Might never know. He closed his eyes. *Not now,* he cautioned, shaking his head. *Don't react to it now. You don't have time.*

He brought to mind Kirstie's photo, the one she'd asked Jaina to show Liam. If he'd had the chance to see it, he could compare it now to his sister's image. As it was, he'd have to content himself with a photocopy of the letter and Liam's birth certificate. Unfortunately, his sister and her daughter had more in common than a striking physical resemblance. Both had given birth while in their teens, and each would have met their Maker way ahead of schedule, leaving a motherless child behind.

He had no proof, of course, that Kirstie had not married Liam's father. But if she had, would the girl have traveled halfway across the country in search of a total stranger... someone to care for her boy?

Connor felt the heat of tears burning behind his eyelids. He hadn't reacted this way two years ago, when he'd given up all hope of ever finding his sister. Hadn't reacted this way nearly two decades ago, when Susan had run away from home after their parents found out she'd gotten pregnant out of wedlock. He remembered how they'd frightened her, wondering if she could ever atone for her sin.

Hundreds of times, he'd wondered why she'd never contacted him. He chalked it up to her overprotectiveness. Susan had no doubt decided that she'd better stay out of the picture for his sake, knowing that their self-righteous parents would have viewed his communication with her as a betrayal of all they believed in and stood for. They'd have made his life miserable. Well, he'd been miserable anyway, so what had Susan's sacrifice accomplished, except to leave a cavernous hole in his life and a nonstop ache in his heart?

Connor swiped angrily at his traitorous, tear-reddened eyes. Had his beloved Susan lived alone and died alone? Nah, of course she hadn't. She'd always been a ray of light in the dark world his harsh and judgmental parents had created for him. She'd been that way with neighbors, kids at school, total strangers. No doubt, wherever she had chosen to live her life, she'd made friends. Lots of them. He could only hope they were with her at the end.

And Kirstie—the niece he didn't even know he had until Jaina Chandelle introduced him to her by way of a brief note—a pretty young girl with everything to live for, including an adorable son. What kind of world was this, where an eighteen-year-old girl could be taken by some-thing as ugly and vile as cancer?

The answer didn't satisfy him.

The same kind of world that turned your parents against their own flesh and blood because she'd made a flesh-and-blood mistake. Whoever said life ain't fair knew his stuff, he decided.

Connor ticked off all the things that might have been different if…

If Susan hadn't gotten pregnant.

If he'd been able to find her after she'd left.

If Kirstie hadn't heard him shouting on the telephone.

Of course, the only reason he even had his list of ifs was because he'd met Jaina.

Jaina… Her image flashed in his mind.

She was totally unlike the many other women who'd had a way of meandering in and out of his life, his ex-wife in particular. Miriam had been a spoiled "wanna-be rich" girl who was happiest aboard cruise ships, in Caribbean ca-banas, on England's shores. She wanted nothing but to live the good life, draped in furs, bangled in gold and jewels, boasting an address in horse country. How had she known, when they'd met at the tender age of seventeen, that Connor would be her ticket to a house full of expensive possessions and a well-stamped passport? It wasn't until he asked her to prove her numerous singsonged "I love yous" by giving him the children she'd promised that he realized her words were nothing but lies, told to ensure a full travel itinerary. "*Why* don't I want children with you?" she'd asked lightly. "It's really quite simple. I don't think you'd make a good father."

The answer hurt worse than any injury he'd suffered to date. What had made him believe that sooner or later, after he'd satisfied her hunger for trips and treats, she'd realize he *was* father material after all? Naiveté? Bullheadedness? Blatant stupidity?

And then one day, his wife had come to him in that coolly detached manner that was distinctly Miriam's and told him she was going to have a child. Why wasn't she shouting for joy? he'd wondered. Why wasn't she leaping in jubilation? No matter, he was happy enough for the both of them. A baby, at long last!

Less than two weeks later, her agonized moans woke him in the middle of the night. He spent the next morning in the hospital's chapel, seeking the strength he'd need to be supportive of his wife. The doctor had found him there, and sitting beside him on the hard wooden pew, he'd explained that Miriam's IUD had caused the miscarriage.

"What IUD?" Connor had demanded. "My wife and I don't believe in birth control."

"I'm sure that as an attorney, you understand that doctor-patient confidentiality prevents me from discussing any details of your wife's—"

"Do you mean to say I have no say in whether or not she used artificial means to prevent pregnancy?"

"I'm afraid that's something you're going to have to discuss with her."

Connor vowed then and there, looking into the doctor's sympathetic eyes, that Miriam had hurt and humiliated him for the last time.

He had taken her home from the hospital and helped her to bed, brought her cup after cup of Earl Grey, brewed the way she liked it and served in a Wedgwood cup. It hadn't been easy, behaving like the devoted husband, because now he had proof that she did not see him as a man, as the head of their household. He began to understand that her secrecy had been a lie, a blatant betrayal, and it had killed their marriage just as surely as her choice of birth control had killed their child.

Miriam did not cry over the loss of the baby. In fact, it seemed not to have affected her at all, emotionally. Within days of the miscarriage, she was back on her feet, laughing, planning shopping trips and vacations, ordering a new sofa for the parlor and shoes from an exclusive New York shop.

She had lied by omission when she'd instructed her doctor to insert the IUD, just as every "I love you, honey" had been a lie. He knew that now. If she'd ever loved him, even a little, wouldn't she have seen that he was suffering, that he was grieving over the baby's death? If she'd loved him at all, wouldn't she have seen how much fatherhood meant to him?

Connor had kept track of the weeks and months, and on the day that the doctor had predicted would have been the baby's due date, he'd driven miles into the country and parked in a secluded spot beneath a willow tree, then stared for hours, dry-eyed, at the Victorian-style farmhouse he'd purchased months ago. He'd planned to bring Miriam here as a surprise after their baby was born. It was his dream house—the perfect place for his new family, where a child could run free, maybe even have a pony.

He didn't fight Miriam a month later when she asked for a divorce. Didn't grieve when the final papers were delivered. It surprised him, when she was gone, that he didn't miss her, not a bit. They'd shared a home, a bed, a life of sorts for nearly ten years after all....

Instead, in the wake of her leaving, Connor experienced a solace like none he'd never known, a peace he hadn't thought possible in this world. If yoking himself to a woman meant giving up that hard-won tranquillity, he'd gladly spend the rest of his days alone. And so, he had not been deeply involved with a woman since. The moment it began to look as if a woman was expecting him to make a commitment to the relationship, he'd ended it.

Every lawyer should be forced to live with a woman like Miriam, he often told himself, for what she'd done to him had left him callous, rigid, insensitive...characteristics that made him a ruthless, determined-to-win attorney.

Connor hadn't shed a tear when his father died of a

stroke five years after the divorce, nor when a heart attack took his mother a year after that. His parents had been cold, withholding people who hadn't shown him or Susan a moment of warmth. They hadn't abused their children physically, nor had they neglected them. In fact, anyone on the outside looking in would have commended Bert and Edie Buchanan for providing their son and daughter with the best of everything…everything but the knowledge that they were loved.

He hadn't cried two years ago when he accepted the possibility that Susan did not want to be found. He'd made the decision to stop looking for her matter-of-factly, from a levelheaded, feet-on-the-ground position.

Until now, he'd convinced himself he had inherited the same gene that made his mother and father frosty, hard-hearted, unreachable. How else could he have suffered so many losses without shedding a single tear?

Until now, he'd never known how much he needed to grieve.

Connor gave in to it. Great, racking sobs shook his body as a lifetime of unspent tears rained down his face.

He didn't know how long he sat there, bawling like a child. He only knew that if not for Jaina, he might have spent his whole life thinking himself abnormal, uncaring, *dead* to such emotions.

But she had breezed into his life, blowing warmth into the pockets of cold aloneness with nothing more than her concern for his nephew.

He didn't know why an unfettered single woman would want the responsibility of raising someone else's child, but Jaina wanted Liam; Connor read it in her eyes, heard it in her voice. If she could love the boy that deeply after just one day with him, how much more would she love him in a month? A year? A lifetime?

He admitted that if she hadn't contacted him, he'd never have known his niece had come looking for him in the first place, wouldn't have known that he had blood kin on this earth at all.

Why, he asked himself, had she risked losing her only opportunity to keep Liam? *Because she's the kind of person who believes in doing the right thing, even when it costs her.* That's *the kind of woman you* should *have married, Buchanan. The kind who puts the needs of others ahead of her own. You might have even had a kid or two by now...or half a dozen if...*

If...

There it was again. One of the smallest words in the English language, yet oh, how large its implications.

Something about her called to everything manly in him. He had a feeling that Jaina had a capacity for love and caring and nurturing like no one else he'd ever known. She might be petite, but he could tell by the way she walked and talked that her strength of spirit more than compensated for whatever limitations God had placed on her body. He liked that, too, and found it far more attractive than the practiced demeanor of a woman who took her physical gifts for granted. She'd probably be the kind of woman who kept an orderly house and cooked rib-sticking meals, who'd make her man believe he'd hung the moon. He'd spent a total of perhaps forty minutes in her presence; how could he be so certain, after such a short time, that she'd be good for him, good for his life?

You're losin' your mind, that's why, Buchanan, he thought, shaking his head. *Finding out you've got family has you living in a fantasy world.*

He sat up, straightened his shirt and tie, wiped his eyes with the hankie he'd used on Jaina's palm. The tiny spot of her blood caught his attention. Remembering the way she'd pulled herself together, despite whatever trauma had put her into the tailspin to begin with, he pulled himself together now.

He shrugged. Sniffed. Knuckled his eyes.

He made himself focus on the boy and wondered what Liam would be like. Jaina had said he was big for his age. Would he be blond and blue-eyed like his mother and grandmother? Would he have Susan's even-tempered disposition? Or might he have inherited his great-grandfather's quick ire? His great-grandmother's judgmentalism? Connor's own heartlessness? *If there's any justice in this world, every one of the bad traits skipped a generation, because life is gonna be tough enough for the kid.*

He took a deep, shuddering breath.

And did Liam cry quickly and easily? Or was he stoic and brave?

Connor could hardly wait to find out.

Funny, he thought, sniffing one last time, *that a full-grown man can have so much in common with a baby.* Except for the other, each of them was alone in the world.

He'd been powerless to help Susan. Hadn't been able to help Kirstie. If he found her—another if—he doubted he could do more than make her last days comfortable.

But he *could* make a difference in Liam's life.

He could, and he *would.*

He had a family at long last.

Family!

Connor would move mountains, fight beasts barehanded, take on every official in the state of Maryland, if need be, to adopt this child he'd never met. He didn't have to *meet* the boy to know he loved him, didn't have to *see* him to know he'd protect him till his own dying breath.

And he'd do it, no matter what—or whom—it cost him.

Chapter Three

"**H**i, Jaina. It's—"

"Connor. I know." She cut a quick glance at Liam, lying on his side in the middle of her living room, sucking his thumb and poking a stubby finger into the quilt's colorful rainbows. Her heart lurched with love for the sleepy boy...and with fear at the sound of the voice of the man who would attempt to take him from her. "So, how's New York?" She asked the question lightly, casually, as if she hadn't noticed that he didn't call last evening as he'd promised.

"Same as always...dirty, crowded, noisy."

Jaina wondered about the feelings of protectiveness and pity that automatically rose inside her when she heard the exhaustion in his voice. *You shouldn't be feeling* anything *for him but mistrust. Remember what Skip said.*

"Sorry I haven't called sooner. It's been a circus up here. I haven't had a minute to myself since I stepped off the plane."

Did he really expect her to believe he couldn't have found one moment to check on Liam's welfare? Following Skip's instructions, Jaina jotted the time and date of his call in a spiral tablet. From now on, every moment the lawyer spent with Liam—in person or on the phone—would be logged in Jaina's Buchanan Book. So far, he was playing right into her hands. She could only hope he'd continue behaving as though everything in his life took precedence over the baby.

Feeling a little two-faced, she put an extra lilt into her voice. "It's a shame they're keeping you so busy. You ought to take advantage of being in the Big Apple. See a play. Tour the museums. Stroll down Times Square. Do something touristy."

"I have a client with business interests in New York. I'm up here once a month, minimum…"

Jaina scribbled that fact in the tablet.

"…and I wouldn't do any of those things even if I *did* have the time."

When his tone switched from exhausted to disgusted, Jaina got a mental picture of him, wrinkling his nose at the idea of doing anything fun. "So you've never seen *The Phantom?*"

"Nope."

"*Cats?*"

"No."

"Why not?" she asked, genuinely incredulous.

"I'd rather sit in my room, watch the news and order room service than watch a bunch of supposedly sane adults romp around a stage dressed up like cats," he replied in a cutting tone.

Jaina's brow rose a little higher. Kirstie was right. He *is* a mean old grouch. And she might have said so if Skip hadn't cautioned her to treat Buchanan with kid gloves…at least until after the preliminary hearing.

"Oh, well I guess musicals aren't your thing," Jaina replied lightly.

"Got that right," he grumbled.

"So, did your audience like your speech?"

He chuckled. "Nobody threw rotten tomatoes, and I didn't hear any snoring. It went all right, I guess."

She reminded herself what else Skip had said. "It'll be harder for him to take Liam if he *likes* you." She'd started working with the public at seventeen when, to pay her way through college, she began singing and playing guitar all around the country. Jaina's easy manner at the mike earned her a reputation for having what was generally referred to as "stage presence." *Just pretend he's some guy in the audience, celebrating his birthday.*

"What was your speech about?" she asked. Skip's advice had very little to do with her interest; *everything* about Connor Buchanan fascinated her, from the beautiful smile he so rarely exhibited to the fact that he, too, seemed to know how to "work a crowd."

"Well, it was called 'The Importance of Effective Closing Arguments.'" There was a long pause before he added, "I seem to have a talent for them, according to the media."

"Why? Because when you're at your best, you can turn a jury around, even at the last minute."

There was another long pause. And then he said, "Been reading the papers, I see."

Jaina thought of the case she'd read about—the surgeon who still had his license thanks to Connor Buchanan's "talents." Suddenly, she didn't care what Skip had said about biding her time, about buttering up the lawyer. "Would you like to talk to Liam?"

A moment of silence ticked by as if he might be considering it. "Nah, it's after ten, and I don't want you to wake him."

At the mention of his name, Liam reached for her. "Mmumm-mmumm," he said, lifting his arms. "Mmummmmmumm."

Buchanan cleared his throat. "He's still up?"

"Yes."

"I thought you said his bedtime was eight."

She sighed at his scolding tone, stroking Liam's hair. "It is, usually. But tonight we went to the park after supper, had some ice cream. Between the long walk, the swings and the slide, plus the extra chocolate sprinkles, he's a little wound up." Worried that Buchanan might read "too permissive" into the way she was caring for Liam, she quickly added, "But it usually doesn't take him more than ten minutes to fall asleep." Just for good measure, she tacked on another truth. "Especially if I rock him with a lullaby."

Another moment of silence. "How do you manage the, uh, quality mothering when you have a diner to run?"

Skip had predicted this question, too, and warned her that Buchanan would try to make the judge see her as a success-oriented businesswoman who couldn't—or wouldn't—make room in her busy schedule for a baby. "I'm already interviewing to hire extra staff and a full-time manager at the diner. I also have my parents to baby-sit anytime I need help. Liam is number one on *my* priority list. Would he be on yours?"

"I think I can make a case for that."

"But that's not the question, Counselor." Lifting Liam from the quilt, she settled into the rocker with him. Immediately, he grabbed the phone cord. "No, no, sweetie," she said, gently disentangling his fingers from the coils, "don't put that in your mouth."

"So, can I talk to him?"

Jaina could have sworn she heard apprehension in his otherwise sure-of-himself voice. Apprehension, and maybe a tinge of uncertainty. "I have to warn you, he doesn't say much, but listening amazes him."

This oughta be fun, she told herself, holding the phone to Liam's ear. A one-way conversation between a defense attorney and a defenseless baby.

"Hey, Liam. Whatcha doin', li'l buddy?"

The child turned his head toward the voice, scraping a fingernail over the tiny holes in the earpiece.

"You bein' a good boy, Liam? Huh? Are ya?"

The baby furrowed his brow. "Dih-dih?" he asked Jaina, pointing at the phone. "Dih-dih-dih?"

"I'm gonna come see you tomorrow," she heard Buchanan say. "What do you think of that? Maybe we'll go to the zoo, see the big ol' lions and tigers, even ride the train."

She'd expected the lawyer to sound stiff and stern, not animated and friendly. Then Jaina remembered he'd behaved similarly when she nearly fainted dead away in his office. But was the warm, gentle demeanor genuine, or rehearsed like his jury-turning closing arguments?

Liam tried his best to stuff the entire phone into his mouth. When it wouldn't fit, he lost interest entirely and focused on Jaina's dangly wolf earrings, which suddenly held far more baby appeal. Then, just as quickly, he spotted the wooden pull-toy truck her father had made him and did several deep knee bends in her lap, pointing toward the quilt. "Mmumm-mmumm. Mmumm-mmum!"

"Sorry," she said, taking the phone. "His attention span is fairly short, especially at this time of day."

"He sounds terrific. I can't wait to see him."

Her mouth went dry and her palms grew damp. He'd been away for days, had promised to call yesterday, then didn't. Now, suddenly, after a brief conversation with Liam, he wanted to see him? *I don't like this. Not one bit.*

"How's tomorrow?"

Her heart thudded with dread. Saturday had always been The Chili Pot's busiest day. She pictured his quiet, elegant office, comparing it to the nonstop hustle and bustle of the diner. He didn't know a thing about the restaurant business and would likely see all the activity and noise as a chaotic mess. And as an unsuitable place to raise a traumatized, abandoned child. "It's a lot quieter midweek, between lunch and supper," she suggested. "If you stop by, say, on

Wednesday afternoon, I can give you my undivided atten—"

"It isn't going to be a social call, Jaina, so you needn't worry about entertaining me. Besides, it isn't you I'm coming to see."

She clenched her jaws together so tightly, her gums ached.

"If the plane lands on time, I should be there by one."

Why had he asked to see Liam tomorrow, Jaina wondered, when his attitude made it perfectly clear it had been an order, one he fully expected her to follow?

"I, uh, I bought a little something for him."

She imagined a Statue of Liberty key chain, an Empire State Building mug, an I Love New York baseball cap, things completely inappropriate for a seven-month-old and probably purchased in his hotel's gift shop. "How thoughtful."

"You doing okay?"

"I'm doing just fine," she said, her voice thick with defensiveness. "I've had to juggle my schedule a bit so that Liam gets my best at all times, but—"

He harrumphed.

Time to terminate this conversation, she told herself, *before you say something that gives him the excuse he needs to take Liam away from you now.* "Have a safe flight."

"Will do."

"See you tomorrow."

"Okay," he said. "Gotta go. I have a call waiting." And he hung up.

Jaina stared at the dead receiver for a moment. Of all the arrogant, pompous—

"Dih?" Liam asked, pointing at the phone. "Dih-dih?"

Fear gripped her heart. It sounded an awful lot like he was saying Da-da. No, you're just imagining it, she assured herself. But the baby was clearly responding to Connor. Had the baby somehow sensed that he and Buchanan were related? Had he recognized something in the man's voice that told him they were family? She picked him up, then hugged him protectively, possessively. "Time for bed, little one," she cooed into his ear. "You've got a big day tomorrow."

Jaina tucked him into the crib she'd gotten from Ronnie's Rent-All and turned out all but one dim lamp. And after dragging her bentwood rocker closer, she did what she'd been doing for five consecutive nights. She slid her hand between the bars and let Liam hold on to her forefinger. If the night ran true to form, he'd fall asleep in minutes, snuggled against her hand, and long after slumber overtook him, she'd continue to watch him until drowsiness overtook her, too.

Jaina woke, wincing at the discomfort of the cramp in her hand. When she sat up in the rocker to flex it, she noticed another knotted muscle in her neck. *How long have I been asleep?* she wondered, stretching as tall as her five-feet-three-inch frame would allow. A glance at the glowing red numerals of her alarm clock answered the question. Buchanan had called shortly after ten and talked all of five minutes. She'd put Liam to bed immediately after his uncle hung up. It was now one thirty-five. No wonder she was stiff and sore. She'd been out for nearly three hours!

Taking a deep breath, she raised and lowered her shoulders, rolled them forward and backward, tilted her head left, right, left again. The alarm clock blinked as it changed to one thirty-six…a silent reminder that its radio music would come on in less than four hours.

In less than *twelve* hours, Connor Buchanan would arrive.

She tiptoed over to the crib, leaned on its oaken rail and smiled. She'd tucked a light blanket around him earlier. He must have kicked it off when he rolled over. Grinning, Jaina shook her head. How can you be comfortable in that position? she asked him silently, covering the round rump that protruded into the air, the pudgy fingers splayed on Winnie the Pooh sheets. She patted that well-diapered little behind…and wondered about the sob that ached in her throat.

It hadn't even been a week since his mother's disappearance. If not for Skip's influence, Jaina didn't know what might have become of Kirstie's innocent little boy. Since the demand for suitable foster parents was far greater than those available, Liam would likely have ended up in some impersonal, overcrowded children's ward. Surely, if that had happened, the doctors and nurses on duty would have given him the best they could, despite the demands of their busy jobs. But a hospital is a place for sick people, not for abandoned youngsters. The day after Kirstie's disappearance, Jaina had taken Liam to a pediatrician recommended by Skip. "The only thing wrong with this baby," the doctor had said, "is that he has no family."

Well, that wasn't entirely true. He had Connor Buchanan….

But despite the age-old cliché, blood wasn't always thicker than water. And the proof—at least in Jaina's mind—was the lawyer's cavalier attitude toward Liam's well-being.

How could he have gone off to New York, knowing Kirstie's little son would be in the care of strangers, without checking on him from time to time? For all he knew, Jaina *was* the overambitious career woman Skip had described, who'd put business ahead of the child's welfare. How did he know she even *liked* children? What made him so certain she wouldn't abuse or neglect the baby? Why did he believe Liam would be in safe hands?

Blind faith must run in the Buchanan family, she told herself, remembering the trusting way Kirstie had left Liam at the diner in the first place. Odd, she told herself, because faith was primarily a spiritual thing, and Buchanan didn't seem the religious type....

Liam sighed in his sleep, a delightful, musical sound that made Jaina's heart throb with love. She hadn't known it was possible to love this deeply in such a short time. Indeed, she didn't know it was possible to love this much at all!

If she was the one who'd given birth to him, she might have understood the all-consuming tenderness she felt for him. If she'd held him in her arms in the delivery room, nursed him, sung him lullabies in their hospital room, she might have had an explanation for the overwhelming fondness beating in her heart. If she'd watched him thrive and grow as she showered him with attention and affection as he struggled to sit up and then to crawl, eager to learn about the world around him, she might have comprehended the powerful sense of devotion she'd developed toward him.

But he'd been with her less than a week. Was there something wrong with her, that she'd so quickly succumbed to this innocent baby's charms? Could there have been such a void in her life that she'd be so utterly filled with love for this tiny being?

There was no denying how lonely she'd been until he came into her life. Lonely for someone to care for, someone to be needed by, someone to spend years of pent-up love on. How strange that she didn't know it, didn't recognize it for what it was until Liam came into her life. He'd filled the emptiness in her soul, in her heart. But what had she done for *him?*

Any foster parent could have provided him with safe surroundings, healthy food, wholesome activities, a clean diaper when he needed it. If Skip had been able to find a home that wasn't already overrun with children, that's exactly the kind of care Liam would be getting. It was only because her best friend believed Liam would suffer less anxiety and disruption if he remained with Jaina as the

investigation surrounding his permanent placement continued that she'd been given this time with him.

Jaina wondered if her mother could be right...that Liam
was God's reward for her stoic acceptance of her barren-
ness.

Jaina padded into the kitchen and poured herself a glass
of lemonade, then unlocked the back door and stepped out
onto the porch. Standing at the rail and looking beyond the
parking lot, she could see rolling hills, pastures and farm-
land, a fence here, a barn there.

As a child, she'd moved every other year on average,
from apartment to apartment on air force bases between
New York and California. It had been fun and exciting—
meeting new people, seeing new sights, learning new
things—yet Jaina had always dreamed of living in a place
surrounded by acres of grassy, tree-lined knolls. Since own-
ing The Chili Pot, she'd been saving every spare dime,
intent upon making her dream a reality. For the time being
at least, she must be satisfied with her vision of the two-
story farmhouse she'd someday call home.

It would have a wraparound, covered porch. She'd paint
the railing and the floorboards white so the bentwood rockers flanking the front door would be clearly visible from
the road, telling passersby that the house and its views were
thoroughly and frequently enjoyed by its owner.

There'd be lots of tall, narrow windows, where she'd
hang gauzy white curtains that would billow gently in the
summer breezes, a gray-with-age split-rail fence, lined by
black-eyed Susans, and a winding flagstone path that would
lead visitors from the crushed-stone driveway to her red-
enameled front door.

Ancient trees would shade the house, creating a cool can-
opy on sizzling August days and a place for birds to build
their twiggy nests in the springtime. Out back, she'd plant
a garden and grow vegetables for freezing and canning,
enough for friends and neighbors, as well as a few to set

out on a table near the road, where a sign would invite city folk passing by to partake in nature's country glory.

If she had that place now, she'd certainly have a better chance at being allowed to adopt Liam. What judge could refuse her, when the home she'd provide for the boy would have a tree house, a swing set, a pond for catching toads, a stream for snagging fish, and a big, bright bedroom overlooking it all.

She had always been happy in her modest apartment above the diner. Soon after moving in, she'd torn off layers of peeling wallpaper and painted the whole place a creamy off-white. She'd taken up the green shag rug, refinished the mellow oak floors and laid down the Persian rugs her family had collected when stationed with her father in faraway places. She'd scrubbed years of grease and grime from the windows and replaced the heavy draperies with tap-topped curtains she'd sewn herself. She'd furnished the rooms with an eclectic mix of comfortable traditional-style pieces, family heirlooms and some interesting old "finds."

But there was only the one bedroom. And no backyard. The only way to reach the apartment was by way of the long, narrow staircase at the back of the diner. Worse… whatever noise was going on downstairs could easily be heard through the floorboards. Then once the sun went down, the chili red neon sign she'd had crafted by an Ellicott City glassblower beamed steadily, casting an orange glow over everything in the living room.

The diner was open 7:00 a.m. to 7:00 p.m. every day except Sunday, but it took two hours to get ready for the public and two hours to clean up after the last customer had gone home. Would a child-care specialist see this as a stable home for a growing boy…or as a virtual three-ring circus?

She should have bought that little farm she'd found last year, she scolded herself, instead of being such a perfectionist. It hadn't been such a bad place; a little time and

elbow grease would have turned it around, just as her efforts had improved the apartment.

But the house had been a rambling ranch, not a stately
Victorian. In place of a cozy wraparound porch, there was
a concrete slab near the front door. She couldn't hang a
tree swing from the branches of the pathetic sapling in the
side yard. The house had a contemporary modern kitchen
and two equally sleek bathrooms. And the only antique that
would have fitted into the low-ceilinged, narrow-doored
house was the player piano she'd found at the Westview
flea market.

But the price had been right, and considering that it was
situated less than a mile from The Chili Pot, the location
couldn't have been better. With a farm to her right and
woods to the left, she'd have at last those wide open spaces
she'd yearned for while living on cramped air force bases.

"You're such a tomboy," her mother would lament
when, as a girl, she'd come home with cuts and bruises
sustained in a rousing game of touch football. "What a wild
one," her father would exclaim when Jaina slunk into the
house with holes in the knees and seat of her jeans…holes
put there by reckless slides into home plate. She'd always
been a spur-of-the-moment girl, a do-it-now, worry-about-
it-later kind of kid.

Except about that house. To make that dream come true,
Jaina had been more than willing to wait.

It had been that very mind-set that prompted her to get
onto her first stage in response to a dare from Skip and sing
with Bobby Pierce and his four-piece band. If she had
known her guitar wasn't tuned to scale, she'd never have
agreed to stand at the mike and croon the tune she'd written
all by herself. Somehow, Bobby's lead guitarist provided
backup to her little ditty, and when the song ended, it had
been the plaudits of the musicians that gave her the incentive to repeat the performance again the very next week.

She had a natural talent with the guitar, they'd said; she could go places with a voice like that, they'd insisted.

And she had. After signing with Artists' Corporation of America, her agent had booked her all over the country. It had been after a benefit performance in Chicago that a record producer approached her about signing a contract. She'd gone to Nashville with the grandfatherly gentleman, done a stint with the Grand Ole Opry and cut a record.

The tune went national, and within the first week, radio stations from coast to coast were broadcasting "Lovin' Arms," the song she'd written about the love of her life, drummer Bill Isaacs.

She'd met Bill during that first year of touring the country, when the agency scheduled her to do a show at a college in Virginia. She'd been slated as the feature act, and Bill headed up the backup band. They had clicked both musically and personally, and when the gig ended, they'd arranged to meet as often as possible.

Like everything else she'd done in her life to that point, Jaina decided in a snap that she loved him, despite his heavy drinking and bouts of bad temper. Her devotion, she'd told herself, would give him the incentive to quit.

And then one night, when his band wasn't booked, Bill drove from Illinois to Wisconsin to spend a weekend with her so they could discuss their future. And in a snap, she knew if he asked her to marry him, she'd say yes.

He had shown up nearly an hour late. If she'd known he'd been drinking, she'd never have gotten in the car with him, but Bill was good at hiding his drunken state. As she later realized, Bill was good at hiding so much of his real personality from her. Or, was it only that she chose not to see his weakness?

As she walked toward the car, something warned her not to get in. She hesitated a moment, and Bill called to her. Hollered at her belligerently and honked the horn. Everything in her warned her not to get into the car with her wild-eyed boyfriend.

In a snap, she'd cast caution aside.

And she would pay for that mistake for the rest of her life.

You're paying for it now, she thought dismally, *big time! If it hadn't been for that night…*

Fear seized her soul.

What if Connor found out about that night? It wouldn't matter one whit that you were totally innocent of any wrongdoing and that the records have been expunged. A lawyer like Connor Buchanan will pounce all over that black mark in my past and use it to take away Liam so fast it will make my head spin.

Jaina gave the view a last forlorn glance and went back inside. After locking up, she stuck her empty glass into the dishwasher and headed for her room. On the way to the extra wide four-poster, she stopped beside Liam's crib. He'd kicked off his covers again, and she gently pulled them up. Tears filled her eyes. As she watched him sleep, Jaina did something she hadn't done in a very long time.

"Dear Lord," she whispered, "I want to do Your will, and I want to keep Liam." Softly, her fingertips traced his cheek. "Please help me find a way to do both."

Her father had been an early riser ever since his air force days, when he'd get up before dawn to climb into a cockpit and "test drive" the latest, fastest, most powerful fighter planes. "I'm at the market," read the note propped against the carving board. "See you by six. Hugs and kisses, Dad." He'd been penning the same words every day for all the years they'd run The Chili Pot together.

The name on the diner's deed said Jaina Clarisse Chandelle, but she had never considered herself sole proprietor. Without her father's keen eye for picking only the best fruits, vegetables and meats, and her mother's knack for creating delectable sweet treats, Jaina's menu would be sparse indeed.

The rest of the staff, she believed, owned a piece of the place, as well. Take Eliot, for example. It had been a risk, hiring the cook; with nothing more than the say-so of Pastor Cummings, she'd given the ex-con a job, knowing full well that he'd spent the past three years at Jessup on charges of car theft. To this day, he proclaimed his innocence, but guilty or not, in Jaina's mind the man had served his time and deserved a chance to prove he'd righted his life.

It had been one of the smartest business moves she'd ever made, and the proof could be found in the crowded lot, where vehicles with license plates from West Virginia, New York, Delaware, Virginia and Maryland's Eastern Shore parked every day of the week. It was one of the best personal choices, too, because in the six years he'd worked for her, the stocky black man had become one of her dearest, most trusted friends.

Hiring Billie had also required a leap of faith. She'd come to Jaina's attention thanks to the pastor's youth rehab program. Billie had been drawn into a gang and couldn't see a way out, until Pastor Cummings had come into her life. A youthful offender, she'd been arrested for shoplifting, truancy, driving without a license and a few other minor offenses. In the pastor's program, she'd decided to turn her life around, get a job and leave the gang. Now Jaina was determined to help her anyway she could. In Jaina's opinion, Billie was the best all-round waitress in the tristate area. She could keep a twenty-party order straight without writing down a single word and balance six plates on one arm while carrying four cups and saucers, stacked one atop the other, in her free hand.

Eliot's cousin, Barney, a recent graduate of Cummings's Say No To Drugs project, could operate and repair every piece of equipment in the diner, from the twenty-slice toaster to the industrial-size dishwasher, from the extra large stove and grill to the walk-in freezer.

And Joy, who had hung out with Billie on one of Baltimore's meanest streets, rounded out the diner's offbeat employee roster.

Until now, Jaina hadn't given much thought to the things they'd done before joining the Chili Pot family. But Connor Buchanan changed all that. Skip had warned her that if Buchanan discovered the dubious résumés of her employees, he'd use them against her in court.

There was a chance, she supposed, that he'd be as broadminded as Pastor Cummings, the way she and her parents had been. But then, they'd had reason to be understanding. Her friends deserved *at least* as much of the fairness and open-mindedness that she'd been given since her release from Jessup.

Would he be fair and open-minded? Jaina was in no position to take chances. Not when Liam's future was at stake.

She crumpled her father's note and tossed it into the trash can. "Dad ought to save himself the bother and carve the message into the countertop," she told Liam. Secretly, she'd have been disappointed if he did, because when she came downstairs from her apartment every morning, finding his brief note was like running into an old dependable friend.

"What're you lookin' so down in the dumps about?" Eliot asked. He'd already toasted several loaves of bread and now stood at the stove, flipping sausage patties in a giant iron skillet.

"Liam's uncle is coming to meet him today."

"A big-time lawyer in The Chili Pot?" the cook said, shaking his head. "There goes the neighborhood!"

"Fortunately," she countered, laughing, "he'll only be here a short while. I don't think he'll drag down the property values in an hour or two."

"Well, he gives you any trouble, you send him to *me*,"

he said, slathering butter onto the last slice of toast. "*I'll* set that legal beagle straight!"

Jaina patted his shoulder. "Thanks, Eliot."

"Hey, what're friends for?"

Billie barged into the room, balancing a plate on one palm. "They're for saving us the last wedge of lemon meringue pie, that's what friends are for," she said around a mouthful. "I love ya, big guy!"

"Aw, now don't go gettin' all mushy on me, girl. I only set that piece of pie aside 'cause I couldn't stand to throw it away."

"I forgot," the waitress said, smiling sarcastically and rolling her heavily made-up eyes, "how much you hate to waste food."

"Don't you sass me, missy, or I'll put you to work choppin' onions. You know what that does to your mascara."

Her blue eyes widened. "You wouldn't!"

Eliot smirked. "I would, and you know it."

Billie faced Jaina, pretending she needed protection. "Help?" she said in a tiny, wavering voice.

"Don't look at me," Jaina said, holding up one hand as Liam inspected the other. "I just write the paychecks. He's in charge of the kitchen…or the onions at least."

Billie chucked Liam's chins. "How's our widdo boy? Did him sweep wike a wock? Did him have boo-tee-ful dweems?"

"Don't talk to him that way," Eliot scolded. "You'll make a sissy out of him. Besides," he added, "I read someplace that it takes young'uns twice as long to learn proper English if they have to learn two languages."

Billie grabbed the salt canister. "What?"

He held up one finger. "English," he said as a second finger joined the first, "and baby talk."

Using her hip to open the swinging door, Billie harrumphed. "When did *you* get so smart?"

"Didn't get smart," he called after her. "Was *born* smart."

"Yeah, yeah, yeah," she said from her side of the door. "And it's gonna snow on the Fourth of July."

Eliot met Jaina's eyes.

"I know, I know," she said on a sigh. "You think she's getting too big for her britches."

"If she spent a little more time on her feet, waitin' tables," he hollered, "and less time warmin' the stools at the snack bar…"

"I heard that, Eliot!"

"Are you two at it again?" Rita asked, waltzing into the kitchen. "Honestly, I feel like I'm back teaching kindergarten again, refereeing all of your squabbles!" She held out her arms, and Liam spilled into them. "How's my boy? Did you sleep well, sweetie?"

"Connor Buchanan will be here at lunchtime," Jaina said matter-of-factly.

Rita's eyes widened and her mouth dropped open. "You invited him *here?* Jaina, what were you thinking?"

"I was thinking we'd better keep him happy so that maybe—Lord willing—he'll see how good we are for Liam and won't throw a monkey wrench into the works and ruin our chances for adoption." Her heart raced as she said it because Buchanan had probably already set his investigative team to snooping into her background.

Rita looked at Eliot. "I guess if you're going to dream, you may as well dream big, right?"

Eliot looked from Jaina's frowning face to Rita's mistrustful expression. "Ladies," he said, carrying his egg tray to the stove, "I have scramblin' to do, so if you'll just excuse me…"

"Chicken," Rita grumbled. "Go ahead, leave me here all by myself."

"I learned long time ago, it ain't smart to take sides. Not when it puts you between two women!"

Rita clucked her tongue, then said to Jaina, "I finally figured out why Buchanan's name is so familiar." She handed Liam a long-handled spoon to chew on. "There was a big article about him in—"

"The *Howard County Times*. I know."

Eliot turned away from the stove long enough to ask, "What did he do? Cheat on his bar exam?"

"Worse," Rita explained. "He defended a doctor whose botched surgery cost a woman the ability to have children. He got the man off."

The cook put his back to the women. "Nothin' wrong with that," he grumbled. "Man's innocent 'til proven guilty. Least, that's what the writers of the Constitution intended for folks in this country."

Jaina stiffened but said nothing. Eliot didn't know about her past so he couldn't possibly realize how deeply his comment had affected her. What he didn't know couldn't hurt her; she'd learned the hard way that when people found out about the accident, things changed. They took a step back. Smiled the way one might smile when speaking to the very young—or the very old. Spoke with a patronizing tone as though they believed anything they said might cause her to snap.

"What's this lawyer fella gonna say when he finds out what your employees were up to before they started working here?" Eliot wanted to know. "You reckon he's gonna use it against you in the adoption proceedings?"

She had never been one to sugarcoat things. "I'm sure he'll try, but he won't get very far. You and Barney, Billie and Joy have turned your lives completely around. If anything, knowing about you will *help* me, not hurt me."

Eliot's brow furrowed. "How do you figure that?"

Jaina grinned mischievously. "Well, my goodness, if I can make honest citizens out of the likes of you guys, think what I can do with an impressionable kid like Liam!"

"Oh, so now you're taking the credit for our reform?" he teased.

Her grin became a gentle smile. "Only if Buchanan forces me to, and even then, only on the witness stand." She took a deep breath. *It's my past that'll hurt me in court, not the Chili Pot employees'.*

"Enough blabbing," Ray ordered good-naturedly, dumping a fifty-pound sack of potatoes on the floor. "Let's get this show on the road. We open in fifteen minutes!"

As usual, eighteen-wheelers, pickup trucks, motorcycles, cars and assorted minivans had already filled the graveled parking lot. They opened the doors at seven, and by quarter past, all the booths and tables in the diner were filled.

Joy took care of the Minnesota family heading for Washington, D.C., and the young Maryland couple who planned to spend the afternoon at Baltimore's National Aquarium. Billie handled the truckers and bikers sitting at tables near the window, Jaina waited on retirees and construction workers lining the snack bar, while Rita monitored the cash register. Barney saw to it that a steady supply of squeaky-clean dishes lined the shelves below the counter, and Ray did double duty as busboy and setup man.

They'd worked it out to a fine science, easily satisfying hundreds of hungry patrons a day, thanks to Ray's "Get 'em in, fill 'em up, move 'em out" policy. If the dishwasher had decided to malfunction any other day, the Chili Pot team would have handled the setback with quiet efficiency, and more than likely, nary a customer would have noticed.

But the machine sprang a leak at precisely the same time as the main drain developed a clog. Barney hadn't touched the central water valve in so long, it took five minutes to locate and turn it off. Meanwhile, the black-and-white-tiled floor seemed to float beneath several inches of foamy, antiseptic-scented dishwater.

The crew tried valiantly to sop up the mess, slinging long-handled string mops, towels, aprons...*anything* they could get their hands on. Customers tiptoed through the suds, their sneakers and sandals and work boots squishing as they made their way to the cash register and out the door. A pigtailed redhead of perhaps five fell *splat* on her behind, raining water on everyone in the vicinity.

"I can't get up, Mommy," she whimpered. "The floor's too slippery."

As her mother held out a hand to help, she joined the girl with a watery *sploosh.* "George," she called, "give us a hand, will you?" To his credit, the poor man tried. A second later, he, too, hit bottom.

"Danny's making fun of us," the little girl whined, pointing at her brother. "Make him stop it, Mommy."

"Danny," the woman warned, shaking a bubbly finger in her son's direction.

The boy clamped his lips together to stanch his laughter. But his efforts were of no avail. His snickers and snorts soon had the rest of the patrons laughing right along with him.

Jaina, balancing Liam on one hip, stepped cautiously toward the wet-bottomed threesome. "I'm so sorry," she said, extending a helping hand to the mother. "Your breakfasts are on us." And as if to punctuate the offer, she became the fourth, turning the damp human triangle into a neat, if soapy square.

Liam slipped from her arms and began crawling through the frothy water, stopping now and again to slap at the foam. His giggles blended with the rest of the happy din.

Connor stepped back onto the wood-planked porch and looked up at the sign. It said The Chili Pot all right, he thought, frowning as he went inside. He didn't know which was wetter—the floor, the diners, or the staff. *Talk about a tempest in a teapot,* he mused, smiling slightly as he looked for Jaina amid the tumble of soggy, cheery people.

His smile froze when his gaze came to rest on the baby on the floor, sitting in a diaper-deep puddle, spattering his own happy face with the droplets that flew from his hands. The baby had Susan's blond hair and his own blue eyes. Liam? he wondered, his mustache tilting in the beginning of another smile.

But what was the child doing in the middle of this mess, unsupervised? And what *was* the mess anyway? It looked like soapsuds, and if it was, they could get into the baby's eyes and—

"Dih-dih-dih," Liam squealed, flapping his arms like a bottom-heavy bird. "Dih-dih!"

Since Liam had been looking straight at Connor when he'd said it, all heads turned, gazes zeroing in on the only dry person in the diner. Connor was the center of attention, but he didn't even notice.

As he moved slowly, woodenly, across the room, his feet seemed weighted down by far more than the water that had seeped into his Italian leather loafers. If he didn't know better, he'd have to say the baby seemed pleased to see him. *But how can that be, when we've never met?*

Chili Pot patrons cleared a path for the tall, muscular man in the dark suit, but Connor didn't notice that, either. The closer he got to Liam, the harder his heart pounded, and when at last he was within reach, he got down onto one knee, seemingly unaware of the inch-deep water, and scooped the baby into his arms. "Hi there, little guy," he said, sliding a crisp white handkerchief from his breast pocket. "What're you doin', taking a bubble bath, or do they have you swabbin' the deck?" he added, blotting Liam's hands and dripping blond curls.

The child looked deep into his eyes as if searching for some clue to a riddle. He popped a fist into his mouth. "Dih-dih," he muttered around it. "Dih-dih."

Lost in the deep blue intensity of Liam's gaze, Connor felt as though he was in a trance. Mesmerized, he stood, balancing the baby on his hip as he blinked silently, unable to tear his eyes from the child's angelic face.

Her voice came to him as if through a long, hollow tube. "Mr. Buchanan? I mean, Connor?"

Hugging Liam a little tighter, Connor turned. He knew before she came into his sight who had called his name. She looked lovely, despite her waterlogged jeans and sneakers, despite the drops raining from her cinnamon curls and clinging to her long, lush lashes.

He swallowed hard, then gritted his teeth, fighting the feeling of powerlessness that was washing over him. He was here to meet his nephew, to establish a routine visitation schedule—as his friend, Judge Thompson, had advised—not to get all googly-eyed over Jaina Chandelle.

"What's the big idea," he demanded, "of leaving the child all alone in the middle of this slop?"

Chapter Four

"I realize how this looks," she said, hands twisting in front of her. "You're probably thinking he might have gotten soap in his eyes."

"But—"

"And you may think he could have fallen facedown in this mess—kids can drown in half an inch of water, you know. He might have—"

"I haven't said—"

"But I had an eye on him every minute," Jaina defended, tucking a damp and droopy curl behind one ear.

"So did I," Rita announced, stepping up beside her daughter.

Ray stood on Jaina's other side, his defensive stance indicating he'd been watching, as well.

Eliot crossed both arms over his broad chest. With a nod of his head, he indicated the kitchen, which was no more than five feet away. "I was right there the whole time."

Joy knocked on a nearby tabletop. "This is my station."

"And this one," Billie said, pointing to the tables across the narrow aisle, "is mine."

The last muffled voice, coming from somewhere under the counter, belonged to Barney. "And I was right here."

"Mmumm-mmumm," Liam said, smiling and waving at Jaina. He leaned forward, nearly tumbling from Connor's arms as he reached for her. "Mmumm-mumm, Mmumm-mmumm."

Connor turned so the baby would be farther from Jaina rather than closer. A second or two ticked by before Liam turned, too. He looked into Connor's face, an expression of confusion and slight mistrust registering in his now serious blue eyes, as if he was wondering why the man who had seemed so friendly would now want to keep him from his mmumm-mmumm. Undaunted by the added distance between him and Jaina, Liam threw his body toward her. Connor winced slightly as though the child's actions had hurt his feelings.

But he did not hand the child over.

"Don't you know anything about babies?" Billie snapped. "Can't you see he wants Jaina?"

"Yeah," Joy agreed. "Give him to his mommy."

Both Eliot and Barney took a careful step forward, their assertive stances telling Connor they were prepared to do whatever it might take to rescue Liam from this stranger. His eyes narrowed and darkened as he searched each serious face.

A moment of silence passed as the row of defensive men and women moved closer. Connor stood his ground. "I'm the boy's uncle," he said through clenched teeth. "What's wrong with you people?"

"Don't make any difference if you're the Pied Piper," Eliot said, "if the kid wants Jaina...."

What's with these people? Connor wondered. He looked at Liam, who had been temporarily distracted from wanting to be in Jaina's arms by the intensity of the verbal sparring. The baby frowned as he studied his uncle's serious face, then stuck a damp, chubby finger into his mouth. "Dih," he mumbled around it. "Dih-dih?"

One look at the little fellow had been all it took to stir a strong territorial reaction; the child was *his* flesh and blood, not these strangers', and the last thing he wanted was to hand him over on some infantile whim. And yet that was exactly what Liam seemed to want. The questions warred inside him: satisfy his own need, or the baby's? He'd never been in a position like this before and didn't quite know what to make of it. Because the real question—in everyone's mind, it seemed—was what was best for *Liam?*

The baby answered for them by giving one last squeal, then diving toward Jaina. Connor's eyes darkened even more as he handed the baby over. "This place is a madhouse. How do you expect to—"

Jaina, hugging Liam and smiling into his face, held up a hand to silence Buchanan. "We've had a minor emergency, that's all. The dishwasher sprang a leak, and the main drain is clogged, so there was no place for the water to go." She met his eyes to say, "I know it seems like a madhouse right now, but things like this don't happen every day. In fact," she said, looking around at her friends for support, "ordinarily, our Chili Pot is a pretty quiet place."

"I'll say," Eliot agreed.

"Downright dull," Billie put in.

"Boring," Joy said.

Ray gave a yawn and Rita stifled one as if to prove it.

Connor met each pair of eyes in turn. "Now why do I find that difficult to believe?"

If Liam *had* been in any danger, it was apparent any one of them would have fought to the death to save him. That fact should have riled him further. So why was he feeling strangely calmed and satisfied?

He pocketed both hands. "I'd call you a 'see no evil, hear no evil, speak no evil' bunch," he said, a half smile slanting his mouth, "but there are too many monkeys…and too many monkeyshines."

Rita stood as tall as her five-feet-two-inch frame would allow and lifted her chin. "We're a family, Mr. Buchanan, and families stick together."

Family. The woman couldn't possibly know what the word meant to him. His smile vanished as he ground his molars together to hide his discomfort. "Right or wrong?"

She narrowed her dark eyes and rested a fist on her hip. "I can only answer half your question since we haven't done anything wrong. We believe what it says in the book of Jeremiah. 'Walk ye in all the ways I have commanded you, that it may be well unto you.'"

"And blessed are those who are blameless," he translated another verse, "who walk in the law of the Lord." He gave her a hard stare. "But unless they've rewritten the Scriptures, Mrs. Chandelle, none of us is blameless…except Jesus."

Rita's mouth dropped open in silent shock.

"What's the matter?" Connor asked Jaina's mother. "Surprised I'm a believer?"

"Well…well, yes, frankly," she stammered. "I suppose I am."

A loud sucking sound captured everyone's attention. "That's got it!" Barney hollered. "The main drain's cleared!" Within minutes, a few puddles were all that was left of the miniflood.

"Mom, why don't you take Liam and Mr. Buchanan up to my apartment while the rest of us clean up this mess. I can't afford for the tiles to lift and loosen and—"

"Of course you can afford it." Rita took Liam. She gave Jaina a look that said, "Watch what you say around this guy, will you?"

"There's lemonade in the fridge upstairs," Jaina told them, heading for the kitchen, "and I baked chocolate chip cookies last night."

Connor didn't miss the understanding expression that connected mother to daughter. It told him they shared a love, deep and abiding, that allowed them to read one another's thoughts, to sense one another's feelings. A spark of envy shot through him for he'd never known love like that, not as a boy and certainly not as a man. Another spark—determination this time—flashed through him. *Liam deserves to be loved like that, and I'm going to see to it that he is!* he silently vowed.

Rita started for the stairs. "Take your time, sweetie," she called over her shoulder. "We'll be just fine." She gave Connor a look that defied him to challenge her and added, "Won't we, Mr. Buchanan?"

Connor's brow furrowed slightly. "Sure. Why wouldn't we be?"

"If you'll just follow me…"

At the bottom of the steps, Connor wiped his feet on a mat that said, "Hi! I'm Mat!" Smiling, he climbed the highly polished wood steps and thought of the moment that Jaina had spotted him in the diner. He could think of only one reason she'd seemed so terrified at the mere sight of him. *Brace yourself, Buchanan. She's going to fight like a mama tiger for that boy.*

His attention was immediately diverted by the paintings that lined the left side of the stairway. Landscapes—farms, mostly—all signed JCC. Though each was a different size and shape, nestled in its own unique frame, one thing repeated itself in every picture: a two-story farmhouse. *His* house!

Did she really think he'd fall for such an obvious plot to gain his approval? Did she honestly believe he wouldn't see through her attempt to win him over?

You're not making sense, man, he chided himself. *No sense at all.* There had to be two dozen paintings here, he began to reason. Even if she'd had time to find out what kind of house he lived in, she hadn't had time to put it into all these paintings, not with running a restaurant and taking care of Liam.

Liam.

He looked up, saw that the baby was staring directly at him. The child wasn't smiling. Nor was he frowning. Rather, he seemed content to merely study the man in the soggy-cuffed pants whose shoes squished with every step. "Who are you?" his big blue eyes seemed to ask, "and what is your interest in me?" Even if Liam had been seven years old instead of seven months, Connor couldn't have explained. How would he describe a feeling so deep and so intense that he himself didn't understand it?

Rita dug in her pocket and came up with the key to Jaina's apartment. "Well now," she said, stepping inside and gently depositing Liam in a fifties-style playpen, "would my boy like a bottle of juice?"

"Dih," he responded, pointing at Connor. "Dih?"

She pulled dry baby clothes from a bureau drawer and began stuffing Liam into them. "Isn't this a pretty dresser?" she said, more to herself than to Connor. "Jaina bought it just last week at a yard sale. Had no idea what she'd keep in it." She gave Liam's tummy a playful poke, smiled warmly when he giggled in response. "And then this little fella came along. I'd say it was the Lord's hand at work if you hadn't—"

Botched up Jaina's plans to be a mommy? he finished silently.

Rita clamped her lips together, then smiled stiffly. "How about a nice glass of lemonade? Jaina makes it fresh-squeezed, you know."

He did his best to mask his annoyance. Fresh-squeezed? In this day and age? Yeah, right. "Lemonade sounds great," he said, his big hand ruffling the baby's golden curls. "Can't recall when I last had fresh-squeezed."

"Keep an eye on him while I pour, will you?" she asked, handing Liam to Connor.

And while she rummaged in the kitchen, Connor meandered around the apartment. "I'll bet you can't find a speck of dust in this place even if you gave it the white-glove test," he whispered into Liam's ear. But it didn't have the look of a room that had been recently scrubbed to impress him. Rather, it seemed to Connor that Jaina lived by the old adage that everything should have—and be in—its proper place.

She'd managed to make the huge space seem intimate, cozy even, by arranging overstuffed sofas and chairs in the center of the room. She'd offset the almost antiseptic white walls and cream-colored upholstery with bright pillows, candles, more artwork....

Here in the living room, as in the stairway, her paintings were of country settings, and the Victorian had found its way into each. In some, the house dominated the canvas; in others, it occupied a background space. Connor stepped up to the one hanging above the player piano. "Look at that, Liam," he said softly, pointing. "See that pretty house?"

It sat in the upper right-hand corner, high on a rocky hillside, and though it was barely larger than a postage stamp, the detail was incredible. Lace curtains hung in every window. Twin bent-willow rockers sat on the covered, wraparound porch, a brass door knocker gleamed from the red front door, a gray-striped tabby lay curled up on the welcome mat, and a cardinal perched on the white picket gate. Except for the cat and the bird, it was *his* house, right down to the rope swing in the giant oak out front. It had been there when he'd bought the house, and although he had no kids—and doubted he ever would—he couldn't bring himself to take it down.

He'd gone to great pains to keep his home address and phone number private. How had she managed to find out where he lived...*how* he lived—in such a short time? She just couldn't have. She hadn't had time to dig up the information and create dozens of paintings in the limited time they'd known one another. So how did she know so much about his house?

It was the most amazing, uncanny coincidence of his life. Or was it a sign of some kind, one he should pay attention to? His cynical side shook off the notion.

"Well, she's no Rembrandt," he told Liam, "but she ain't bad, is she?"

The baby wasn't in the least bit interested in Jaina's artwork. Wasn't interested in Connor's critique, either. Kicking both feet, he reached for the piano keys. "Mmumm-mmumm," he said. "Mmumm-mmumm."

Connor sat on the piano bench and placed Liam's fingers on the keys. "Ready for piano lessons, little guy?" he asked, chuckling.

"Dih." With surprising deftness, Liam gently depressed the keys one at a time. "Dih," he said again as the pleasant notes drifted throughout the apartment.

Connor's eyes were drawn back to the picture. She couldn't have known it was his house. If she had, she wouldn't have put it on a hillside in one painting, in a valley in the next, on a rocky outcropping in another.

Something happened to him as he sat there, gazing at Jaina's creation, something simultaneously wonderful and frightening. He'd gotten the same sensation when she'd nearly fainted in his office and he'd held her in his arms for the tick in time it had taken to help her to a chair. He'd put his hands on *her,* so why was *he* feeling touched?

The sensation washed over him again, the feeling that she'd known him, and he her, for a long, long time. He'd never experienced anything quite like it before, didn't know if he *liked* the experience. For even while the connection made him feel as though he belonged, it made him feel vulnerable, out of control.

He shook his head, held Liam a little tighter, kissed the top of his head. *Get hold of yourself, man,* he cautioned himself, *'cause one thing is certain. If you want to win in court, you'd better stay in control.* Complete *control at all times.*

Connor stood and headed for the French doors on the opposite side of the room. Outside, a wide deck overlooked a thick stand of yellow and white pines that swayed in the steamy breeze. Liam, who'd caught sight of a toy in the playpen, began to bounce up and down. "Buffoo?" he asked, a finger aiming in the direction of the desired plaything. "Buffoo?"

He put the baby back into the playpen, and the child grabbed what appeared to be a hand-carved wooden truck. An assortment of new toys surrounded him. If she'd brought in a playpen, no doubt she'd also secured a crib, a high chair, a car seat...everything a social worker would deem necessary to care for a baby Liam's age. Connor ruefully shook his head and lifted one eyebrow. He had to give her credit. She was good, real good. She'd gone to a lot of trouble to make herself look like a woman who deserved to win a Mother of the Year trophy. Either that, or...

Did he like and admire her...or didn't he?

"Dih-dih," Liam said, holding up his arms.

Connor picked him up again. "Can't make up your mind whether you want in or out, eh?" he asked, gently chucking the baby's chin. "I know the feeling."

Liam offered him the truck.

"Say, this is nice. Where'd you get it?"

"My husband made it for him," Rita explained. She'd entered the room, holding a baby bottle in one hand, balancing a tray on the other. "He's very handy. Fairly artistic, too."

"So that's how Jaina comes by her talents." He nodded toward the paintings. "Did she study art in school?"

Rita giggled. "No, no. Didn't have time for art lessons. Everything you see is the result of God-given talent."

"Can't help but notice that the same house is in every picture. Is that where she grew up?"

Liam, having seen the bottle, began flapping his arms. "Buffoo. Mmumm. Dih!" he said, reaching for it.

Laughing softly, Rita took the baby from Connor's arms. "No, but she would have loved to. It's her dream house."

"Her…"

"Her dream house. You dream, don't you, Mr. Buchanan? Every Sunday, she combs the real-estate section of the newspaper, looking for something that even comes close." She headed for the bedroom. "One of these days, she's going to find it. I wouldn't be the least bit surprised if when she does, she sells The Chili Pot and spends the rest of her life painting and growing flowers."

Connor pocketed both hands and nodded. He could almost picture her in that house, long, thick hair tied up in a ponytail as she stood, paintbrush in hand, at her easel, fresh-cut flowers from her garden in vases all around her…. He'd bought the place, held the deed to it, but could it have been intended for *her?*

"Would you like to see where Liam sleeps, Mr. Buchanan?"

He blinked himself back into the present, then followed Rita through the arched doorway. Several things—from the sensible way she'd dressed each time he'd seen her to her obvious belief in hard work—made him believe the furnishings would be plain and simple. Instead, an ornate four-poster dominated the space. A mahogany chifforobe and matching bureau stood side by side against one wall, a small writing desk and chair against another. A thickly napped blue Persian rug dominated the center of the gleaming hardwood floor, while wide-slatted wooden blinds covered the double-hung windows. Here, as in the living room, she'd brightened the backdrop of creamy white walls with multicolored afghans, lamp shades and knickknacks.

Liam's crib stood beside her bed, and next to it, a low-seated, broad-backed rocker. The beady black eyes of a fuzzy teddy bear peeked out from the baby blanket folded neatly over one chair arm. He could picture her sitting there, tucking the blanket around Liam, who'd be snuggled against her bosom, chubby fingers wrapped around her slender ones, hugging the bear as she rocked him to sleep.

It was a lovely picture.

Too lovely.

Cut it out! he scolded himself. *You don't even know the woman.*

Rita snapped the blinds shut, throwing the sunny room into chocolaty darkness as Liam settled in for his afternoon nap.

Connor followed her back into the living room. "Should I close the door so our talking won't keep him awake?"

"He sleeps like a log."

She said it like a woman who knew Liam well. A pang of guilt shot through him. *He* was Liam's blood kin; *he* should be the one spouting everyday facts about him.

When she'd come into the room earlier, Rita had placed the tray, bearing a plate of cookies and two glasses of lemonade, in the center of the coffee table. She leaned down and helped herself to a cookie and a glass, settled on one end of the couch and tucked her legs up under her. "Have a seat, Mr. Buchanan. Jaina won't be much longer, I'm sure." Smiling fondly, she shook her head. "She can't stand to be away from the baby for more than a few minutes. Sometimes it seems like he's permanently attached to her hip!" A soft, motherly chuckle punctuated her statement.

He settled into the overstuffed chair, where he could see the bedroom doorway. "I may not have been the first to admit it, but I'll admit it now. Jaina's been good for the boy. It's obvious she's doing everything she can for Liam. I don't know how I'll ever repay her."

Rita's smile vanished, and in its place she wore an angry frown. "Repay her?"

"I assure you, I didn't mean that as an insult. I only meant that I appreciate what she's done…what she's doing—" he glanced at the bedroom doorway "—at least until the legalities are finalized."

The woman lifted her chin. "You sound awfully sure of yourself, Mr. Buchanan. How can you be so certain the courts will appoint *you* Liam's legal guardian?"

He shrugged. "I'm his only living relative. It's been my experience that in cases like this—"

"Please don't take this the wrong way," she interrupted, "you being a lawyer and all, but I know you've read Kirstie's note. She made it clear where she wanted her son to live." Rita tilted her head slightly to add, "Doesn't that matter to you at all?"

Connor leaned forward, balanced his elbows on his knees and clasped his hands tightly in the space between. Only then did he meet Rita's eyes. "Please don't take this the wrong way, *you being Jaina's mother and all,* but we can do this one of two ways. The easy way, or the hard way."

There was no question in his mind that Mrs. Chandelle understood his meaning. He watched as she glared openly at him, lips trembling as she struggled to keep a civil tongue in her head.

The door opened, then closed quietly. "I see you've put Liam down for his nap," Jaina said, breezing into the room. "It's a little early. But then, he had quite a morning, so I suppose it's all right." She smiled at Connor. "Did you two have a nice visit before he conked out?"

He had made up his mind on the way over here to take a hard-line approach toward the woman who wanted to deprive him of a life with Liam. Despite his resolve, he returned her friendly smile. "We had a few minutes."

"Isn't he the most precious thing you've ever seen?" Her eyes sparkled, her smile sweetened, her voice sang.

His back stiffened in reaction; he'd been the unwilling victim of womanly charms before. Had been the victim of not-so-charming wiles, too. He'd learned the hard way that smiles, tears, pouts and venomous glares could be turned on and off like a water faucet to ensure that the so-called ''lady'' would get her way. He didn't know why Jaina wanted Liam, but she did. To stop the ticking of the proverbial biological clock? To fulfill some typically female need to win?

Looking into her open, honest face, Connor was forced to acknowledge another possibility, another *probability:* she genuinely loved the baby.

He'd dismissed his earlier suspicions about her. He considered character judgment part of his business, and she didn't seem the type who would deceive him. Well, he wouldn't hurt her, either…if he didn't have to.

Connor didn't relish the idea of waging judicial war against this diminutive woman who seemed to care so deeply for his nephew. She either loved him, he thought, or she'd missed her calling and deprived Hollywood of one of the world's greatest actresses.

She glanced at his half-empty glass. ''Would you like a refill?''

Connor blinked. Met her eyes, and again smiled against his will. ''No. It was terrific, but I've had plenty, thanks.''

She sat on the other end of the sofa. ''Well, what do you think of him?'' Grinning like a proud mama, Jaina enthused, ''Isn't he adorable? And what a smartie! He'll be talking and walking long before other kids his age, I just know it. And the doctor—''

''The doctor?'' he interrupted. ''Is everything all right?''

Jaina waved his concern away. ''Of course it is. I didn't mean to scare you. It's, well, he'd been through so much, what with the long trip and all, that I thought it would be a good idea to bring him in for a checkup.'' She shoved a damp curl behind her ear. "I mean, what if something was wrong and Kirstie was too distraught to notice?"

"Wrong? Like what?"

She shrugged. "Nothing serious, really, but a milk intolerance, for instance." Another shrug. "It's such a relief knowing he's perfectly, one hundred percent healthy."

Milk intolerance? He'd never even heard of such a thing. Under the same circumstances, Connor doubted he'd have thought to take the baby to a pediatrician. A male versus female thing? he wondered. He'd heard the age-old theory that mothers were natural-born nurturers. Not that he knew it from personal experience, his mother being as cold as she was and all.... "How many people know about Liam? In a professional capacity, I mean."

"The doctor—" she began counting on her fingers "—and the police, of course."

"The police?"

"Sure. Liam was exhausted that first night, so the very next morning, I called a friend of mine—he's a social worker with the Department of Social Services, you know—to find out what I should do. Skip came right over, told me to call the police so there'd be a record of how the baby came to be in my, ah, possession."

"You have a friend with the Department of Social Services?"

Jaina nodded. "I've known Skip since..." She hesitated. "For years," she finished carefully.

Connor made note of the way her smile faded and the bright light in her eyes dimmed during her moment of hesitation. She was hiding something...something that seemed to be causing her a great deal of discomfort, and he aimed to find out what. He had enough familiarity with adoption proceedings to know they were rarely cut-and-dry. Just as in custody cases, folks would sometimes fight ruthlessly over a child, with both sides willing to wage full-scale, no-holds-barred war to win. Connor didn't like the idea of putting Jaina through that. But if that's what it took…

Because he was a practical man, if nothing else. Sure, he owned a fifteen-room house on a three-acre property in one of Howard County's most prestigious neighborhoods. And true, his legal practice provided him with more money than he could spend in his lifetime.

But he was divorced. Had developed a bit of a reputation for being a ladies' man. Even his peers called him a shark because he'd defended clients accused of the most heinous crimes—spousal abuse, murder, kidnapping—and secured acquittals more often than not.

He was realistic enough to know he'd have a fight on his hands, trying to beat a woman like Jaina Chandelle in a courtroom. If the judge issued his decree based solely on outward appearances, she'd win hands down. Pretty and petite, with an angelic voice and the smile of a saint, she was a hard worker who could prove to the court that she had an army of friends and relatives standing by to help if and when she needed it.

The way he saw it, if he wanted Liam—and Connor wanted him more than anything—he had no choice but to use every weapon at his disposal. And the secret she harbored, he believed, might very well be the deadliest weapon of all.

He'd faced enough hostile witnesses in his day to know how far to push, how hard, and when. This was not the time for confrontation. "So," he said, smiling, "what does this Skip person say your chances of adopting Liam are?"

Her gentle expression hardened, and Jaina sat up straighter. "He advised me to keep you away from Liam, if you want to know the truth," she snapped, "but I didn't think it was fair, to you or Liam."

Connor expelled a bitter chuckle. "Not fair? Why?"

She seemed amazed he needed to be told something so

obvious, so elementary. "Because you're *family,* of course."

That word again. Connor bristled as it echoed in his ears.

"I may be cutting my own throat to admit this," she began slowly, "but I happen to love that little boy more than I imagined it was possible to love another human being. You can ask my mother. I didn't want to keep him…at first."

That surprised him, and he said so.

"It's true," Rita confirmed. "She was dead set against the idea."

"But…why?"

Focusing on her hands, clasped tightly in her lap, Jaina took a deep breath. "I…I have my reasons," she said softly. Lifting her gaze to his, she continued, "It was past closing time when Kirstie left the diner. I couldn't shuttle him off to some institution that late at night." Sighing heavily, she closed her eyes. "It was supposed to be one night. Just one night."

"You don't have to tell him any of this, sweetie," Rita interjected, patting her hand. "He's—"

"He's Liam's uncle," she stated matter-of-factly. Jaina sandwiched her mother's hand between hers. "He deserves to be a part of the boy's life."

"So what made you change your mind?" Connor asked quietly. "About keeping Liam, I mean."

She gave him a whimsical smile. "He did." She cut a glance toward the bedroom where the baby was napping.

Rita gazed lovingly at her daughter. "She didn't have a crib that first night, so she dumped her clothes out of a dresser drawer and lined it with a quilt. And would you believe this girl spent the night on the floor?"

"Because I couldn't leave him," Jaina defended.

Connor's eyes narrowed. He hoped they'd rehearsed this little skit just for him because if Jaina was sincere… "But you'd only be, what, three or four feet away."

"I know. But everything about him fascinated me. The way his chest rose and fell when he breathed, the way he puckered his lips now and then, the sweet little sounds he made... He was just so...beautiful!"

There's a time and a place for everything, he reminded himself, biting back anger that seemed to have no source, yet pulsed through him like jolts of electricity. "So you're intent on taking this to court."

In place of the smile was a look of strength and determination. "I know it sounds silly after just a week with him, but I don't have any choice."

Connor stood. "Then I hope you have a good lawyer."

Rita frowned. "Good lawyer? Ha! I believe that's the best example of an oxymoron I've ever heard."

Jaina turned to her mother with a warning glance. "Mom, please..."

Connor ignored Rita's insult. "I only meant that legal battles can be lengthy and expensive, Mrs. Chandelle."

"I have the rest of my life," Jaina asserted, standing and looking at him hard. "As for money, I've saved a little for a rainy day."

He acknowledged that he'd be doing his own research, that he'd be representing himself. The hearing would cost him next to nothing, but Jaina...

Guilt hammered inside him as Connor walked toward the door. "I'll get started first thing in the morning, then."

"Started?" Rita asked. "Started on what?"

"Paperwork. Call my office and let Pearl know who your lawyer is, so I can mail him the filings."

Jaina stood near the door, wringing her hands in front of her. "Will your...your paperwork spell out where Liam will stay in the interim?"

"It will." For motives he could neither name nor understand, he felt like a heel for causing her even a moment's fear. "Don't worry, I won't bother filing for temporary custody because the judge more than likely will decide Liam should stay right where he is, until the final court date anyway.'' He met her eyes. "Frankly, I think that's best for him, all things considered.''

She nodded, then sent him a trembly smile. "I appreciate your honesty, Connor.'' Jaina extended a hand.

Connor hesitated, unable to believe she could bring herself to do such a thing under the circumstances. She had a surprisingly strong grip for a woman her size. Another item on his "Reasons To Like Jaina Chandelle'' list.

"I just want you to know,'' she said, "that if I win, you'll always be welcome here.'' She straightened her shoulders. "I hope you'll extend me the same courtesy if you—''

"If he wins,'' Rita snapped, "Liam loses.''

Again he pretended he hadn't heard Rita's barb. He was still holding Jaina's hand and could barely believe it when he heard himself say, "You can see him anytime you like. That goes without saying.'' One of the first rules a defense attorney learns is to keep his strategies to himself. So why had he exposed so much of his plan to the enemy?

She released him and stuffed the hand he'd held into her apron pocket. "Would you look at me?'' she asked, running her other hand through still-damp curls. "I'm a soggy mess. What must you be…?'' Biting her lower lip, she sent him a nervous smile. "You won't use this against me in court, will you?''

He returned the smile. "What…that as for your being a mother, I think you're all wet?'' Jaina nodded, and he read the hopeful expression on her face. "I fight to win, and usually I do,'' he admitted, "but I believe in fighting fair. If I win, it'll be because I deserve to. Dirty tricks will not be on the agenda.'' His earlier thought—of using her secret against her—resurfaced in his mind. *Dirty trick,* he asked himself, *or semantics?*

She opened the door. "I'll call your office, then, once I've hired someone.''

"Good. And I'll call you to arrange another visit with Liam soon." He glanced toward the bedroom. "He's quite a kid."

Jaina agreed. "Speaking of kids...have you had any luck locating Kirstie?"

"The investigator I hired did some computer tracking, found out who her doctor was. She'd been going for treatments twice a week before coming to Maryland." He looked at Jaina, at Rita, then Jaina again. "She hasn't been back."

Rita's hands flew to her mouth. "Oh, no. You don't suppose that means..."

Connor slowly shook his head. "I don't know...I hope not."

Jaina laid a hand on his forearm. "We'll all pray that you find her." She squeezed the arm gently. "She needs to be with family at a time like this."

There was that word again. Connor stepped into the hall.

"If you find her, will you let us know?"

He nodded. "Sure thing."

This wasn't the way he'd intended for things to go. Not even close. He'd planned to leave here, feeling secure in the knowledge that he'd made her see how futile it would be to fight him for Liam. And what had he done instead? Advised her to get a good attorney!

He started down the steps, stopped, then turned to face her. *Say something businesslike,* he told himself, *something to end things on a professional note, like "Don't wait too long to get a lawyer."*

He met her big dark eyes—eyes still damp with concern over his niece's disappearance—and was reminded of what she'd told her mother. "He's Liam's uncle," she'd said in her no-nonsense way. "He deserves to be a part of the boy's life." The memory of that killed the last of his resolve.

"Thanks, Jaina," he said instead.

"For what?"

You really don't know? he asked silently. *For being you!*
"For the lemonade, the hospitality, letting me see
Liam...."

With him now two steps down from the landing, they
were eye-to-eye. She smiled. "Anytime. When Liam becomes mine, I know I'll need to provide a place at my table
for his closet kin. You know where to find him. No need
to call first, because—"

"I'm family?" He didn't miss her hopeful statement.

"Exactly."

It was as though someone had sneaked up behind him
and nailed his shoes to the step. Connor couldn't seem to
make himself turn away from her warm gaze.

"Well," she offered, rescuing him, "I'd better change
into some dry clothes and get back to work."

He hurried down the steps. "Thanks again."

"No thanks necessary," he heard her say as he stepped
into the diner, "but you're welcome all the same."

"'Fear not, for I will be with you,'" Connor recited
Isaiah quietly to himself, "'the rivers shall not overwhelm
you, and when you walk through fire, you shall not be
burned, nor will the flame consume you.'"

He wondered if, within the pages of his Bible, he'd find
a passage that assured him protection against falling in love
with the enemy....

Jaina locked up The Chili Pot and turned out the lights
as Liam babbled nonstop in her arms. She felt Connor Buchanan's presence as she climbed the stairs. Though there
was no physical evidence that he'd been in her apartment,
it seemed he'd left a sliver of himself here, a fragment
there, to remind her of him.

Soon, she'd be standing toe-to-toe with him in a courtroom, fighting for Liam. The dilemma: how to defend herself against a man she genuinely liked.

Though she considered herself a peaceable sort on the whole, Jaina had participated in her share of disputes, debates, and arguments. Calm, reasonable discussion, she believed, could only take place between rational, mature individuals. If an adversary didn't respect her right to express an opinion, she wouldn't respect his. She'd never started a fight, but she'd never run from one, either. "If you have right on your side," her father had always asserted, "you can't lose."

But was she right to fight for Liam?

Or did Buchanan have right on *his* side?

"'The way of the righteous is level,'" she quoted Isaiah. "'Thou dost make smooth the path of righteousness. In the path of judgments, Lord, we wait for Thee.'"

As she got Liam into his pajamas, he cooed and gurgled contentedly. She felt as though he'd been a part of her life *all* of her life. Taking care of him had seemed natural and normal—routine—and no more work than brushing her teeth or combing her hair. What would her world be like without him, now that she'd grown so accustomed to having him near?

She couldn't bear thinking of the possibility.

If she lost the court battle, would Buchanan really allow her to remain a part of Liam's life? Why should he? She wasn't blood kin.

But he *had* to, she thought, biting her trembling lower lip. "I'll just have to believe in the power of hope," she said softly. God had promised to be her steadfast anchor, her forerunner, her refuge, hadn't He?

After filling a baby bottle with milk, she microwaved it for a few seconds to take off the chill, screwed on the top then shook it well. Nestling in the chair where Buchanan had sat mere hours ago, she held Liam close.

He wrapped both hands around the bottle, sucking greedily from the nipple. "'Hush, little baby, don't say a word,'" she crooned. "'Mama's gonna buy you a mockingbird.'"

Smiling with his eyes only, Liam continued to drink.

"'And if that mockingbird don't sing, Mama's gonna buy you a diamond ring.'"

She finished the song, and another, and halfway through the third lullaby, his eyelids began to flutter as he struggled to stay awake. But soon his jaw relaxed and he let go of the nipple, setting a gurgling stream of tiny bubbles loose in the bottle. Jaina got slowly to her feet, tiptoed into the bedroom and eased the baby into his crib. He stirred slightly, then settled into a peaceful sleep. She gazed at his sweet face and tears filled her eyes. "In my heart, he's already mine, Lord. If You truly don't want me to have a child of my own, please know that I'm available for this one."

Several years ago, in an attempt to comfort and console her, her pastor had suggested she read Psalm 113:9. The verse had not given her hope, had not provided solace as she fretted about whether she'd ever marry and have children like a normal woman.

She found solace in God's Word, and in doing His work, teaching Sunday school, helping to prepare children's services, preparing food for the potluck suppers and labeling products to be sold at white elephant sales and volunteering for the pastor's various rehabilitation programs. Helping others, she discovered, kept her mind off her past and her lost dreams.

Now, with Liam safely sleeping in the next room, Jaina took the black leather volume from the shelf and found the verse. "'He gives the barren woman a home,'" she read softly, "'making her the joyous mother of children. Praise the Lord!'" The verse that had once been the source of bitter tears now gave her hope as she took heart in the possibility that with Liam she had a chance, at least, at motherhood.

Carrying the Holy Book to the overstuffed chair, Jaina did something she hadn't done since she was a little girl.

Every night before turning in, instead of getting on her knees and asking the Lord to bless her parents, her stuffed animals, her teacher, like so many other Christian children, she'd sit on the edge of her bed, the Bible in her lap and, closing her eyes tight, let the book fall open on its own. Her forefinger would draw an invisible spiral that started above her head and stopped on a crisp, gilt-edged page. Only then would she open her eyes to read what she believed to be the verse the Lord had chosen for her and think about how the passage fitted her life.

When she opened her eyes this time, Jaina's finger was resting on Genesis 2:18. "'It is not good that the man should be alone.'" She closed the book, opened it again, read the first verse she saw. "'Oh that his left hand were under my head,'" she read from the Song of Songs, "'and that his right hand embraced me!'" Another flip of the wrist provided a line from Proverbs. "'House and wealth are inherited from fathers, but a prudent wife is from the Lord.'"

This wasn't working the way it used to, Jaina thought, smiling wryly at every romance-related passage. She decided to give it one more try. This time, the Bible opened to Ecclesiastes, 4:9. "'Two are better than one, because they have a good reward for their toil. For if they fall, one will lift up his fellow; but woe to him who is alone when he falls and has not another to lift him up. Again, if two lie together, they are warm; but how can one be warm alone?'"

She had a strange feeling these verses *were* messages from God. But why? And what had He intended her to learn from them?

Jaina reread the last verse. "'Two are better than one...'" Did it mean that together, she and Connor would be better for Liam than either of them could be alone?

The thought struck a reverberating chord in her heart. Strange as it seemed, the idea *did* make sense....

Stop it, she commanded herself. *Stop being a silly, overly romantic girl! Grow up and face the music. If you want this child, you're going to have to fight for him.*

Still...the idea of raising Liam *with* Connor instead of against him had a certain appeal that she hadn't thoroughly embraced. For one thing, if they had a...*relationship*...he might not be so certain to dig up her sorry past.

Jaina hadn't felt much like reading the Bible since the tragic night that had changed the course of her life. Her faith had been badly shaken, her trust all but snuffed out, because the way she saw it, God had gone back on His word. He'd promised that if she believed a thing strongly enough, it would be done. Well, she had believed He would help her, so why hadn't He? Confused, angry, afraid and hurt because she believed He'd abandoned her, she'd turned from Him. Until now, nothing had seemed important enough to encourage her to reestablish a relationship with Him.

Liam's well-being was important enough. It was more important than *anything.*

She wanted so badly to be his mother—legally, not just in her heart. But she also loved him enough to want what was best for him. Was *she* best for him, a woman with a tainted past? Or was Connor Buchanan?

All her life, she'd heard that the surest way to solve a problem was to lay it at the foot of the cross. Jaina closed the Bible and returned it to the bookshelf, confident for the first time in a week, because it was right to leave the matter in the Lord's capable hands.

Something told her that sooner or later, God would let her know what He wanted her to do—fight for Liam, or step aside and let Buchanan raise the boy, or suggest the "togetherness" idea.

Her father had a favorite Bible verse. "He will not let

you be tempted beyond your strength, but with the temptation will provide a way of escape, that you may be able to endure it.''

She would adopt First Corinthians 10:13 as her own chosen verse. Because, she admitted, slipping into bed, if the Lord decided it was Buchanan who should parent Liam, Jaina was going to need all the strength she could muster.

Chapter Five

Jaina ran a hand through perspiration-matted hair and said a quick prayer of thanks that he'd phoned instead of dropping by as she'd suggested. Her evening of weeding the flower beds out back had cost her one bruised knee, two broken fingernails and a scraped palm. She hadn't minded Skip seeing her this way when he'd come over earlier, so why did it matter what Connor Buchanan might have thought of her appearance? She searched for a reason she could live with. *Because Skip's opinion of you won't affect the judge's ruling, that's why.* There was a lot of truth in that, but not the whole truth....

"Sorry to be calling so late," he said, breaking into her thoughts, "I thought I'd take a chance Liam might still be up."

If she didn't know better, she'd say he sounded lonely. But how could that be? she wondered. He was...he was *Connor Buchanan!* "I'd wake him for you, but he's had quite a day. I bought him one of those big blue wading pools, and he splashed away the whole afternoon. And tonight, he had his first gardening adventure."

He chuckled. "I'll bet he dug in for all he was worth."

Jaina giggled. "Those petunias didn't know what hit them. I found dirt in crevices I didn't even know he *had!*"

They chatted about the heat and humidity, about the Orioles' chances of playing in the World Series, about the Ravens' star quarterback sustaining an injury that might keep him from supporting his team in the fall.

"So, what do you guys do to celebrate the Fourth of July?"

Jaina thought she detected a note of hopefulness in his voice but couldn't determine if he "hoped" to have Liam all to himself, or "hoped" she'd include him in the family's plans. "We have all sorts of traditions," she said. "For one, we start the day with a red, white and blue breakfast."

"Red, white and blue?"

"Raspberries, blueberries and whipped cream on our pancakes. Then we head for the parade. No matter where we were stationed, Dad always managed to find us a marching band and a majorette. Then it's home again for hot dogs and burgers on the grill. And once our bloated bellies deflate a bit, it's off to the fireworks."

"Sounds like fun."

The hopefulness in his voice had turned to disappointment, she detected. Surely he didn't really expect her to invite *him.* Her mother would probably ring her neck for asking, but…

"What do *you* do on the Fourth?"

There was a long pause before he said, "Once in a while, I take Pearl up on her invitation to spend the day with her family."

"Only once in a while?"

"She has four kids, eleven grandchildren and four great-grandchildren."

"Goodness, she doesn't look old enough to be a great-grandmother! What's her secret?"

"She claims to walk two miles a day, and her kids tell me she reads like it's going out of style."

"If that's what keeps her so young and alert, I'm going to walk and read more, starting right now!"

Connor laughed. "She's a dynamo all right."

"So…why would you ever avoid spending time with a woman like that?"

"Because she's got a huge family. Sometimes it seems like half of Ellicott City is packed into her yard."

"But…that sounds wonderful."

"It is, in a way." He hesitated. "But it's hard being around all those people when you're not related to a single one."

Connor Buchanan, big news-making attorney, wishing for a family? Jaina couldn't believe her ears. Surely he had parents, siblings other than Kirstie's mother… "I only spoke with Pearl once, and the conversation was admittedly brief, but I got the distinct impression she's the kind of woman who goes out of her way to make folks feel like part of things. I'm sure if she knew you were feeling uncomfortable, she'd—"

"She's a doll, and I know she means well. Trouble is, the more effort she puts into making me feel a part of the family, the more obvious it is that I'm *not*."

She heard him take a deep breath.

"We didn't do picnics and cookouts and parades when I was a kid. Ever. I don't know how I could miss something I never had but…" He paused. "Family stuff scares me to death."

He was either genuinely miserable or doing an excellent job of faking it. But why would he pretend? Some of her most pleasant memories were rooted in family gatherings. No one should be deprived of such happiness. "Why does it scare you?"

If not for the sound of his sigh, she might have thought he'd hung up. "Because," he said, breaking the lengthy silence, "sometimes I wonder if it'll ever be mine to enjoy, except from the sidelines."

If he was anything like her father, Buchanan would rather die than discover he'd made her feel sorry for him. She knew how to comfort her father at times like this, but Jaina had only exchanged a few words with Connor Buchanan. She wanted to say something soothing, but she didn't know him well enough to choose the right words. What if what she said insulted rather than reassured him?

Hold your tongue, Jaina. You can't risk riling him.

But even as she thought it, Jaina knew the reason she didn't want to hurt him had nothing to do with the adoption case. She didn't want to hurt him because she was beginning to feel a strong emotional attachment for him. Already.

He began to chuckle softly.

"What's so funny?"

"You."

Me? "But I didn't say a word."

"It wasn't what you said. It's what you *didn't* say."

"I don't get it."

Another long moment passed. "Maybe I'll stop by to see Liam on the Fourth. Just for half an hour or so."

Pursing her lips, Jaina ran the options through her mind.

She could say it wasn't a good idea for him to see Liam on such a busy day. She could tell him to come on over just for a while as he'd suggested.

Or she could do what she knew to be the right thing, the Christian thing. "Look, why don't you plan to spend the day with us? I'm sure Liam would love it, and I could use help lugging him around. He's a solid little guy even if he is only seven months old, you know."

He was holding the phone with his left hand. She knew because the quiet was so complete she could hear the ticking of his watch.

Finally, he said, "The whole day?"

"Why not?"

Again, silence.

What if he has plans? she asked herself, feeling her cheeks redden. *He's a good-looking, successful guy. Maybe he's turned Pearl down because…* "If you…if you have a date, feel free to bring her along," she said. It surprised her a little to admit how difficult it had been to say that. Surprised her a lot to admit to feeling jealous. Jaina forced a note of cheeriness into her voice that she didn't feel. "The more, the merrier, I always say."

"I don't have *plans,*" he said, overemphasizing the last word. Then, in a softer, almost pleading voice, "Are you sure it'll be all right?"

He reminded her of the seven-year-old she'd found wandering the Columbia Mall a couple of weeks back. She'd stayed with the boy until Security found his mother. He'd fought tears the entire time, repeatedly apologizing for being such a bother. "Why wouldn't it be all right?" she asked Connor.

"Well…I get the feeling I'm not one of your mother's favorite people."

Put a hammer in the man's hand, Jaina told herself. *Can he hit the old nail on the head, or what!* In this case, a fib was far kinder than the truth, and so Jaina said, "She doesn't know you very well, that's all."

"Neither do you."

He loved Liam. At least, she was pretty sure he did. How else could she describe the look that came over his face whenever the baby was around? "I know enough."

"What can I bring?"

"Just yourself, and a big appetite. Mom always goes overboard with the potato salad."

"Okay, then. What time does the parade start?"

"Nine. But it's in Catonsville, and that's a twenty-minute drive from the diner. You'd better be here by at least seven."

"What!"

"You want a red, white and blue breakfast before we stake out curbside seats, don't you?"

Chuckling again, he said, "Yeah, I guess so."

"Then be here by seven. The diner is closed for the holiday, so we'll have the whole day to ourselves."

"I'm looking forward to it. I'll bring the gift I bought for Liam in New York. I left it in the car last time I was there and forgot to get it in all the, uh, confusion."

She remembered the stern, disgusted expression that had darkened his handsome face when he saw the soggy hullabaloo in the diner. "I'm sure he'll love it, whatever it is."

"It's kinda big."

She'd pictured the trinkets folks generally brought home from New York, most of which could fit in a shirt pocket. "How big?"

"Your height, and maybe three times your width."

"Good grief, Connor!" she said, half-laughing, "a toy that big for a baby this small? What were you thinking!"

"Truth is, I *wasn't* thinking."

"When you get here, come to the back door. It won't be locked."

"Gotcha."

"By seven, then."

"Right. Seven."

Jaina hated to hang up, but she couldn't for the life of her understand *why*. "G'bye," she said.

"Bye."

They seemed to be enmeshed in a contest of wills, each daring the other to hang up first. Grinning mischievously, Jaina said, "See you day after tomorrow." She quickly added, "Of course, you're welcome to stop by, or call, or both, before that."

"I know."

"They're calling for rain on the Fourth, you know. Maybe you should bring a jacket."

"Gotcha."

She smiled. "Connor?"

"Yeah…"

"Hang up, okay?"

He chuckled. "Okay."

And he did.

Jaina cut the connection and hung up, glancing at the calendar. A day and a half till the Fourth of July…

She pictured him in his crisp gray suit and sodden wing tips, slogging through the inch of water that had flooded the diner floor. He was kinda handsome, if you liked the button-down type. Did he own any casual clothing… sneakers, shorts, a T-shirt? She hoped so, because wouldn't he look funny at the barbecue in a dapper suit?

Her smile faded as she realized she faced a much more serious question. How would she tell her mother she'd invited the fox into the henhouse? We might not even have to leave the diner to see fireworks, she thought, grinning halfheartedly.

By accepting the invitation, Connor was effectively deep-sixing any case he had against her for being an unfit guardian. He shouldn't like her. Didn't want to like her. Had no reason to like her.

But he did.

She'd been taking such good care of Liam. Showering her parents with love and respect. Treating the men and women who worked for her like family, and from what he'd seen in the moments before Rita led him upstairs to Jaina's apartment, her customers got the same treatment.

Hard *not* to like a woman like that, he thought, tapping his pencil against the legal pad he'd been doodling on, especially with those big brown eyes and a smile that could melt a polar ice cap.

Connor didn't know why he'd accepted her invitation. Visiting Liam was one thing—how else could he ensure the child would get to know him?—but spending a major holiday with Jaina Chandelle was another matter entirely.

He had feelings for her—a hard fact to admit.

But *why?* Because he was lonely? Connor didn't think so. He'd been lonely for years, and it had never inspired him to willingly lay his head on a legal chopping block. *And that's exactly what you'll be doing if you don't get your emotions in check,* he warned himself.

Did she realize that when she aimed that loving, motherly smile at Liam, she made Connor want to fill that dream house of hers with children...*their* children? Did she understand that the sound of her laughter reminded him of birdsongs and wind chimes and a myriad of other delightful, musical things? Did she know that when he looked into those big brown eyes of hers, he wanted to take her in his arms and kiss her?

Connor sighed. She'd stirred up a vat of trouble, that was for sure. Trouble with a capital *T* if he didn't get a handle on his emotions...

Maybe *she* hadn't stirred up the feelings. Maybe what he felt was merely the result of decades of feeling like an outsider. Maybe seeing her with Liam, dispensing maternal warmth and affection...maybe *that* was what had awakened his incredible yearning to start a family of his own.

He remembered the natural, easy way she'd plopped Liam onto her right hip and dotted his chubby cheeks with a hundred sweet kisses. Connor had wanted to stick his head between hers and Liam's to find out for himself if those pink lips felt as soft as they looked.

And what about the time he'd watched her comb slender fingers through the baby's curls? What would it be like, he'd wondered, to have those hardworking yet tender hands rearranging *his* hair?

Once, when Liam had started to fuss for no apparent reason, she'd cuddled him close and looked deep into his eyes. "Aw, don't be grumpy, sweetie," she'd cooed.

"Let's see your beautiful smile. That's it! Where's that shiny new tooth of yours, huh?" Her lovely voice alone would have been enough to soothe the child, but her hands and her lips had gotten into the act, and in no time the baby's whimpers became happy giggles. Standing on the sidelines with his hands in his pockets, Connor had had to force himself to stop wondering what life might be like if she loved *him* that much.

She was everything he'd ever wanted in a woman, and then some. What was wrong with him anyway, that he'd never been able to attract someone like her, someone stable and secure, someone who seemed to like him for who and what he was rather than what he could buy her, or what he could do for her, or where he could take her?

But *was* she so different from all the other women he'd known? *Did* she like him for himself?

Or was the gentle, caring way she treated him directly related to the fact that she wanted something from him?

Liam.

Oh, Lord, he prayed, *don't let it be that.*

Connor closed his eyes and conjured up her image. She was so tiny that the top of her curly-haired head barely reached his chin. His fingertips would probably meet if he wrapped both hands around her waist. He had a dim childhood memory of Christmastime, when his grandmother roasted chestnuts in the fireplace; the sheen and glow of their mahogany shells had fascinated him. Jaina's hair was exactly the color of those chestnuts.

She didn't seem strong enough to lift a basket of feathers, but he'd seen her heft a fifty-pound sack of potatoes as if *it* were the basket of feathers. And her hands... He'd exchanged handshakes with men whose grip didn't possess such power and strength. And yet she'd touched his arm so gently, so tenderly when he told her there'd been no word about Kirstie, that if he hadn't seen it, he might not

have known she'd touched him at all. To have that sweetness aimed in his direction…

Knock it off, Buchanan! Running a hand through his hair,
he took a swig of coffee. *Best thing to do is stop focusing
on her and start focusing on what's good for the kid.* Made
perfect sense, since sooner or later, he and Liam would be
sharing the house.

The house…

Her mother had told him about Jaina's dream. *You
oughta just marry her…make her dream come true and
avoid a court battle at the same time.*

The idea struck him like lightning, knocking him back
in his chair. Talk about comin' out of left field… He swiveled to face the windows. The view of parked cars, shaded
by saplings, was hardly distracting enough to push the con-
cept from his mind. *Marry her? Are you out of your ever-
lovin' head?*

But he couldn't shake it loose.

For the rest of the day, when he least suspected it,
thoughts of Jaina pummeled his mind. As he was sched-
uling a meeting with Judge Thompson, he suddenly envi-
sioned her on his front porch, smiling and waving goodbye
as he headed for the office. Instead of writing "Tuesday,
2:30" in his appointment book, he'd called out, "Pearl, did
you get those tickets for the Toronto Blue Jaina…uh…the
Blue Jays game?"

He called a client to inform him about a postponement,
then had a mental picture of Jaina standing in the foyer of
his house, arms spread wide in welcome when he came in
from work. He almost said "Ah, but it's good to be home,"
into the answering machine. While dictating a letter for
Pearl to type, he imagined Jaina snuggled on the sofa, reading to Liam. He had to rewind the tape and erase the line
that went something like "I couldn't have ordered a better
life if the Sears catalog had a 'Terrific Wives' section."

And when he imagined her in his kitchen, feeding Liam

mashed potatoes and strained carrots, he nearly slammed his fingers in a file drawer.

If he kept this up, he thought, reaching for his coffee, no self-respecting judge would let him adopt a goldfish, let alone a kid.

The telephone rang, startling him so badly he nearly overturned his mug. "Yeah?"

"Hey, Buchanan. How're things?"

Connor balanced an ankle on a knee. "Fine, O'Dell, and you?"

"Well, there's good news and there's bad news. Whaddaya want first?"

He could almost picture Buddy O'Dell, the potbellied, Dallas-born private eye whose impish grin seemed painted on his face. "The usual," Connor said.

"Okay, bad news first." O'Dell proceeded to fill Connor in on the search for Kirstie. He'd reached a dead end at a small hospice in a Chicago suburb. She'd been in Lombard as recently as last week, the detective explained. Rumor had it she'd gone to Milwaukee to spend her last days with a friend. "I followed that lead, but either the friend isn't home or she's avoiding me. I have a couple feelers out in Racine and Kenosha in case they're headed south on their way back to the hospice."

Connor nodded sadly. "If we don't find her..."

"I know, Boss, I know."

There was no mistaking the sympathy in the man's voice. Connor stiffened his back. "So what's the good news?"

"It's about the lady who has your great-nephew." Connor listened as O'Dell rattled some papers. "Says here that once upon a time, she was a singer. Toured the U.S. all by her li'l self with nothin' but a twelve-string guitar to keep her company."

"A singer?"

"Yup. Little over ten years ago. She was doin' pretty good there for a while. Folks musta liked her 'cause she made return performances in just about every place she was booked.''

Connor couldn't seem to wrap his mind around that news. "A *singer?*"

"Uh-huh. She even cut a record. Made the top ten back in the late eighties. Then she dropped out of sight, just like that."

Connor heard the unmistakable *pop* of snapping fingers. "She quit? After a hit recording? Why?"

"Arrested."

Every muscle in his body tensed. "Arrested?"

"We must have a bad connection."

Connor frowned. "Why do you say that?"

"'Cause you keep repeating everything I say."

He cleared his throat. "Why was she, uh, arrested?"

"Seems the guy she was seeing at the time—drummer name of Bill Isaacs—was having some trouble with booze.''

"Spare me the details, O'Dell. I get the picture." He'd been clamping his teeth together so tightly, he was beginning to get a headache.

"I don't think you do."

Connor ran a hand over his face. "There was an accident, wasn't there?"

"Uh-huh. Bad one."

Connor's heartbeat doubled. "Was Jaina hurt?"

"Yep. Spent a week in intensive care, another two in a private room, then six months in physical therapy."

Connor clenched his fists until the joints began to ache. "And then what?"

"A stint in the pen."

"What!" Connor clenched and unclenched his jaw. "She got in the car with a drunk. There's no crime in that. She probably didn't even know he'd been drinking till it was too late."

There was a considerable pause before O'Dell spoke

again. "Seems she was in the driver's seat when the cops showed up. She claimed she was trying to drive back to the hotel when Isaacs lost it and grabbed the wheel, and... Well, the rest is in the report."

Connor replied with a deep sigh.

"Can I ask you a question, Boss?"

"You can *ask*."

"Are you sweet on this li'l gal? Not that I blame you, 'cause I've got a picture of her here, and she's right pretty, but..."

Sweet on her? Did he have to tack a Texas cliché onto everything he said? "This is business, O'Dell. Period. She's the lady my niece left her baby with. If I hope to adopt the boy, I need to know as much about her as possible."

"Didn't mean to pry. It's just that your reaction to the news was—"

"Believe it or not, even a coldhearted defense attorney like me can feel a pang of pity when he hears about the suffering of others."

"Yeah, well, whatever..." Then, "You want I should fax this stuff to you?"

"Do that. And Buddy?"

"Yeah?"

"Keep your mouth shut about this. I don't want the information falling into the wrong hands."

"Consider my lips zipped. You want me to head on home?"

"Nah. Give it a couple more days. Maybe we'll get lucky and one of your leads will turn up something on Kirstie." He breathed a deep sigh, then said in a gravelly voice, "I don't want her dying alone."

"I could always hire couple a locals. Three heads are better than one and all that."

"Whatever you think best," he said distractedly.

Connor hung up, then buzzed his secretary. "I'm ex-

pecting a fax,'' he announced when Pearl answered.
''When it comes in—''

''I know, I know. Don't read it, don't touch it. It's top
secret, right?''

''Right.''

''I'll buzz you the minute it arrives.''

After thanking Pearl, Connor spent a few restless minutes
shuffling folders around his desk and pacing from one side
of his office to the other.

Finally, Pearl entered with O'Dell's report. Connor
nearly grabbed the papers from her hand. ''Hold my calls,''
he instructed.

Connor quickly scanned the report, which included old
news articles, police records and also records from Jaina's
internment at Jessup. Connor didn't know how O'Dell had
gotten them, but there they were. The date O'Dell had
given him was emblazoned on his brain, and he aimed to
find out all he could about the night of Jaina's accident. It
took nearly an hour of cursoring, but he finally found what
he'd been looking for.

According to an old article, Jaina had spent seven months
in the hospital, and after her release, she'd spent another
six at the Women's Corrections Center at Jessup. There had
been an operation, too. ''Injured Convict Under Suicide
Watch,'' that headline said.

Connor's heart pounded as he skimmed some medical
records from her prison file. ''Surgery performed by Dr.
Thomas Stewart to correct internal injuries sustained in a
head-on collision on Interstate 94 in June of this year may
have rendered Jaina Chandelle incapable of having children... Chandelle was extremely depressed upon learning
of her condition.''

Rubbing his forehead, Connor sighed. ''Poor kid,'' he
said under his breath.

He quickly flipped through other pages, noting her de-
scription as a ''model prisoner,'' then paused to skim

Jaina's arrest record. The officer who'd taken the police report recorded that Jaina had claimed that Isaacs pulled the wheel away from her, causing the accident. Other than that, her "jacket" was clean. *One of those "guilty by association" cases, looks like to me,* Connor thought. He closed the file and set it aside on his desk.

He stared down at the file. *This* was the secret he'd suspected she'd been hiding. *This* was the weapon he needed to beat her in court. He should be feeling elated, confident. So why didn't he?

He tried to focus on his work again. But it was no use; he couldn't concentrate on anything but Jaina. O'Dell had called the report a bad news/good news kind of thing, but in Connor's opinion, there hadn't been anything good about it.

He sat back in his chair and linked his fingers behind his head. Until now, he hadn't really understood Jaina's deep and sudden attachment to Liam. But if she believed she'd never conceive a child of her own, it made perfect sense that she'd latch onto one that had literally been dropped in her lap.

And now he understood why that single case of his that she'd read about had pushed all her buttons.

But Connor had taken an oath on the day he became an attorney. In it, he'd sworn to fairly and honorably defend all citizens protected by the Constitution. He didn't believe in much these days, but he believed in that.

The harsh, unfeeling upbringing of his Bible-wielding parents had caused him to leave organized religion behind long ago; if his mother and father were typical examples of devout churchgoers, he'd just as soon not call himself a Christian. He worshiped privately in his own way and found, during his one-on-one sessions with the Almighty, that whether social, political, personal or religious, *any* issue could be put to the Golden Rule test. If *he'd* been brought up on similar charges, would he want to be stamped "guilty" without benefit of a fair trial?

Each time such a case crossed his desk, Connor forced himself to answer that question because how would he face the man in the mirror if he wasn't willing to give every defendant the benefit of the doubt? He firmly believed in the basic precepts of the Constitution. Among them, that no matter what crime a man is accused of, every U.S. citizen must be considered innocent until proven guilty in a court of law by a jury of his peers. Anything less, and anarchy would prevail.

His heart ached for Jaina. A familiar "I want to *do* something about that!" sensation plagued him, as it always did when he heard a story like hers. But, as usual, he felt paralyzed because, much as he wanted to right every wrong committed against the innocents of the world, he could not. The best he could hope to do, given his powerlessness, was to go back to basics: the Golden Rule.

If *he* had survived Jaina's ordeal, how would he want her to deal with *him?* Would he want her to back off, let him win Liam simply because he'd lived through some tough times? Or would he want her to treat him as an equal, with no more rights—and no fewer—than she had?

The answer was obvious. He would not add insult to injury by treating her like a victim because, in truth, she was anything but. She had turned tragedy into triumph, had risen above her past and emerged victorious. Out of admiration and respect for that, he owed it to her to treat her as an equal.

Besides, he wanted Liam to be a full-time, permanent part of his life. True, he'd mostly felt that way at the start because the baby was kin—his only connection to family—but within moments of his first encounter with the bright-eyed, smiling little boy, Connor had been captivated. Liam had stolen his heart, and there was no escaping that fact. The love he felt for the child was like none he'd felt before, and *that's* why he wanted Liam now. If he had to hurt Jaina to make Liam his...

He'd represented parties on a great many custody suits and couldn't recall one that hadn't been hard fought, that didn't end up causing hatred or, at the very least, bitterness between the parents. How could he even consider putting Jaina through that when he felt...

But exactly how *did* he feel about her?

Connor knuckled his eyes and sat up abruptly, knowing that to acknowledge the truth was tantamount to legal suicide. His head and his heart were clashing.

You're falling for her, old boy, falling hard, said his brain.

FallING, his heart asked, *as in "You're gonna"? Or fallEN, as in "Man, are you in trouble"?*

What's the difference? his brain demanded.

If you have to ask, answered his heart, *it's already too late.*

Dear Jaina,

I've been staying in Milwaukee with some friends that I met in the hospice. They told me a man has been poking around, asking a lot of questions about me. I told them to ignore him.

You're the only person I know who would have any reason to send someone looking for me, and I think I know why. It's because you don't want me to be alone right now. I'm not a bit surprised that you would go to such lengths to make my last days happy and comfortable. It's even more proof that you're exactly the right person to raise my little boy.

I know that some people will say I'm a terrible mother for leaving my son with a woman I had never met before. They just don't understand! I didn't want to leave him at all! So when they say it, you just tell them that in my heart you were never a stranger! Be-

cause as soon as I found out I was going to die, and
Liam might end up in some of the same horrible places
I grew up in, I spent hours on my knees, asking God
to help me make sure that wouldn't happen.

I know it sounds crazy, but I believe He put me in
your diner because He had chosen you to be Liam's
new mommy. God wouldn't steer me wrong. Especially not at a time like this!

So please don't worry about me, Jaina, because I
really am fine. I'm not in any pain, and I'm not afraid
of what's about to happen because, as God said,
"Your years will end like a sigh."

I think that it's a real blessing that Liam is so young.
If he was older, I'd probably be all worried that he
might miss me. As it is, I can go to Jesus without a
care in the world for I know my baby boy couldn't be
in better hands. Plus, I know that you'll help him understand why I did what I did, and that you won't let
him forget me.

They say there's a special place in heaven for people who do angelic things on earth. You are one of
those people, Jaina. God bless you, and thank you
from the bottom of my heart.

                                        Kirstie Buchanan

Jaina thanked God that she'd had the presence of mind
to put Liam to bed before opening the envelope. Though
there had been no return address, she had immediately recognized Kirstie's unique handwriting, and something had
told her the contents of the letter would not be easy to
accept. She stared through her tears at the colorful balloons
Kirstie had drawn in the upper left-hand corner. They
seemed to bob and float on the page. She was far too young
to meet her Maker, Jaina thought, sighing.

Kirstie was dying when she'd come into the diner. When
she'd penned this message, the end was closer still. For all

Jaina knew, the girl had already joined her Father in heaven. It seemed terribly unfair that a beautiful young woman should be separated from her child for any reason, but *this*...

If only Jaina could find her! She'd do everything in her power to make the girl comfortable, until the end came. And surely if Kirstie wrote a letter, or made a tape, outlining her desire to have Jaina raise Liam....

Why did life have to be so hard? she wondered.

But Jaina knew better than to ask why, because her own experiences had taught her that there were no satisfactory answers to questions like that.

Jaina had heard it said that human suffering was a test from God, that it must be endured so He might humble and discipline His children, to make them worthy to spend eternity with Him. *You need to take a lesson from Job,* Jaina told herself, *because he managed to accept all the anguish tossed at him without question or complaint.* Still...she wanted to believe there was a better way, an easier way for God to read Kirstie's heart than cancer.

Jaina went to the bookshelf and pulled down her copy of *Don't Blame God.* She'd purchased the book years ago while searching for healing of her own wounded spirit. The text had not brought her comfort despite the fact that she'd read it cover to cover several times. Maybe *this* time, she'd find the answers she sought.

The book opened automatically to page 179. "God cannot be blamed for sickness, disease, tragedies, and trials," Michalski had written, "any more than He can be blamed for sin."

He cannot be blamed for tragedy any more than He can be blamed for sin, Jaina reflected. If He created the universe and everything in it, didn't He also create sin?

No. Jaina couldn't pin that one on the Lord. He'd blessed His children with something He hadn't given a single other creature: free will. Unlike the beasts of the field and the birds in the sky, He expected His children to exercise that free will rather than act upon instinct. Crime was the direct result of the actions of people who chose to do evil. No one had forced Bill Isaacs to get drunk and then get behind the wheel of a car; no one had forced Jaina into his car that night. The accident that altered her life was no one's fault but her own, she reasoned, for she had *chosen* that path.

It wasn't as easy to explain something like cancer. The answer to that—if an answer existed—could only be found through prayer. A lot of it. But…did she remember how to pray? Did she even *want* to remember?

She'd been a devout girl, a prayerful young woman. But Jaina had not conversed with God in a long, long time. Not, in fact, since that night. Why would she, when she believed He didn't listen to her pleas?

Her fifth-grade Sunday school teacher had given this homework assignment: "Find a Bible passage you can call your own. Memorize it, so that when trouble comes your way, or you're afraid, or your faith is tested, you can recite it, and it will renew your strength."

It took hours of searching before Jaina had come across the verse in Psalms that had always soothed and calmed her, even on the stormiest of nights: "…when the waters of the sea roar, and the mountains shake with the swelling thereof, be still and know that I am your God, your refuge."

Jaina closed her eyes and huddled in a corner of the sofa, hugging her knees to her chest. Until that awful night, she'd believed wholly and completely that she was a child of God, that He loved her with all His might and would never leave her alone and unprotected.

Don't do that, she warned herself. *Don't let yourself remember….*

But in the blink of an eye, she was transported back in time to Menomonee Falls, Wisconsin, and the nondescript room management had provided as part of her week's pay for entertaining guests in the hotel lounge.

There was Bill's car, an old yellow boat of a thing that had been around since the late seventies. She'd thought it odd that he hadn't greeted her with his usual kiss to her cheek, but dismissed it. Bill was often withdrawn and surly when his band was out of work.

It wasn't until he steered the car onto the highway that she realized he'd been drinking. "Pull over," she said, "and let me drive."

He shot her a withering glance. "Nobody drives my baby. You know that."

"Yes, but you've been drinking, Bill, and I think...."

"I haven't had that much. I'm fine."

They drove in silence for a moment or two before Jaina turned in the passenger seat. "You have two choices, Bill Isaacs. Stop this car and let me out, or pull over and let me drive, because I have no desire to die in a...."

"Okay. All right. Calm down," he said, a hand in the air to silence her. Both brows rose as he considered his alternatives. One look at her no-nonsense expression seemed enough to convince him to steer onto the road's shoulder.

"Nice and easy now," he instructed as she made a U-turn and headed back for the hotel. "Hey, where you goin'?" he demanded, reaching for the steering wheel. "We haven't had our talk yet."

Jaina didn't know why the Lord would turn a deaf ear to her pleas. She only knew that if Bill continued jerking on the steering wheel, they'd end up....

When she came to, she couldn't feel anything from her waist down, couldn't see past the white-hot pain that filled her head each time she opened her eyes. She remembered the way Bill's big hand had clamped over hers on the wheel, the way trees and fence posts whizzed by at breakneck speed as the car lurched toward the ravine beside the road. Her screams were still echoing in her ears as she lay there, gasping, panting as those last terrifying seconds ticked through her memory in sickeningly slow motion....

The sudden jerk of the car as it tilted right, the sound of branches and rocks pummeling the undercarriage...

...the giant tree, looming closer, closer.

She had no idea a vehicle that could hum so quietly while on the road could make such a hideous sound upon impact.

Then blackness, and total silence.

Had it been minutes, or hours, that she lay there in the dark, paralyzed, terrified? Jaina only knew that at the sound of distant sirens, she began to cry tears of relief, softly at first. By the time the paramedics yanked open the door that groaned in protest, her sobs had blocked the questions hammering in her head: Where's Bill? Is he all right?

Two days later, Jaina learned she was being accused of vehicular manslaughter. The authorities didn't believe her when she said Bill had jerked the wheel, sending the car careening out of control.

Jaina didn't know exactly when she'd stopped hating herself. The self-loathing was restricted to those times when she stupidly allowed herself to glance in a mirror. When she saw the scars twisting and turning across her abdomen, *then* she hated herself. *Then* there was no escaping the fact that in that moment in time, she'd made one terrible decision, and it had cost her the ability to have children...the one thing she'd always wanted more than anything else in the world.

She pressed a hand to her stomach. Even through her pajama top, Jaina could feel the disfigurement that would be a permanent reminder of that night. Thanks to the operation, performed in haste by a surgical resident mere hours after the accident, a child would never grow in her womb. They'd made the decision without discussing it with anyone—not her parents and certainly not Jaina—and the surgery that had saved her had, in her estimation, destroyed her.

She'd never been a particularly vain woman. Even now, as she ran her fingers over the thick, ugly scars, Jaina knew the deformity wouldn't have bothered her...if it wasn't a reminder that she'd never have her own children.

Liam whimpered in his sleep, rousing Jaina from the horrible memories. She ran to him, scooped him up, held him tight. "You're all right," she crooned into his ear. "I'll never let anything hurt you, I promise."

It's what she had expected the Lord to do that night—scoop her up in His Almighty embrace, put a stop to anything that could harm her—and promise that she'd always be safe in His protection.

She carried Liam to the living room and snuggled with him in the recliner. The Bible was still on the coffee table where she'd left it, open to the verse in Psalms that had given her such peace as a child.

Anger and disappointment made her turn her face from it. She focused instead on Liam's sleepy eyes. He was so much like the way she'd been before that night: vulnerable, innocent, completely dependent on bigger, more powerful beings for care and protection. But that night had changed her dramatically and forever.

Never again would she trust those who claimed to be wiser than her. Never again would she have faith in mere words. Actions, life had taught her, were stronger and more powerful than any promise ever made.

Except one. "You can always count on me, sweetheart," she said, kissing his forehead. "I *promise*."

They had a lot in common, Jaina and this helpless baby. He needed her.

And more than anything, she needed him.

Chapter Six

The phone was ringing when Connor unlocked the office door, and he fumbled with his keys, briefcase and file folders in an attempt to grab it before the answering machine picked up.

He glanced at the digital clock on Pearl's desk. Eight fifty-five. She didn't get in until nine sharp. He had this theory that she stood just outside the door every morning, tapping her toe and staring at the minute hand of her watch, waiting for it to hit the twelve before making her entrance.

"Law office," he droned, dumping his load on Pearl's armless chair.

"G'morning. It's Jaina."

As if she had to identify herself. He'd thought about her—and her past—long into the night. Connor's heart lurched at the sound of her musical voice. "I didn't expect to be talking to you until tomorrow morning."

"I didn't expect to be calling, but…"

He noted the careful pronunciation, the slow pace of her words. "Is Liam all right?"

"He's fine. In fact, he stood on his own for the first time last night."

Spoken like a true mother, he thought, grinning, proud of her boy's latest achievement. Connor felt a pang of guilt, knowing that her mothering days were quickly drawing to a close...thanks to the paperwork he'd filed the prior afternoon.

"The reason I called," she said slowly, "is because I got a letter from Kirstie in yesterday's mail. I thought maybe you'd like to..."

O'Dell had tracked the girl as far as Milwaukee but hadn't been able to get any further in his search for Connor's niece. Every night since she'd left Liam with Jaina, the last thoughts in his head before drifting off to sleep had been of Kirstie. Every night except *last* night, when he'd lain awake thinking of that article about Jaina.... "Does she say where she is?"

"No, she still doesn't want to be found."

"Does she say how she's doing?"

"She's doing all right. Why don't you stop by sometime today," she suggested gently, "and read it for yourself?"

He drew a quick breath through his teeth and winced. If only he could; it would be an opportunity to see Liam...*and* Jaina. "I wish I could, but I've got a packed schedule... back-to-back appointments before lunch, a hearing this afternoon. I can't come to The Chili Pot, but..."

He wondered if she was wearing her shoulder-length curls in a ponytail at the nape of her neck as she had the day the diner had flooded, or if she'd let it hang free, the way she'd worn it for the meeting in his office. *Wild and free,* he hoped.

Jaina ended the long pause. "But what?"

"But if you let me buy you lunch," he finished, "we could kill two birds with one stone."

"I suppose I could get away for an hour or so. Where should I meet you?"

"Ever been to The Judge's Bench?"

"No, but I've passed it a hundred times when I've been on Main Street looking for bargains in the antique stores."

Antiques. She had an eye for them all right, and a flair for knowing how to show off their finer qualities, as evidenced by the way she'd scattered them throughout her apartment. Maybe one of these days, he'd bring her to the house, see if she'd be interested in helping him fix it up....

Very recently, thoughts of her had distracted him from his work. Now, the image of her, arranging and rearranging things in his house was having the same effect.

"When?"

"When what?"

"When should I be there?"

"Oh. Right." He adjusted his tie as if that would set his mind straight. "Why don't I call you when I wrap up my last appointment, so you won't end up waiting...in case the meeting runs overtime."

"That'll be fine." It was her turn to hesitate. "Is this...is this a fancy place?"

He didn't believe there was a woman alive who didn't ask that question when invited to a new restaurant. He smiled, picturing the way Jaina might dress for work: kicky little skirts or blue jeans, but with a bright scarf or a strand of colorful beads for added flair. "A black robe will be fine."

She laughed softly. "Not that I have anything against basic black, mind you, but maybe I'll just wing it."

"I can tell you this. You'll stand out like a sore thumb if you wear anything dressy."

"It's just...I thought with a name like The Judge's Bench, it'd be crawling with guys and gals in suits and ties and Italian loafers, you know?"

"Nah. Just ordinary folks like you and me." He felt a bit strange saying that because, in his opinion, there was nothing ordinary about Jaina Chandelle.

"Good. Then I won't have to change."

"Call you around noon, then."

"Okay. And Connor?"

"Hmm...?"

"Just so you won't worry...Kirstie says she's not alone. She's getting some medical care, too."

Then why couldn't Jaina wait until tomorrow to show him the letter? he wondered. "Don't *you* worry. I won't."

Connor was still sitting on the corner of Pearl's desk, staring at the receiver, when the secretary breezed into the room. "You have to talk into the end with lots of holes," she said in a scolding tone, "before anything will come out of the other end."

He blinked. "Morning, Pearl." Squinting, he wrinkled his nose. "Er, what did you say?"

Pearl shoved her purse into a drawer and grabbed the phone from his hand. "Never mind," she said, hanging it up. She opened the appointment book. "I'll pull the Adams file for you. They won't be here until nine-thirty. You have plenty of time to go over your notes."

Nodding distractedly, he gathered his things and headed for his office. He stopped in the doorway. "Pearl?"

"Hmm?"

"Would you get me the Adams file? They'll be here soon, and I want to go over my notes."

Frowning, she propped a fist on an ample hip. "Sure thing, Boss." Then, pursing her lips, she studied him through narrowed eyes. "You okay, Mr. B.?"

"Who, me?" He smiled. "I'm fine." He knitted his brow. "Why do you ask?"

She shrugged. "No reason, just asking."

He sent her a halfhearted smile, then disappeared into his office.

"If I didn't know him better," Pearl muttered, "I'd say he's been bitten by the lovebug."

"Did you say something, Pearl?"

"Sometimes we old folks talk to ourselves, that's all."

But he didn't hear a word she'd said. Pearl knew it because the last thing she saw before pulling out the top drawer of the filing cabinet was Connor Buchanan, staring off into space, thick mustache slanting above a silly half grin.

She rummaged in the drawer, withdrew a folder labeled Adams. "Here you go," she said, handing it to him.

He met her eyes. "Isn't that incredible? I was just about to buzz you, ask you to bring me this very file."

Shaking her head, she raised one brow. "Just doin' my job, Boss." And as she closed the door, Pearl put a hand over her mouth and giggled softly. "I hope he's not planning to drive anywhere today," she said under her breath, "'cause I don't think the insurance company covers fender benders caused by bug bites."

With Liam safe in his playpen in the far corner of her room, Jaina prepared for her lunch date. She hadn't been out with a man in nearly two years, unless she counted going to the movies with Skip as a date, and she didn't. But then, this wasn't a date, either. *Because Connor Buchanan doesn't care a fig for me!*

She looked at the rumpled pile of clothing in the middle of her bed. Jaina had tried on every summery outfit she owned, as well as a few that would be more appropriate in the spring or fall. *You should have stayed in the diner till it was time to leave,* she scolded herself, *because then you'd have been too busy to think about anything so silly as what you'd wear.*

Jaina slumped to the floor and leaned against the wall. What would he think of a woman whose clothes were more suited to McDonald's than a fashionable café in town? But what did Connor Buchanan's opinion of her wardrobe matter? *Liam* was the reason he'd come into her life, and Liam would be the only reason they'd continue to communicate.

Liam, and for a little while longer, Kirstie....

She thought of the way he'd sounded when she told him about Kirstie's letter. The joy and relief in his voice made it clear that he really cared about a girl he'd never met...a girl he hadn't even known existed two weeks ago. As well he should, considering that Kirstie had been his beloved sister Susan's daughter. But how did he feel about the fact that Kirstie would soon be gone, and the only family he'd have left in the world came in the form of a tiny, gurgling package called Liam Connor Buchanan?

If only she could get a message to Kirstie! Jaina would love to tell her that she'd made a terrible mistake about her uncle. Because though Connor might have appeared to Kirstie as grumpy and mean, he was nothing of the kind. He had a giving nature, and the proof was in the way he behaved around Liam.

She'd seen plenty of men attempt to communicate with babies. Most seemed to feel it wasn't macho to make silly faces and noises. And then they wondered why kids didn't react well to them! It was no surprise that Liam had taken an immediate liking to Connor. But then, any man willing to speak two octaves higher than usual—while wiggling his brows and making funny noises—was pretty much guaranteed a happy and affectionate response.

He'd be a wonderful father someday, she thought. Jaina's wistful smile gave way to a worried frown as she thought of his desire to be a father to Liam. But hopefully, not any time soon.

Buchanan was young, vital, handsome. Why hadn't he married, had a few children of his own? she wondered. If he had a wife and family like most other men his age, maybe he wouldn't be so intent on having Liam.

The door opened, providing a much needed escape from her frightening reflections.

"Hey, girl, what's shakin'?"

"Skip! What are you doing, stopping by in the middle

of a workday? Is this where my tax dollars are going?'' she teased.

"You need to get a new writer, pal, 'cause that joke's gettin' old.'' He chuckled. "Say…I'm gonna be here around lunchtime. Since I'm with Social Services, what say I offer you *my* services. Whatcha doin' for lunch?''

Ordinarily, she'd have jumped at the chance to spend an hour or two with her best friend. "Today?''

"No,'' he said teasingly, "the second Tuesday of next month.''

"I'm sorry, Skip, I'd like to, but—''

"Why am I always the last to know about your love life?''

"If I ever *get* a love life, you'll be the first to know,'' she said dully. "This isn't a date.'' The words had spurted from her mouth so quickly, even she didn't believe she'd actually said them.

"Hmm, what was that old line out of Shakespeare? Something like me thinketh thou protesteth too mucheth?''

She took a deep breath and started over. "Seriously, it's a business lunch.''

"What kind of business?''

"Well, I got a letter from Kirstie Buchanan yesterday and—''

"The girl who dumped her baby in your diner?''

Jaina frowned. "She didn't 'dump' him. She wrote to let me know she's doing fine. She didn't want me to worry.''

"Mighty big of her,'' he grumbled, "considering it's *she* who oughta be worrying…about whether or not her kid's okay, about whether or not you're a serial killer, about—''

"Skip,'' she interrupted, "be fair. You know the circumstances as well as anyone. Kirstie is barely more than a child, herself, and she's dying. What did you expect her to do?''

"Oh, lemme see, I dunno. Put him into a home with two

loving adults, where maybe he had a chance of becoming a permanent part of a real family?''

''You don't have to be so sarcastic. You read the letter. Her own mother died when Kirstie was young, and the poor girl got bounced around by the system for years. She didn't want that for Liam.''

There was a long pause before he muttered, ''I don't know why you're mad at *me*. I don't make the rules. And I know the system isn't perfect. Besides, I haven't really been looking for foster parents. I thought you wanted—''

Jaina sighed heavily and rolled her eyes. ''Then I wish you'd told me that before. Every time my phone rings, you know, I think it's going to be you—''

''Thanks a heap, kiddo. Didn't know you cared so much.''

''You didn't let me finish. I was about to say that every time the phone rings, I'm afraid it's you, calling to say you *have* found someone to keep Liam until—''

''Until the final adoption hearing is scheduled?''

''Yes. Until then. I'm really nuts about him, Skip, and every day that he's with me, I love him more.'' She sighed again. ''How do foster parents do it?''

''Do what?''

''Take a child in, treat it like their own, then hand it back whenever Social Services snaps its collective fingers.''

''To my knowledge, we've never done *anything* collectively. But to answer your question, it's just as hard for foster parents to give up the kids we place with 'em as it'll be for you to give up Liam. The difference is, it's something they accept because it's part of the job, which is to do what's best for the child.''

His matter-of-fact comment seemed to freeze the blood in her veins. It may have been good advice, but it sure did hurt.

She chose to ignore his dig. ''Do you really think that I'll have to give him up?''

"Yes…and I think *you* think so, too."

Jaina might have denied it if a sob hadn't choked off her words.

"When there's a healthy, well-adjusted relative in the picture, the court awards that party custody…if that's what the person wants."

A glimmer of hope sparked in her. "What do you mean…'if that's what the person wants'?"

"Well, sometimes a cousin, a grandparent, whatever, will go for guardianship instead of full parental rights, either because the kid's parents are still in the picture, or maybe because they're in some sort of bad trouble and the relative is hoping that when things straighten out, the kid can go back home to them. And sometimes, folks plain don't want the expense and bother."

"But…but Liam doesn't *have* anyone except for—"

"Exactly. So if Buchanan wants to adopt the kid, they're gonna let him. He's a close blood relation, and the way the state sees it, a kid is usually better off with family than anybody else. Face it, pal. You're fighting a losing battle. As long as he hasn't killed anybody lately, Connor Buchanan, Esq., is gonna be a daddy in a little while."

"But he isn't married, and his schedule is frantic, and he lives alone, and—"

"Change the 'he' to a 'she', and you could be describing yourself," he gently reminded her.

"I have my parents to help me. And loads of friends. Who has Buchanan got?"

"Not 'who,' but 'what.' He's got money. I don't mean to sound vulgar, Jaina, but whatever he doesn't *have*, he can *buy*. He has, as they say, 'the wherewithal' to take care of the child."

She ran a hand through her hair. "Is that the reason you wanted to go to lunch, Skip? To rain on my parade?"

"Course not, but…" He paused, then patted her hand. "Okay. Here's my honest, professional opinion. If Buchanan wasn't in the picture, I'd bet my last paycheck the judge would let you adopt, considering—''

''Considering what?''

''That his mother left the…left Liam with you and wrote that heart-tugging note and—''

''You really think Buchanan will win?'' she broke in, unable to get her mind off a comment Skip had made moments ago.

''It's rare, *real* rare, for a woman in your position to get custody.''

''It's rare, but it happens from time to time, right?''

She could tell from Skip's expression that he was torn. Part of him wanted to help her by not offering any false hope, while another part couldn't resist the pleading look in her eyes.

''Well, I shouldn't be telling you this—it wouldn't be right to give you false hopes—but a couple years back, I handled a similar case. Remember that woman who found a baby in the trash can behind her apartment building?''

The story had been in all the papers and on the TV news for days, Jaina recalled.

''Well,'' Skip continued, ''she brought it to the hospital, and the whole time the docs and nurses were checking its health, she stayed right there. When they gave the little guy a clean bill of health, she told 'em she wanted him.''

Jaina said, ''I don't remember how it turned out.''

''She got him.''

''Was she…?''

''Wasn't married, owned a cleaning service, lived alone…the works.''

''Oh, Skip,'' Jaina sighed, ''do you think…?''

''See, this is just what I was trying to avoid. Listen to me, Jaina. *That* kid didn't have a relative waiting in the wings, so unless you're planning to get rid of Buchanan, it's apples and oranges.'' A few moments of silence ticked by before he said, "So, who are you having lunch with? Your lawyer?"

"No…"

"It's high time you started planning a strategy, to discuss the girl's letter and all. Who'd you hire? Maybe I know him and can put in a good word."

"I don't have a lawyer yet."

"Jaina! What're you waiting for?"

"When I need one, I'll get one. I'm hoping that in the meantime, Buchanan will realize I'm in a better position to—" The sight of him smacking his palm against his forehead silenced her.

"I can't believe this," Skip said. "Don't tell me your business lunch is with—"

"Yes, Connor Buchanan."

"Are you out of your ever-lovin' mind? Consorting with the enemy? You have no chance of beating him in court, and you're gonna—"

"Hold on a minute, *pal.* 'No chance'? Just a minute ago, you said I had a slight chance. Which is it? C'mon, 'fess up. You know how important this is to me."

He moaned quietly, then said, "Jaina, don't do this to me."

"A little thin-skinned, aren't you, Skip? Especially since I'm still wiping the dirt off my face."

"Huh?"

"After you rubbed my nose in it," she explained, impatience ringing in her voice.

"I didn't mean things to sound that way at all," he said. "It's just that we've been good friends a long time, and I'd like it to stay that way."

She rolled her eyes. "Really, Skip," she said on a mocking laugh, "what could you possibly have to say that would threaten our friendship?"

"All right, but don't say I didn't warn you." He took a deep breath. "You're doing the right thing for all the wrong reasons. This attachment you have for Liam? In my professional opinion, I think you've turned him into a substitute.''

''Substitute? For what?''

''For the babies you think you can't have,'' he said quietly.

As her heart thundered, Jaina's free hand clenched and unclenched. *The babies I* think *I can't have?* She would have shot his opinion down if the words hadn't frozen in her throat.

''It's perfectly understandable, but it isn't healthy, not for you *or* for Liam. You'll only end up brokenhearted again.''

''Again?''

''The way you were when Bill...when he—''

''You haven't had any trouble speaking your mind so far. Go ahead. Say it. When Bill died and left me to pick up the tab.''

''Stop it, Jaina. That's not what I meant and you know it.'' He breathed an exaggerated sigh. ''Look, I have a meeting with my boss and I haven't even pulled the case histories yet. Can I call you later so we can finish discussing this?''

''We've already finished discussing it.''

''There you go again.''

Jaina emitted a low growl of frustration. ''What does *that* mean?''

''You can't hide from the truth because it'll find you every time.''

''What truth am I hiding from *this* time, Dr. Freud?''

Skip chuckled. ''Go ahead, insult me if it helps.'' He cleared his throat as if preparing for the seriousness of what he was about to say. ''When they take Liam from you— and it's pretty likely they will—it's gonna break your heart. *Those* are the facts, and pretending they don't exist won't make them go away.''

Go away. That's *what I'll do. I'll take Liam and head out of town.* No, that wouldn't solve anything. Not for Liam, certainly not for her.

She bit her lower lip to stanch the sob aching in her throat. It seemed as if Skip was deliberately trying to hurt her. But why? Why had he told her the story about the woman who'd adopted the baby she found in a trash can? Why give her some small hope to cling to, then retract that hope entirely?

"I know I'm being rough on you, Jaina, but what kind of friend would I be if I lied to you? I know how these things play out. I see it everyday." He paused, looking as genuinely contrite as she'd ever seen him. "Would you have preferred it if I lied to you and said it was all going to work out just fine?"

She shook her head. "No... I guess not. At least now I know what I'm up against." Then, in a stronger voice, "Are you coming to the parade with us tomorrow?"

"Wouldn't miss it for the world."

"According to my watch," she said, forcing a lilt into her voice, "you have to get ready for your boss."

A slight pause, then Skip said, "You know I love ya, don't you?"

Her eyes filled with tears, but she managed to say, "Yeah, I know." But she didn't know anything of the kind. She seemed to have made a habit of developing close ties with men who were bad for her. "You don't want to be late. Now get going."

"See you tomorrow," Skip said cheerily, and left.

Jaina glanced over at Liam, sitting in the middle of the playpen, trying to decide between his squeaky red fire engine and the yellow plastic dump truck she'd bought him. She cried softly as Skip's warning reverberated in her ears. She didn't want to lose Liam.

That first night, as she lay on the floor beside him, a thousand worries had kept her awake. Did he understand, in some instinctual way, that he'd been abandoned? Did he sense that his mother was dying? And if he did, Jaina had wondered, how would she assure him he'd be well cared for, always? Because what did she know about babies? Would she know if, when he cried, his tears were from hunger or gas…or fear?

When he woke fussing the next morning, Jaina couldn't explain it, but something had told her that a clean diaper and a sweet song was all it would take to calm him. And it had. From then on, knowing when he needed a nap or if a hug was called for seemed as natural as inhaling and exhaling. In just two weeks, he'd become the center of her world.

One of the hardest things about having been told she might never be able to have children of her own was the fear that if she adopted a baby, as everyone advised her to, she couldn't love the child as deeply or completely as a baby she'd given birth to herself. Jaina's feelings for Liam were proof that love for a child could be all-encompassing and all-consuming, no matter what. If she couldn't keep him…

The accident hadn't killed her, but it had come close. Neither had the subsequent physical therapy—though at times, as she struggled to regain the use of her legs, she thought it might. And somehow she'd managed to keep body and soul together, even after stepping into the hideous orange jumpsuit at Jessup. Those six months had changed her forever, had hardened her in so many ways. Being tough, she learned early, was the only way to survive. Innocent? Guilty? What did it matter to women who'd been sentenced to two, five, *twenty* years? Jaina got through it by dipping into a reserve of inner strength she hadn't known she possessed. It never ceased to amaze her that no matter how many times she went to it, the well always seemed just full enough to provide the fortitude to go on despite the hardship. Only recently had she come to realize that it had been kept full by the love of Almighty God.

But how deep *was* it? How much more could she take from it? The ultimate test, she believed, lay just ahead. If Skip was right, if Buchanan succeeded in taking Liam from her, it would require so large a draft of courage and endurance, that the well might just run bone-dry.

When Connor called, as promised, to tell her he was leaving for the restaurant, he thought she'd sounded sad. That was odd, he told himself, remembering their brief conversation, because she'd seemed pretty up when she phoned him earlier. Could it be that she knew what he'd been up to? That he'd had a detective on her heels? That he'd started the machinery to take the baby from her?

Perhaps this motherhood thing was beginning to wear thin. She'd lived a full and busy life before Liam came along; maybe the added stresses and strains of taking care of him day in, day out, were proving to be too much. Which, in his opinion, would be a blessing in disguise because Connor wasn't looking forward to taking the baby from her.

He set the scene in his mind: Jaina, teary-eyed and trembly-lipped, arms outstretched as he walked away with his bawling nephew. His heart beat double time and he winced, forcing the picture from his mind. He ran a hand through his hair. If thinking about it made him feel like such a heel, what was it going to be like when the real thing happened?

And it *was* going to happen because he intended to raise that boy as his own. He didn't want to fight her; that would mean dredging up her past. He knew hers was just the kind of story that media vultures were always hunting for. And he'd do everything in his power to prevent that, but...

He spotted her just then, crossing the street from the parking lot to the restaurant. Thoughts of fighting her were forgotten as he smiled unconsciously. Connor liked the way she walked, head up and shoulders back, each fluid stride causing her glistening chestnut brown curls to bounce a bit. Somehow her slight limp did nothing to distract from her grace. She raised a hand to tame windblown bangs, frowning slightly when they refused to cooperate. She'd worn a jean skirt cut a few inches above her knees, topped by a white summer-weight sweater. He noted a brown braided-leather belt around her slender waist and matching sandals on her tiny feet. Cinderella couldn't have looked as pretty at the ball, he thought.

She saw him then, at the table on the other side of the window, smiled and raised a hand in friendly greeting.

He stood to remove his jacket and hung it on the back of his chair. "I hope you haven't been here long," she said, settling into the seat across from him. "I left as soon as we hung up."

"No, not at all," he said. "I've only been here a few minutes." Connor hadn't felt this awkward since high school, when he asked the homecoming queen to accompany him to the spring dance. "I have to admit, even if I'd been here an hour, it would have been worth the wait. You look lovely today."

Jaina blushed, then fanned her face with the menu. "I, uh, the air conditioner in my car isn't working very well. I think it must need servicing. Freon. Something…" She took a quick look around the place, ran a finger down the food list. "You've eaten here before. What do you recommend?"

"They make a mean crab cake, and their pizza isn't half-bad, either."

She took a sip of water from a squat, red-rimmed tumbler. "There's no price beside the crab cake platter." Narrowing her eyes, she leaned across the table. "'Market price.' What kind of nonsense is *that?*" Clucking her tongue, she lifted her chin. "Mine is $9.95 year-round, period."

Chuckling, Connor waved the waitress over. "I'll have a glass of iced tea. Jaina?"

She laid the menu beside the small butter plate. "Make it two," she said. Then, looking around conspiratorially, she wiggled her forefinger to summon the woman closer. "How much are the crab cakes today?"

The waitress looked left and right. "Eight ninety-five," she whispered, "and they come with French fries and a side of coleslaw."

Jaina's brows rose. "Wow, a whole dollar less than mine."

"Well," Connor said, "you know what the sages say."

"You get what you pay for," they said in unison, laughing.

As the woman left to get their drinks, Connor commented on the weather, and Jaina repeated last night's Orioles score. He asked if she'd heard about the dockworkers' strike. She wondered if he'd seen the article about the president's latest diet. Once the waitress had delivered their tea, Jaina opened her purse and sat back, smiling a bit.

"What?"

"This feels strangely like déjà vu. Except the last time I did this," she said, pulling the letter from her purse, "we were in your office."

"True." He cocked a brow. "How'd you sleep last night?"

"Fine, thanks, and you?"

"Like a rock, as usual. Did you have breakfast?"

She tilted her head to the side and looked at him curiously. "Why…yes."

"Good."

Jaina nodded slowly. "Ahhh, I get it. You're worried I'll pass out again," she observed, grinning mischievously, "and make a scene in front of all your lawyer friends."

He chuckled. "They've already observed a young

woman in my company making scenes. Then again, a swoon would be a refreshing change."

Her smile faded. "I apologize for that business in your office. I wish I could explain it. Sometimes the strangest things remind me of…" Eyes wide, she bit her lower lip, then hid behind the menu. "So, you say you've had the crab cakes here?"

Though she'd left her remark unfinished, he knew where she'd been headed, thanks to O'Dell's report. And because of what he'd read on his own, he understood for the first time that he must have said or done something that day to remind her of the accident. Whatever it had been, *that's* what prompted the fainting spell. He shrugged one shoulder. "I've had better, but then, I've had worse."

She nodded again, and he took a swallow of his tea. He'd heard enough testimony, both in private quarters and on countless witness stands, to know what went on inside a women's prison. He'd always felt many differing emotions when listening to ex-cons tell their stories. Some he thought deserved exactly what they'd gotten. Others he'd believed couldn't possibly have deserved the punishment meted out in a court of law. But he'd always managed to keep his reactions to himself, to keep a safe emotional distance, because they'd all been virtual strangers.

But he knew Jaina. Knew her well enough to believe he might be falling in love with her. That anyone had used and abused this diminutive lady caused a roiling that started deep in his gut and ended at his tightly clenched fists. The muscles of his jaw flexed and his eyes narrowed. If he could've gotten his hands on that Bill guy, he'd have… *You're a hypocrite, Buchanan,* he told himself, heart pounding with shame, *because what you're planning is going to hurt her more than—*

"Connor? Are you all right?"

He met her dark eyes, reading genuine concern on her

pretty face. Connor wrapped his hand around the glass of tea. "I'm fine. Why?"

Jaina blinked several times before answering. "You looked…" She grinned. "You looked like you were ready to commit a homicide." Jaina feigned a look of terror. "Not a very smart place to murder someone, what with all these cops and judges and prosecutors around."

He chuckled.

"So, who was the victim—me?"

The question made him sit up straighter. "Why would I want to hurt you?"

She laid the envelope beside the web-covered candle in the center of the table. "Because I'm going to fight you for Liam."

Connor licked his lips. Nodded. He took another sip of the tea. "I can think of less messy ways to stop you."

He saw the fear that widened her big brown eyes and winced inwardly. *Well, you knew this wasn't gonna be easy,* he told himself.

"You wouldn't kill me to get Liam," he said, and seeing the mischievous grin that lifted one corner of her mouth, added, "would you?"

Narrowing her eyes, Jaina wiggled her brows. Smiling gently, she reached across the table and touched her index fingertip to his forehead. "That's for me to know," she said, her thumb cocking a pretend gun, "and you to find out."

"Wow," he said, laughing. "I can't remember when I've last heard that 'me to know' line. Not since third grade, I'll bet."

"'You make me feel so young,'" she sang, forefingers waving in the air.

His smile diminished a little in response to her singing. It had lasted a second, perhaps less, but it had been enough to make him want to hear more. He could almost picture her, microphone in hand, eyes closed, standing in the spotlight and crooning a ballad. "So tell me," he asked, non-chalantly picking up the letter, "how's my little man to-day?"

"Terrific. Did I tell you he's learned to stand?"

"That must be a sight," he said, sliding Kirstie's note from its envelope.

She scooted her chair back. "He uses the coffee table for balance, gets into a standing position, like this." Jaina stood beside the table, oblivious to the curious glances of nearby diners, spread her feet shoulder-width apart and assumed the position. "His arms go up and down like he's going to take off, then he leans forward, bobbles back and forth, side to side, and *plop!*" Air whooshed from the cushion as she landed on the seat of her chair. "Good thing his bottom is well padded!"

Jaina lifted her shoulders in a dainty shrug. "I declare, you just gotta love him!"

Unfolding Kirstie's letter, he wondered what it would feel like to have her saying that about him. "What do you think...should I read this before or after we eat?"

"Maybe it'd be best if you waited." She inclined her head, studying his face for a moment. "You don't seem like the type who has a weak stomach, but..."

He returned the letter to its envelope. "As my old granny used to say, I'm as strong as an ox."

Jaina clasped her hands beneath her chin. "Is she still with you?"

Connor shook his head, then took a sugar packet from the tray on the table and folded all four corners down. "No. She died when I was about twelve."

"Any grandparents left at all?"

He unfolded the corners. "Nope." And meeting her eyes, he asked, "You?"

"I'm afraid it's just my parents and me."

He folded the corners in the opposite direction. "No siblings?"

"Mom has a heart condition. She didn't find out until she was in labor with me. From what I hear, the delivery nearly killed her. The doctors told her if she got pregnant again, that'd be the end of her." Jaina took a deep breath, staring out the window for a moment. "So she had her tubes tied, and that was that."

He shook his head. "That's too bad. Would your parents have wanted any more kids?"

Jaina met his eyes. "Dad wanted four, she wanted six. The thing was, they'd have needed ten kids in order for both of them to get their way."

She smiled, but it never quite made it to her eyes, he noticed. Something dark and sad glittered in the brown orbs, something akin to bitterness.

"Yeah, it would have been nice to have brothers and sisters," Jaina admitted. "But my mother's alive, and so far she's healthy." She swirled the clear plastic straw around in her tea, setting the ice cubes to tinkling against the glass. "I used to think I'd like four or five myself."

Her long lashes, dusting her cheeks as she stared into her drink, reminded him of the woolly caterpillars that appear in the fall, signaling winter's approach. "Used to?"

Jaina stared into the whirlpool she'd created in the tumbler. A spark—anger? regret?—glittered hard and cold in her usually warm eyes. "Things happen, you know? If you don't go with them, they'll knock you flat."

And you know something about that, don't you? It took all the strength he could muster not to leap from his chair and wrap her in a big protective hug. His heart ached for her, for all she'd suffered and survived, because good people like Jaina shouldn't have to endure such hardship.

"So, are you folks ready to order?" The waitress stood beside the table, looking from Connor to Jaina, order pad in one hand, ballpoint poised in the other.

Connor's eyes never left Jaina's. "Two crab cake platters. Broiled, not fried. And onion rings instead of French fries.''

''Need refills on your tea?''

He continued staring into Jaina's face. ''Sure.''

''Back in a jiff,'' she said, and left them again.

Something told Connor to fold his hands on the table, the way his fifth-grade teacher had taught him, to keep him from fiddling with his pen or the corners of his textbook. But he didn't listen to the warning. Instead, he reached out and grasped Jaina's hand, then gave it a gentle squeeze. Under the circumstances, it was the best he could do because he couldn't very well admit that he'd found out what she'd lived through and admired her for it. Maybe someday…but not yet.

He half expected her to withdraw her hand and tuck it out of sight in her lap. Jaina surprised him by placing her free hand atop his, effectively sandwiching his hands between her own. Smiling sweetly, she gave his knuckles an affectionate little pat, and he read it as a silent thanks for his understanding.

Her fingers felt smooth, cool, soothing, against his skin. He wanted to rest the fingertips of his other hand on her delicate wrist, walk them up her slender arm and pull her close, closer, until he could press a kiss to those smiling lips.

As if she could read his mind, her lips spread into a wide grin. ''You're good, Buchanan. I'll give you that much.''

He gave her a puzzled look. ''Good? Good at what?''

She arched a brow and tilted her head, before shooting a taunting glance his way. ''Distractions are probably very influential with members of a jury, but they're not quite so effective with the unsequestered.''

One corner of his mustached mouth rose. ''I don't get it.''

The warm light in her brown eyes cooled. ''Romancing

me isn't the answer. I love him, and if I have to, I'll fight for him."

He'd been so lost in the moment, he hadn't caught her meaning until now. Then, as understanding dawned, he tightened his grip slightly and asked softly, "What makes you think I'm romancing you?"

Jaina's heart thundered suddenly in response to his question. The challenge in his words was matched only by the impact of his intense gaze. She withdrew her hands, hid them in her lap. "I'm sorry," she said quietly. "That was out of line."

Connor crossed his arms over his chest and sat back. "No. I'm the one who's sorry."

She tried but couldn't make sense of the peculiar expression that had hardened his features. She watched him pick up the envelope, then pretend to be engrossed in the postmark.

"So, Kirstie's still in Milwaukee, I see."

Unable to speak, Jaina only nodded. She'd grown accustomed to keeping an arm's length from men. Pulling away had become a knee-jerk reaction. Clothing hid her scars, but she was aware of them always, and could feel them even through bulky sweaters. If she let a man hold her hand, he might think it was all right to pull her into a casual hug. What if, as his fingers rested on the small of her back and his thumbs pressed against her stomach, he felt the scars? Jaina didn't know what she'd do if she read disgust—or worse, revulsion—on his face.

Keeping a safe emotional distance served another purpose. People tended not to look too closely at folks they didn't care about; if she let a man into her heart, he might just see everything else.

But she hadn't withdrawn from Connor's touch. Hadn't *wanted* to, and that surprised her. It was something she'd give some careful thought to at home later, when she was alone....

"Here ya go," the waitress sang out, depositing their plates in front of them. "Ketchup? Mustard?"

"None for me," Connor said. "Jaina?"

"No thanks." Jaina smiled up at the woman.

"Okay, well, just flag me if you want to see the dessert menu."

Their eyes locked as they replied in perfect harmony, "Just coffee, please."

The waitress gave them her best "the customer is always right" smile and walked away.

They made small talk as they dined, discussing everything from the weather to the high cost of living in Howard County, Maryland. Connor finished eating first, and the way he laid his knife and fork on his plate reminded her of the ceremony made famous by naval academy cadets. They'd stand facing one another, sabers crossed high as a newly married fellow student and his bride walked beneath the shimmering steel archway. Marriage? What was she doing thinking about *marriage?*

They were on their second cup of coffee before Connor picked up the envelope again. "Well," he breathed, "here goes. Shall I read it aloud?"

She shook her head. "I've read it a dozen times already. I'll just take this opportunity to find the ladies' room."

A gentleman to the hilt, he half stood as she rose from her chair. "Don't be long," he said, nodding toward the letter. "I might need you to hold my hand."

He wasn't kidding. She could see genuine apprehension in his blue eyes. "You know," she said, sitting down again, "I think I'll just take advantage of Miss Manners's newest rule and reapply my lipstick right here at the table." She slid a compact from her purse, popped open the lid and glanced into its small oval mirror. "Well, what do you think of that?" She snapped it shut again. "I don't need a touch-up after all."

The look of relief on his face sent her heart into overdrive. Jaina didn't know how to react to that, either, and hid her surprise by pretending to sip coffee from the thick earthenware mug.

She sat back and watched him scan the neatly penned lines of Kirstie's letter. For some time now, she'd been questioning her feelings for him. Did she think of him nearly every hour of the day—and quite a few hours of the night—because he might take Liam away from her? Or was the baby's delighted reaction to him the reason Connor seemed to be constantly on her mind? Were the memories of his compassionate reaction to her dizzy spell in his office what prompted the soft sighs and the quickened heartbeat that accompanied thoughts of him, or had remembering the way he'd clowned for the baby caused the response?

How do you feel *about him?*

She'd posed the question at least a thousand times in the weeks since Kirstie left Liam at The Chili Pot. If he truly was everything he appeared to be—warm, thoughtful, caring of his nephew—she could love him. But if he was the kind of man who could take Liam from her...

Chin resting in her palm, she'd been staring out the window, only half-seeing the people who sauntered past the restaurant. The sound of rustling paper roused her from her reverie, and she glanced up in time to see Connor struggling to stuff the letter back into its envelope.

Was that a tear in his eye? And was she mistaken or had his lower lip trembled?

Yes, the content of his niece's letter had obviously moved him deeply. His valiant effort to hide his emotions moved *her*. Dozens of times, her mother had said, "A man wears pride like a badge of courage." Jaina averted her gaze so that when he looked her way, he wouldn't know she'd seen his moment of vulnerability. He'd likely view it as a moment of weakness; she'd seen it as proof of his capacity to love.

Love.

It explained everything, including the question she'd asked herself a thousand times.

And created a list of new questions yet to be asked.

Chapter Seven

Connor walked Jaina to her car, relieved her of the keys, and unlocked it. After climbing inside, he revved the motor and turned the air conditioner to full blast. "Keep me company for a few minutes while it cools down in there," he said, slamming the door.

Because she'd hoped there would be a reason to extend their time together, she didn't bother to remind him that her car's air conditioner had been on the blink. She felt safe and protected in his company. Strange, since he was the one person who could do her the most harm. She leaned back on the sedan's fender and glanced up. "Looks like rain. I sure hope the weather does whatever it's going to do tonight. I'd hate to see the Fourth of July festivities get washed out."

"Me, too. I've never had a red, white and blue breakfast."

Laughing, she said, "Mother Nature can control the parade and the fireworks, but she can't dictate what I'll do in my very own kitchen!"

"Seven at the latest? Rain or shine?"

Crossing her arms in front of her, Jaina gave an assertive nod. ''Yep.''

Connor shrugged out of his suit coat, hooked the collar on a forefinger and slung it over his shoulder. ''I didn't figure you for a four-door kind of girl,'' he said, patting her car's roof.

''What sort of girl *did* you figure me for?''

''I dunno. I guess I saw you in something sporty and low-slung, with a convertible top. Or maybe one of those four-wheel-drive things.''

Almost from the day she got her learner's permit, she'd wanted a shiny red four-wheel-drive vehicle. ''And why's that?''

He loosened his tie and unfastened the top button of his shirt. ''Because you seem too easygoing, too down-to-earth for a sedate sedan.''

Connor draped the jacket over his forearm and began unbuttoning one shirt cuff. The coat nearly slid to the pavement several times before Jaina intervened. ''Funny you should mention that,'' she said nonchalantly, neatly folding the sleeve back once, twice, then smoothing it. ''I've always wanted a Jeep. Or one of those goofy-looking things the army guys drive.''

''A Hummer?''

''Right!'' She unbuttoned his other cuff. ''The only thing I like better than off-roading is horseback riding...mainly because it's quieter.''

''Horseback riding, eh?''

''If I do say so myself, I was quite the little equestrian when I was a girl.''

''Did you compete?''

She breathed an indignant huff. ''You mean, you didn't see the trophy on the mantel in my living room?''

''Sorry,'' he said, smiling. ''I must have missed it.''

''I don't see how.'' She finished rolling the second

sleeve. "It's three feet high." She patted the cuff. "All set!"

The tawny mustache tilted above a rakish smile. "Thanks. You're a natural-born caretaker, aren't you?"

Jaina didn't know if it was the weather or his compliment that sent a rush of heat to her cheeks. She tore her gaze from his blue-eyed admiration, pretended to be interested in the sidewalk sale in front of a shop up the street. "I wonder if they still have that sideboard?" she said. "I've been drooling over it for ages. It'd be perfect for my front hall. Every now and then I check to see if the price has dropped."

His grin broadened. "Let's check it out." He reached into the car, turned off the motor, then he gestured for her to lead the way.

Jaina had never liked walking in front of anyone because it only called attention to her limp. She would have said Connor hadn't noticed it, but he'd asked if she'd sprained her ankle that day as she left his office. Either he didn't mind it, or he was one fine actor!

They walked side by side in companionable silence until they reached the storefront, where Jaina continued her charade of being interested in the items on display. "I have a set of these," she said, pointing to the spire-shaped salt and pepper shakers. "They don't hold much, but they look so pretty when the table's all set for dinner."

"They'd look great in your house."

"My apartment, you mean."

"No. I mean your house. The one in all your paintings."

Her flush deepened. "Good grief. You noticed them?" She hid her face behind her hands. "It was a birthday surprise. Mom hung them all up one day while I was at the market." Jaina came out of hiding to add, "It's embarrassing as can be, but what could I say after she'd gone to all that trouble?"

"Embarrassing? I think they're very good."

She rolled her eyes. "Please." And then, "Funny how therapeutic something like painting can be when…" A hard little laugh punctuated her unfinished sentence. "I'd never picked up a paintbrush before…" She shook her head, then started again. "Before I knew it, I was surrounded by paintings. Big ones, small ones, rectangles and squares and ovals…" She laughed softly. "I used to watch that guy on PBS. You know the one…with the bushy red hair?"

"'And a happy little tree lives right here,'" Connor said in a perfect imitation of the television artist.

"That's the one!" She giggled. Sighed. "I'd stand there watching him, trying my best to duplicate whatever he was working on that day." She shook her head and gave a wry little smile. "Strange the way that house popped up in everything I did."

"Not so strange. It's your dream house, isn't it?"

One hand flew to her throat. How did he know that? And then it dawned on her. "My mother talks too much sometimes."

"Funny thing," he continued as if she hadn't spoken, "how much that house looks like mine."

"You have a dream house, too?" she blurted.

"I don't know how dreamy it is, but it's where I live."

Jaina gasped. "You live…you live in a house like the one in my paintings?"

Connor nodded. "Wanna see it?"

Her eyes widened. "Now?"

"Why not?"

"Well…well," she stammered, "for starters, I thought you had to attend some kind of hearing this afternoon."

He glanced at his watch. Frowned. "I've got exactly twenty minutes to get back to the office, pick up the files and head over to the courthouse."

"Well, then," she said, smiling, "you'd better get a move on."

"I could pick you up after work, drive you and Liam over there. If you're not busy, that is."

Me? Busy? Jaina almost laughed out loud. She didn't know what had inspired the invitation, but it pleased her nonetheless. Did he want to show Liam the room he'd be sleeping in? Or did he want *her* to see it so she'd know firsthand how well he could provide for the baby? Either way, Jaina's curiosity was piqued. "I'll bring supper," she volunteered, "so Liam won't get off his schedule."

He began walking backward toward his own car. "Pick you up at five?"

"We'll be ready." She watched him climb into the sleek silver sports car. If it hadn't looked like rain, would he have put the top down? she wondered. And then something else occurred to her, and she half ran toward his car. "You'll have to leave your car at the diner."

He leaned out of the driver's window to ask, "You have some objection to foreign models?"

"There's no back seat in this thing. Where would we put Liam's car seat?"

Connor pursed his lips. "Good point." Grinning, he added, "See? It's like I said...you're a natural-born caretaker."

She'd almost asked it the last time he'd paid her the compliment. *What have you got to lose?* she asked herself. "If you really feel that way, why do you want to take Liam away from me?"

Jaina felt his gaze sweep over her face. When his eyes met hers, he said, "I don't *want* to take him, Jaina. I *have* to." She was about to ask why again, but thought better of it as he revved the sports car's powerful engine. "See you at five," he called out, then drove away.

The answering-machine light was blinking when they walked into his kitchen. Still reeling from the similarity between his house and the one she'd dreamt of for as long as she could remember, Jaina watched as Connor reached for the Play button and Liam tugged his earlobe. "Easy, little guy," Connor said, gently prying open the baby's fingers.

She thought of what he'd said just before he'd driven away from the parking lot earlier. A fierce possessiveness overtook her, and Jaina stepped up and held out her arms. "Here," she said, "I'll take him while you do that." Liam's shirt had ridden up, exposing his round tummy, and Jaina adjusted it.

Connor read aloud the bold black letters on the front of it. "'Actually, I'm a rocket scientist.'" And laughing, he played the message.

"Better be careful," a gravelly voice said, "because when you least expect it, you're gonna get yours!"

Scowling, Connor flushed. "Don't tell me *this* is starting again."

"What's starting again?"

He shook his head, jerking a thumb over his shoulder at the phone. "Threats."

"You've been threatened before?"

"Only a few thousand times." He shrugged. "Actually, that one was tame compared to most. It sorta goes with the territory."

She frowned. "I presume you've notified the police."

"Yeah. And I'll give you three guesses what they said."

"They want to assign someone to guard you?"

He perched Liam on his shoulders. "Ain't she the sweetest, most innocent li'l thing you ever did see?" he asked the baby.

"Well, at least they must be going to guard you part of the time," she pressed. "Right?"

Connor shot her a crooked grin. "Gosh, you're cute when you're being naive."

Jaina felt a blush creep into her cheeks. "Then…they're going to increase the patrol cars that pass by your—"

He hissed a stream of air through his teeth. "Don't make me laugh. I'm a defense attorney, remember? I'm the guy who puts their collars back on the street."

Liam heard the hissing sound Connor had made and tried his best to emulate it.

"But...but you're so isolated, way out here in the country. Are you safe, all alone like that?"

"So far...and I'm keeping my fingers crossed."

"Then why aren't you doing something about it?"

Connor unfolded the portable playpen she'd brought along, and Jaina put Liam into it. Together, they emptied the mesh bag that held his toys. The baby squealed with glee as stuffed animals and rubber balls rained down upon him.

"How 'bout a glass of lemonade?" he asked.

"I'd love some."

"I have to warn you...it isn't fresh-squeezed," he bantered.

While he put ice cubes into glasses, Jaina poured. "You can't change the subject that easily, Connor."

He heaved a deep sigh. "It's a long story."

"Liam doesn't have to be in bed until nine. We have four hours by my watch." She put their glasses on the kitchen table, sat, then crossed her arms over her chest. "I'm listening...."

He took the seat across from her, leaned both elbows on the pine surface and, for the next half hour, compelled her attention with the tale of his life in the courtroom, first as a prosecutor, then as a defense attorney. "Didn't matter much which side of the courtroom I was on; in the opinions of the defendants, I helped some, I hurt some."

Jaina wondered whether or not to tell him she had been a defendant. "This is a free country, certainly they're entitled to their opinions. But what they're doing is wrong. And what's that old adage? 'Two wrongs don't make a right.' You can't let them get away with this just because you feel sorry for them."

"It isn't pity, Jaina. It's guilt."

"Guilt? But you were only doing your job!"

"True, but I'm not God. What if, in a few cases that I prosecuted successfully, the defendant really didn't deserve to go to prison? If the evidence said otherwise I had to do my job. Still, my presence is a constant reminder of their years behind bars."

She studied his face and saw that he meant it. The more Jaina learned about Connor Buchanan, the better she liked him. If only there was some way to convince him to let her keep Liam. If only there was a way they could share him.

"If you're in danger…so would Liam be…if he lived here."

He considered that for a moment. "You've got a point. But he doesn't live here."

"Yet." She brought the subject back to the phone call. "How do you know so much about how they feel?"

He stared at his hands, folded on the tabletop. "I was a prosecutor before I became a defense attorney. The things I saw and heard…" He shook his head and gave her a long, penetrating stare. "And how is it you can be so forgiving?"

Jaina flinched. "I…I…I'm afraid I don't…"

He leaned forward, both hands now pressing down on the tabletop. "Yes you *do*." He cupped her hands in his own. "You understand perfectly, because you lived it yourself. Why aren't *you* bitter and angry? Why don't *you* blame all men for what one man did to you?"

She began to tremble. It started in her fingertips, then reverberated to her limbs, her shoulders, her hips. Surely he could feel it, as tightly as he was holding her hands. *He knows about…* But *how* did he know? Had it been something she'd said or done? Was the past written on her face like a scarlet letter? One thing was sure: if he knew about the surgery, he knew everything that had led up to it, too.

Jaina's heart thundered, because if that was true, Liam was as good as gone.

"Who told you?" she asked, her voice a thick, hoarse whisper.

He broke the intense eye contact and, staring at their hands, said, "I just know, okay?"

Jaina glanced at Liam, playing happily in the playpen. "I should start supper. He'll be hungry soon." She stood, then nervously began rummaging in the cooler she'd filled with Chili Pot food. "I think we'll start with a nice salad, and then we'll have some of Mom's famous minestrone before we eat the spaghetti. There's a wedge of cheesecake in here somewhere," she rambled, jostling jars and plastic containers around. "I'll let you set the table since this is your kitchen and you know where things are. If you'll just get me a saucepan so I can heat the—"

In a heartbeat, it seemed, he was beside her, gently encircling her wrists with long, strong fingers. "Jaina," he breathed, "don't."

Don't what? she wanted to demand. Unable to meet his eyes, she focused on their hands. *What must he think of me?* she wondered as her trembling intensified.

Connor lifted her chin on a bent forefinger. "Look at me."

Slowly, she raised her gaze.

"I'd never hurt you, not in a million years."

You're going to take Liam from me, and that'll hurt worse than anything I've ever...

There was a hitch in his voice when he asked, "Do you believe me? That I'd never intentionally hurt you, I mean?"

The same instinct that could have saved her—if she'd listened to it that night with Bill—pinged inside her now. For a reason she couldn't explain, she wanted to say "Yes, I believe you," for no reason other than that he seemed to need to hear it. But it was a lie. He would hurt her, *inten-*

tionally, when he took Liam. Jaina looked into his eyes, sparkling with expectation and hope.

She nodded.

Connor looked toward the ceiling and heaved a great sigh. "Thank God," he whispered, his voice quaking, "thank God."

Slowly, he lowered his head. That time in his office… she'd worried he might kiss her. This time, she knew he *would*. In the instant, that tick in time before it happened, thoughts churned dizzyingly in her mind.…

For the first time since they'd met, she saw him as more than the savvy legal shark whose no-holds-barred approach to law had likely won him a thousand cases. It was evident in his square-shouldered stance, his no-nonsense gait, his matter-of-fact voice, that he was a man unaccustomed to losing. Until now, she believed he viewed Liam as the trophy to be won at the end of a long, arduous battle, or property to be claimed, like a lost dog or a wallet that had fallen from his pocket.

When Jaina read the yearning in his crystal blue eyes, she was reminded of the reason he'd offered for having avoided most of his secretary's get-togethers. Adopting Liam wasn't about ownership, she realized. And it wasn't about winning, either. It was about love, about family, about the need to feel he *belonged*. With nothing more than a forlorn expression, he'd awakened feelings in her she didn't know could exist.

He stood a head taller than her, outweighed her by at least fifty pounds. Clearly, he didn't need her protection. And yet protecting him was precisely what Jaina wanted to do. She felt compelled to stand in front of him, to defend him against anyone who threatened him.

She guessed him to be in his early thirties, and by all outward appearances, he seemed to have done a fine job taking care of himself physically. The house, though sparsely and plainly decorated, was spotless, the yard around it as manicured as a golf course. Yet she wanted to cook for him, clean for him, turn this house into a haven that would welcome him at the end of a long, hard day.

And though she could tell by the taut set of his lips and his lantern jaw that he was trying hard to hide it, Connor looked sad and lonely, and she wanted to wrap her arms around him, whisper soothingly into his ear that everything would be all right…that she'd *make* everything all right.

She was surprised by the tenderness welling up inside her. For one thing, she'd never felt anything like it before; for another, *this* was the man who wanted to take Liam from her. To feel such things for him…

Yes, he was going to kiss her.

And she welcomed it!

When his arms slid around her, she felt the protective wall she'd spent years building around herself begin to crack. He pressed her to him, gently, tenderly—as if the action was, for him, more a gesture of comfort than passionate need—and the wall crumbled around her feet.

His hands, so strong and sure as he tended to her cut that day in his office, trembled now as he embraced her. She felt the thrumming of his heart, steady and sure against her chest, and the faint quaking of his fingers as he combed them, slowly, lovingly, through her hair.

He leaned back slightly, holding her at arm's length, and silently searched her face. She read his soft gaze and understood that he saw her not as a scarred woman with a limp, not as a woman with a sordid past, but simply as a woman, a *whole* woman, with yearnings and dreams that matched his own.

Jaina had thought that, in her twenty-eight years, she'd experienced every emotion known to humanity…love, hate, fear, gratitude. She'd accepted others at face value many times, but she'd never experienced it herself. Not like this. It was new, brand-new, this wonderful sensation that came with knowing that someone who wasn't obliged by blood ties to accept her unconditionally, as her parents did, *accepted* her, scars and limp and history and all!

Overwhelmed with gratitude—to God? to Connor? Jaina didn't know—she felt her heart begin to pound. Hesitantly, she lifted a hand to trace his beard-stubbled cheek with the backs of her fingers. Oh, what a face it was. Square-jawed and high-cheeked, it was hard angles and raw planes, completely masculine. And yet, beneath the thick sandy blond mustache, a tenderhearted smile, and in the bright blue, long-lashed eyes, a shimmering tear.

She wiped it away with the pad of her thumb, smiling shakily through tears of her own. A silent prayer of thankfulness whispered in her heart, and she bowed her head, humbled by the breathtaking freedom Connor had given her. Freedom from feeling she'd been tainted by the violence of that fleeting, long-ago moment. Freedom from believing that the sharp edge of that instant in time had cut her out of the normal things in life, had destined her to spend her life alone, remembering, reliving, regretting her immature, injudicious decision....

It seemed as natural as breathing to press her cheek against his hard, broad chest, to wrap her arms around his narrow waist. Jaina stood in the shelter of his embrace and reveled in the utter peace that surrounded her.

Connor kissed the top of her head, her temple, her cheek. His eyes met hers, and she read the longing there. The same pining beat in her own heart, and she willed him with her gaze to continue, to touch her lips with his.

But she couldn't speak past the sob that blocked her voice.

Since her release from prison so many years ago, every time a man had let her know, by his expression, by taking her in his arms, by saying point-blank that he wanted to kiss her, fear had made her stiffen, step back, call a quick halt to anything that might lead to emotional or physical intimacy. What if the same poor judgment that had allowed

her to get into the car that night had also affected her ability
to discern between the right man…and another like Bill?
And what if he was with her only because he believed her
to be defiled to the point that she'd be, as several had put
it, "easy pickin's." Equally fearsome, what if, in those rare
instances when the man had no knowledge of her disgrace,
he found out about it and judged her contaminated?

She had no such things to fear from Connor. He'd spent
the bulk of his career dealing with the worst society had to
offer after all. He'd have gone into another area of the law
if he didn't believe every murderer, robber and rapist had
an inalienable right to be considered innocent until proven
guilty. He would not judge her sullied. At least, not until
all the evidence was in.

And he knew. The evidence *was* in!

The knowledge made her feel safe. Secure. Sure.

His tenderness that day in his office, the gentle way he
handled Liam, the respect he showed her mother—despite
the fact that Rita was always so hard on him—was rooted,
Jaina believed, in a good and decent heart that beat strongly
with compassion and thoughtfulness. She sensed he was the
type who'd teach his children to pray for those less fortunate, who'd help them learn to field a grounder, and who'd
sit proudly in a dark auditorium while his youngster mas-
sacred Beethoven's Fifth. Patiently, lovingly, he'd assist
with homework and mean it when he recited timeworn clichés like "The world is your oyster" and "Look before
you leap" and "Sticks and stones may break your bones
but…"

She had never been the bold and brazen type. Despite
the fact that she'd gone onstage, wowing audiences, she'd
always been a bit shy. It was almost as though the microphone and the guitar had been props that helped her believe
some invisible barrier existed between her and the crowds.
Like the clown who hides behind his makeup and the pol-

itician who hides behind his speech writers, Jaina hid behind her talent.

No one was more surprised than Jaina when she bracketed his face with both hands, her thumbs drawing lazy circles on his cheeks. Holding his gaze, she slid her hands to the back of his neck, guided him near, nearer, until she felt his warm breath on her lips, until she felt the softness of his mouth against hers.

A dizzying swirl began churning inside her, eddying through her being, until her heart beat like a war drum and her pulse pounded like a jackhammer. She *wasn't* damaged goods, *hadn't been* ruined forever by that night. Connor knew—she didn't know how, but he *knew* about her sorry past—and yet he wanted her. It was a glorious, miraculous feeling. Her pastor had been right when he'd advised her to stop ridiculing herself for feeling so afraid every time a man got too close. "None of them has been the *right* man," he'd said. "When the mate God has chosen for you comes along, fear is the last thing you'll feel."

Connor Buchanan was that man!

Groggy with joy, Jaina began to laugh and cry at the same time. *Thank you, thank you, thank you,* she repeated—to God? To Connor? Both?

"Oh, Jaina," he gasped, hands on her shoulders, "I'm sorry. I'm so sorry that I got carried away. I don't know what's wrong with me." He grimaced as though in pain. "And I promised...I swore you'd always feel—"

Shaking her head, she placed her fingertips over his lips to silence him. Her tears had sent him the wrong message, she realized. "Shhh," she managed to say, "it's...it's not you. I'm...I'm not crying because...I'm afraid," she haltingly replied. "It's...because I'm...*relieved!* I thought...I was...that something was wrong with me."

He looked into her eyes, and as understanding dawned, he drew her close. "Ah, Jaina," he said, "there's not a thing wrong with you. *Nothing.*" He cupped her chin in a palm, and with a perfectly straight face, said, "Well, there's *one* thing wrong with you...."

She bit her lower lip and braced herself for the awful truth.

"You're not mine."

Skip darted into the kitchen. "I thought I'd *never* get you alone," he whispered. "Awright, Jaina, 'fess up. What gives?"

She met her friend's green eyes and said in her best Southern belle voice, "Why, Skip darlin', whatevah do you mean?"

He regarded her with a sidelong glance. "Connor Buchanan, that's what I mean. He's been makin' cow eyes at you all day long. What's goin' on between you two?"

Her heart pounded at the mere mention of his name, just as it had all through the long, lonely night. "I think the great generals would say we've declared a truce." She licked her lips and smiled, thinking of that kiss.... "Connor and I have decided it's in Liam's best interests if we try to get along."

"So it's *Connor* now, is it?" He raised his dark eyebrows. "That sounds very cozy."

She didn't like his insinuation. "Don't be ridiculous. We're...we're—"

"Friends?" The sarcasm in his voice rang like an Oriental gong.

"We're becoming friends. Yes."

"Aha. And my old Aunt Bessie is a horse."

Jaina clucked her tongue. "Shame on you, Skip. Bessie can't help it if she's a bit overweight."

He frowned. "You can't distract me that easily, pal. I know what's going on between you and our attorney friend, and if you ask me, you're making a big mistake."

"First of all," she snapped, "I *didn't* ask you." Propping a fist on her hip, Jaina added, "And secondly, it's obvious from this nonsense you're spouting that you haven't the foggiest idea what's going on.''

''Oh, don't I? *That* guy,'' he said, thick forefinger jabbing the air, ''is the only thing standing between you and permanent custody of Liam. And I've seen the way you look at that kid. I believe you'd do *anything* to keep him.''

Her eyes widened and she gasped. His insinuation had become a full-fledged accusation. ''We've been friends for ages. You know better than that.''

He raised a brow. ''I thought I did.''

Leaning forward, she aimed a threatening digit at his nose. ''Listen, *pal,* I'd never do anything so underhanded to get something I want!''

''Not even something you want as badly as you want Liam?''

She met his challenge head-on. ''There's nothing I want badly enough to make me—''

He held up a hand to silence her. ''Save it for the courtroom.''

Jaina couldn't believe her ears. This wasn't like Skip at all. If she didn't know better, she'd say he was acting like a jealous suitor. Did Skip really think she was so desperate to keep the baby that she'd resort to…to *that?* Hadn't he learned anything about her in all the years they'd known one another? ''I have hamburgers to make,'' she said flatly, turning away from him. ''If you're going to help, wash your hands and grab some gloves. Otherwise…''

Connor entered the room, grinning and rubbing his palms together. ''I'd be happy to help,'' he began. His smile faded as he took note of the surly expressions on their faces. ''Sorry, guys. Didn't mean to interrupt.'' Walking backward, he headed for the door, hands up in mock self-defense. ''I'll just—''

''No. *I'll* 'just,''' Skip interrupted, his voice brittle with bitterness. He shoved the screen door open. ''You know what they say, two's company, three's a crowd," he grumbled.

"Skip, don't be silly!" Jaina's retort crackled.

The door slammed as Skip stomped down the steps.

"What was that all about?" Connor asked when Skip was out of earshot.

Jaina cut the end off an onion. "He thinks," she began, the blade hovering inches above the vegetable, "that I'm using my feminine wiles to trick you into letting me keep Liam." She quickly carved parallel slices three-quarters of the way through the onion, then deftly turned it ninety degrees and repeated the process.

Remembering the way she'd responded to his kiss, Connor swallowed. *Skip thinks she'd...*

He stopped himself. He didn't know Skip from a hole in the wall, so why should he take anything the man said to heart? He stepped up to the sink, turned on the faucet and tested the water temperature before grabbing the bar of soap on the counter. "So...are you?"

The knife split the onion in two, stopping with a dull *thunk* on the battered cutting board. She held his gaze for what seemed a full, agonizing minute. A slow, mischievous grin drew up the corners of her mouth, glittering in her dark, long-lashed eyes. "Am I *what?*"

He looked from her eyes to her lips, and it took every ounce of control he could muster to keep from kissing her right where she stood. One side of his mouth lifted in a sly grin. He decided to rearrange the question slightly, see what her reaction might be if he caught her off guard. *Play it safe,* he decided, his smile broadening, *at least until she puts that knife down.*

"*Are* you using your feminine wiles?"

"No."

"Just as well," he said, though every male fiber in him wished she'd said yes. He shrugged. "'Cause what would a scheme like that get you in the long run?" Their kiss simmered in his memory. Anything she wanted, he admitted, regretting her quick denial even more. Anything she wanted.

She laid the knife on the cutting board and crossed her arms over her chest. "You, for starters."

"Me?" He chuckled. "What would you want with me?"

She tilted her head and raised an eyebrow. "If we were...*together,* I wouldn't have to fight you for Liam, now would I?"

He wished he'd known her longer, wished he knew her better, so he could determine if that flash in her eyes meant she was teasing...or not. Connor didn't want to believe she was like every other woman he'd known—capable of underhanded and deliberate manipulation—but there was too much at stake, and he simply couldn't afford to discount the possibility.

Despite his concerns, his grin broadened. "But, Jaina," he drawled, taking a step closer, "what would you do with me *afterward?*"

To his surprise, she said, "Why, I'd honor my marriage vows, of course. Which would be to your benefit."

Laughing, Connor moved closer still. "And why is that?"

She gave a nonchalant little nod of her head. "I'm right handy with an iron for one thing, and you wouldn't believe how fast I can sew a button onto a sleeve. I believe cleanliness really *is* next to Godliness, and if I do say so myself, I'm pretty good in the kitchen."

If that kiss in my *kitchen is any indicator, I agree!* "So you're saying we should get married? Avoid the courtroom altogether?"

She picked up the knife again. "I'm no lawyer, but if I'm making any sense at all of Skip's advice, a stable, married couple would have an easier time trying to adopt Liam than two people who are—"

"Footloose and fancy free?"

"Cliché, but yes, being single will make it harder."

"Much harder."

He watched her turn the onion on its side so she could carve quarter-inch slices through the grid pattern she'd already cut into it. Tidy opaque squares avalanched onto the cutting board. "I guess your dad served some KP time in the service, eh?"

Jaina's hands froze. "Excuse me?"

"He's retired air force, right? I'm just assuming he did kitchen duty at some point in his military career and taught you that nifty little trick."

She looked at the cutting board, at his face, at the board again. "As a matter of fact," she said, her voice trembling slightly, "my father *did* teach me this nifty little trick." Jaina met his eyes. "But the only KP he did was during barbecues."

She straightened, and he read the pride in her stance and on her face. "He was a test pilot."

"I know."

Glaring, she all but slammed the knife down. "Of course you know." Her mouth formed a taut line as she pointed to a shelf above his head. "Would you mind handing me that bowl?"

Connor placed it on the counter, and while she filled it with chopped onions, he sighed inwardly. Her marriage talk had been a joke, nothing more, he believed. Which was too bad, since it made sense. A *lot* of sense.

It actually *would* make the adoption process a lot simpler if they were a couple. Besides, he could see what a wonderful mother she was. He wanted Liam, wanted him badly. But he wanted Jaina, too. *To be Liam's mother, of course....*

The mental pictures he'd gotten at the office—of her seeing him off in the morning, welcoming him home again in the evening, caring for Liam, for *him*—flashed through his mind. He'd dismissed the feelings those images had aroused. Feelings of warmth and comfort, of peace and passion. Feelings born of the knowledge that, in her eyes, whether rich or poor, he was *okay* just the way he was.

After discovering his ex-wife's betrayal, he'd made a promise never to get serious about another woman. There was no point since they all had a similar plan: lure him into their web with whatever deceitful means they deemed necessary, wrap him securely in their silken lies and leave him there to hang.

It had been a halfhearted promise at best. Because if he was honest with himself, Connor had to admit he'd been searching for the right woman all his life. If he'd listened to his own gut instincts, he'd have admitted way back then that Miriam hadn't been that woman; if he'd heeded his own good advice, he wouldn't have wasted all those years. Maybe now he'd have his dream—a devoted wife and a house full of rambunctious kids.

Why *not* marry Jaina? he asked himself. Then he'd—

"Tell me something, Connor."

"Hmm?" he said distractedly.

"How *do* you know so much about me?"

He repeated her question in his head. She'd been honest with him—at least he *thought* she had been—and he saw no point in being evasive. "I hired a private detective."

Her glare intensified, and she faced him head-on. "A private detective," she echoed.

He nodded.

"So you know—"

"Everything," he finished. "And it doesn't make a bit of difference to me." It was true after all. He'd read the reports, and in his opinion, none of it had been her fault. And even if some of the blame *did* belong on her shoulders—and he refused to accept that as a possibility—she could be forgiven her mistakes because she'd only been nineteen or so at the time. In the years since then, she'd accomplished a great deal.

Rage blazed in her eyes. She turned abruptly away and

grabbed a handful of raw hamburger. "Well, it's *going* to make a difference." She rolled the meat into a sphere, then slapped it flat between her palms. Setting the burger on a plate, she plucked off another lump of beef and smacked it into a patty. "How are you going to feel when the judge says you can't have Liam...because your wife is an ex-con?"

"Not a problem. I'll adopt Liam first, and *then* we'll get married."

"Slick, Buchanan," she said.

"Excuse me?"

"You get me to hand him over just like that, and once the papers are filed..."

He was focusing on the fact that she'd said "when," not "if." Then he noted her determined expression. He'd heard all his life that love was blind. Not till that minute did he realize it was stubborn, too. "If that happened, I wouldn't be thrilled," he admitted, "but..." Could he say it? Dare he admit how he felt? *But I'd feel like a lucky guy all the same, because I'd still have* you.

Practice makes perfect, he thought, knowing that he'd always made a habit of thinking first and speaking later. He'd always kept a tight rein on his emotions, something he was grateful for right now. Because what he wanted didn't matter. Much as he wanted—no, needed a life with Jaina—Liam needed a secure home, a stable parent *more*. If there was a chance, even a slight one, that her background might cost him a life with the child...

Connor cleared his throat. "I suppose you're right." Several silent seconds ticked by before he helped himself to a fistful of meat. "How many of these things do we need?"

He glimpsed the flicker of pain that glimmered in her dark eyes before she answered.

"Ten more oughta do it. 'Cause we have hot dogs and potato salad and baked beans and—"

She stopped speaking so suddenly that he wondered if

maybe something had blocked her windpipe. He looked up in time to see her wiping her hands on a towel.

"I, uh, I'll be right back," she stammered. "Can you hold down the fort for a few minutes?"

"No problem," he said as she dashed away.

Before she'd run off, the room had seemed warm and sunny, despite the storm-threatening skies. As the door between the kitchen and the diner hissed shut behind her, Connor acknowledged that without her, his world was as dark and bleak as a windowless cell.

Jaina stood in the ladies' room, palms flat on the countertop. "What were you thinking?" she asked the woman in the mirror.

The answer was clear: she *hadn't* been thinking. If she had been, would she have suggested they get married? Would she so boldly have suggested she'd make some lucky guy a pretty good wife?

Not in a thousand years, she admitted. *Not in a million years.*

She turned away from the mirror and covered her face with both hands. *He knows what you are.* He knows, and yet he'd said he didn't care, that it didn't matter.

But how could it *not?*

There hadn't been much point in trying to keep her past a secret throughout her life; the accident and everything that had happened on the heels of it had been in the papers for weeks afterward. Like Eliot and Billie and Joy, she'd been forced to learn to live with the sneers and whispers that so often followed her when folks found out her past was not spotless. Some of her friends and co-workers really *had* been headed down the wrong path. Jaina, on the other hand, hadn't been guilty of anything but empty-headed gullibility.

To her knowledge, no one had tried to pass a bill that made foolishness against the law; if they had, six months in Jessup wouldn't have been nearly long enough because it had been blatantly stupid to get into that car with Bill! She'd suspected *something* was wrong that night and hadn't heeded her own inner warnings. That in itself deserved severe punishment, didn't it?

But when would she stop paying for her naiveté? Hadn't the injury, the months of physical therapy, the long, dark days in prison been enough? What of the supposedly life-saving surgery that had more than likely killed her chances of having children, leaving her stomach so contorted with scars it looked like a relief map? And what about the limp she tried so hard to disguise? How much more pain must she endure before she'd atoned for her transgression? When would she have done enough penance for her foolishness, and be set free at last from the humiliating, oppressive burden that was "the past"?

Jaina blotted her eyes on a brown paper towel and blew her nose. She couldn't remember the last time she'd felt so sorry for herself. In the hospital? During rehab? In Jessup? She sighed, remembering that long ago, she'd decided that self-pity was an ugly, egocentric waste of time and emotion. It had not furthered her recuperation, had not erased Bill's brutal death from her mind, hadn't wiped visions of the accident from her memory. And it hadn't cleared away the charges filed against her by the state.

Self-pity hadn't done her any good then, and it wouldn't do her any good now.

A verse she'd often read during her self-pitying days now came to mind. Jeremiah 20:7-18 had given her a sort of perverse comfort, for reading the ragings of that holy man, she'd felt less alone, less forgotten; if even God's chosen few had, from time to time, been furious with the Almighty, was she so different, for being angry because, in her mind, He'd let her down?

As a child, she'd learned that God loved all his children equally, no matter what. He had a capacity for love and mercy far beyond man's understanding, her Sunday school teachers had said, and promised to forgive and forget every sin…provided the sinner admitted culpability and confessed it with a contrite heart.

Connor, for all his insistence that her past didn't matter, was a flesh-and-blood man. She didn't know how long it would take, but sooner or later, she feared, he'd see how wrong he'd been and put a safe, permanent distance between them. It would break her heart when that happened, and she honestly didn't know if she could survive another crushing blow to her soul.

Jaina faced the sink again, patted her cheeks with cold water and ran now damp fingers through her hair. *He* had run his fingers through her hair last evening she remembered. And hiding her lips behind her palm, she tried to forget the sweet, soft kisses he'd pressed to her mouth.

She'd made a complete fool of herself, she acknowledged, and making a fool of herself was getting to be a bad habit. A habit she'd break, starting now.

Jaina stood as tall as her five-feet-three-inch frame would allow and took a deep breath. *You go out there and try to forget about that kiss, 'cause it's a sure thing he will.*

Maybe he could forget, but *she* wouldn't.

Because it was too late.

She'd already opened the door to her heart and let him in.

Chapter Eight

Liam lay sound asleep on his tummy, a thumb in his mouth, oblivious to the brightly colored explosions overhead. Jaina and Connor were on their backs on either side of him, their murmured oohs and aahs harmonizing with those of other spectators enjoying the fireworks.

"I've been giving a lot of thought to what you said earlier," Connor remarked.

Jaina got up onto one elbow, smoothed a wrinkle in the red plaid blanket beneath them. "What, specifically, did I say?"

Connor now, too, levered himself up. "That we should get married."

In the rainbow of light that drizzled from the sky with a prismatic glow, he watched her dark eyes widen, her full lips part, her delicate hand flutter at her throat.

"It…it was a joke," she stammered, her voice shaking. "I never intended for you to take me seriously."

Connor had a feeling that if it hadn't been so dark, he'd have witnessed a deep blush coloring her cheeks. In the time he'd known her, he'd learned that she found it difficult to stretch the truth even a bit. "That's too bad," he said.

"I was really lookin' forward to telling all my pals down at the law library that the prettiest woman this side of the Mississippi proposed to me while—"

"Whom do you know west of the Mississippi?"

Laughing, he said, "I didn't take you seriously." But he hadn't thought of much else since, he admitted silently. It made sense. Perfect sense. They had a lot in common, for one thing. She was a terrific mother, for another. They both wanted what was best for Liam. Granted they didn't know each other well, but...

He'd been telling himself the idea only seemed so appealing because he didn't have the stomach to fight her. Here, now, gazing into her sparkling brown eyes, he admitted the truth: He didn't want to fight her...because he *loved* her.

He couldn't name the precise moment in time when he'd first realized it. That day in his office, when she'd breezed past him, trying like crazy to hide the limp? When he'd called her from New York, and she'd asked all those caring, wifely questions about his well-being? In the diner, when he'd watched her orchestrate the cleanup of the miniflood with calm finesse? Climbing her stairs, when he'd noticed the paintings of her dream house?

What about the horrible accident she'd survived...and everything that had been a consequence of it? And the way she'd defended him to her mother, saying he had a right to see Liam anytime he wanted to because he was *family*.

And her reaction to his kiss...

She'd seemed so tentative at first, so shy and uncertain. He loved the pluck and spirit that had moved her beyond her fear; it was the same drive and determination that had helped her survive an ordeal that might have crushed other women.

He loved the open-armed attitude that had allowed her to welcome an abandoned baby into her heart, into her life, as if he were her own. Loved her levelheaded matter-offactness, her mind for business, her old-fashioned work ethic...

To put it simply, Connor loved everything about her, from her curly brown hair to her size-five feet. Pride prevented him from admitting it, though, because what if she didn't feel the same way about him? He believed there were just two things he couldn't survive at this point in his life: losing Liam, and losing Jaina.

He could only hope that in time—provided he could convince her to agree to his plan—she'd grow to love him, too.

It wasn't completely implausible, was it? Because throughout history, marriages of convenience had prevented wars, secured fortunes, saved businesses, ended family feuds.

If Jaina could admit she *liked* him now, there was reason to hope that someday she'd love him, too.

Wasn't there?

He looked at her, and his heart lurched with hopeful possibilities. It was certainly worth a try. Besides, he added, marrying her would certainly solve a whole slew of problems.

Connor slipped his hand behind her head, fingers playing in the soft waves at the nape of her neck. He didn't know how long he'd been staring into her eyes, lost in his moment of whimsy. He only knew that he wanted this beautiful, bighearted little woman. Wanted her to be Liam's mother. And if the doctors were mistaken—and he'd move heaven and earth if only he could prove them wrong—he wanted her to be the mother to his children, *their* children. But even if the medical professionals were correct, and Jaina could never have babies of her own, he still wanted to face all the joys and trials of life beside her, forever.

He smiled and, leaning forward, placed a light kiss upon her forehead. She'd closed her eyes as he drew near, and Connor backed away slightly to study her face.

He took note of thick, dark lashes, finely arched brows, the gentle slope of her nose. The fireworks' showy hues illuminated her lovely features, accented the soft, feminine roundness of her cheeks and the delicate point of her chin with shimmering, sparkling light that glowed scarlet to emerald to gold. It was as though the state fair's Strong Man had clutched his chest, tightening and twisting. Oh, how he wanted to wrap his arms around her and never let go.

Her lashes fluttered like miniature wings, sending his heart into a pulsing, pounding rhythm that echoed in his ears. He had snickered at the age-old cliché, borrowed and repeated too many times to count by men for whom poetry seemed like a foreign language, but when at last she opened her eyes and he gazed into the depths of those dazzling spheres, Connor understood for the first time what it meant to feel like a drowning man, caught in the powerful vortex of a whirlpool.

"We're missing the finale," he heard her whisper.

Finale? What did he care about eye-popping, eardrum-splitting thunderflashes? The real rockets were exploding in his heart.

Connor watched her profile, resplendent in the rich, radiant color reflected from the sky. Moments later, he, too, looked toward the heavens, pretending to be engrossed in the percussive display until Liam stirred between them.

The baby sat up and knuckled his eyes. Unfazed by the noise above him, he crawled into Jaina's lap and pointed at the booming bouquets above. Her smile, in response to his delight, was tender and sweet, her voice, in reply to his excited squeals, laughingly lively. She wrapped her arms around him, took his tiny hand and pointed it at the sky. If Connor didn't know better, he would have assumed they'd been together since the baby's birth.

That's where he belonged, Connor told himself.

And if he could find a way, that's where the little boy would stay.

                         *   *   *

Jaina woke to the trilling of the phone and mumbled a groggy "Hullo" into the mouthpiece.

"Hey. It's Skip. How ya doin'?"

"Fine," she said around a yawn. "And you?"

"Look. I won't beat around the bush. I called to say I'm sorry. I didn't mean to be so hard on you yesterday. Forgive me?"

One hand covering her eyes, Jaina shook her head. "Yeah, I guess so." She stretched, thinking of their argument. Had he called to pick up where he'd left off? Jaina hoped not. She didn't like confrontation, though Skip seemed to handle it fine. But then, she supposed, he was a counselor and trained to handle difficult emotional discussions.

"So," she asked now, stifling another yawn, "where'd you go after you left the diner yesterday?"

"Home." He cleared his throat. "I had some thinking to do."

Jaina chuckled. "Uh-oh. That's not a good sign. I'll bet you have a wicked headache this morning."

"I forgot how mean you can be first thing in the morning."

"If you don't tell me why you're calling at this hour…"

"Hey, be nice. I was up all night, thinking up ways to help you."

"Help me?" She stretched. "Help me what?"

"I kinda hoped you'd invite me over. You know, to discuss it in person."

She sat up, pressed her fingertips against her forehead and glanced at the clock. "It isn't even five yet." Furrowing her brow, she added, "I thought you liked to sleep till noon on the weekends."

"I'm too excited to sleep. I want to run this idea by you, see if it cuts the mustard."

She swung her legs over the edge of the bed. "I have to

shower and dress, feed Liam his breakfast. I suppose you could meet me in the diner in, say, forty-five minutes.'' She narrowed one eye to ask, ''You sure it's not too early? Because I'd hate for you to fall asleep behind the wheel and—''

''Trust me,'' he insisted, ''I'm wide awake.''

She'd known him long enough to recognize excitement in his voice when she heard it. ''Give me a hint. Did you get a raise? A promotion? Find the girl of your dreams?''

There was a considerable pause before he said, ''I'll tell you this. It's about you.''

Jaina laughed. ''Me? What could I possibly have to do with—''

''Nothing. Everything. I mean…'' He exhaled an exasperated sigh.

''You want me to have your favorite breakfast ready when you get here?''

''Are you kiddin'? I haven't had French toast in ages. I'll be there in *half* an hour!'' An hour later, Jaina was helping her father unload the morning's delivery of milk when Skip blasted through the diner's back door. He grabbed her hand. ''Come with me,'' he said, panting as if he'd run a marathon.

''Skip,'' she scolded gently, ''I'm right in the middle of—''

''This is important, Jaina.'' He glanced at the rest of the staff and lowered his voice. ''I need to talk to you in private.'' He gave her arm another tug. ''It won't take long. I promise.''

Her father gave Skip a quick once-over. ''What's got you so riled up this morning, son? I don't think I've seen you this excited since…'' His forehead furrowed slightly. ''Why, I don't believe I've *ever* seen you this excited.''

Jaina wriggled free of Skip's grasp. ''I hate to be a party pooper,'' she said, tapping her watch, ''but we open in less than an hour.'' She looked at Skip. ''You've known this bunch of nuts for years. They're family. You can say anything in front of them.'' She went back to unloading the truck. A touch of impatience rang in her voice when she said, ''Skip, would you please just spit it out?''

He took a deep breath. ''I'm offering you the opportunity of a lifetime.''

''What opportunity?''

''Me!''

''You?'' Jaina frowned. ''I don't get it.''

''How long have we known one another?''

She shrugged. ''We met in the third grade. If you don't count all the times Mom and Dad and I were transferred back and forth before we settled down here, I'd say twenty years.''

''How'd you put up with him that long?'' Eliot wanted to know.

''Sometimes it wasn't easy.''

''In all the time we've known one another,'' Skip asked, ''have we ever had a fight?''

They hadn't fought, Jaina admitted, because she'd chosen to overlook his bad behavior. ''How 'bout the one we had on the Fourth of July?''

''I don't mean little stuff like that,'' he interrupted, waving her comment away. ''I mean serious disagreements.''

She gave the question a moment's thought. She hadn't considered his attitude toward Connor, toward her keeping Liam, ''little stuff.'' Far from it.

But it seemed he'd taken her silence to mean they'd had no serious disagreements. ''Of course not. I'm the most even-tempered man you know.'' Skip began counting on his fingers. ''We both like baseball, hate sour pickles, and neither one of us misses the six o'clock news unless there's a national emergency.''

Things she had in common with thousands of total strangers, she reflected. ''So what's your point?''

''Well, you're not gettin' any younger—'' he glanced at

the baby ''—and the ki…I mean Liam here is in a dandy fix.''

Oh, no, she thought, her hard-beating heart rattling her rib cage, *I know where this is going.* Clasping her hands beneath her chin, Jaina closed her eyes. *Dear Lord,* she prayed, *let this be a dream, and when I open my eyes, the alarm will be buzzing….*

Of course he hadn't been serious. How could he *possibly* have been serious? For as long as she'd known him, Skip had been a tease. Maybe this was one of his practical jokes. Jaina hoped so, because if it wasn't…

She'd always tried to be a good friend to Skip, and he'd always been there for her, too. But marriage? To a man she didn't love? That wouldn't be fair to her or to Skip. Out of the question! Yes, she'd been accused of a crime, had served time for it, but Jaina believed that even *she* deserved a better life than that!

Connor couldn't believe his ears. He stopped dead in his tracks just outside the diner's open back door, unconsciously clenching his hands into tight fists, his molars grinding like unoiled gears. *Why, that little twerp is gonna ask Jaina to marry him!*

Even before taking his self-imposed vow to keep a safe distance from women, he'd never had reason to be jealous. Not even when his lady friends played the age-old game of passing off another man as Connor's competition. Each time they tried that tactic, it had failed miserably, and they'd stormed off in a huff when he failed to react to his so-called challenger as they'd hoped he would.

Well, he was jealous now!

He'd never been a violent man, and Jaina's old pal had never done anything to him. So why did he feel an overwhelming urge to punch Skip in the jaw?

Connor had stopped by the diner this morning to propose. He'd been up all night, thinking about how much sense it made. Despite the way she'd laughed off the idea.

Perhaps he could convince her that marrying him was the best solution for everyone concerned.

Now he understood why Skip had stomped out of the diner yesterday. He must have interrupted his proposal. If he'd known he had a rival, he might have posed the question sooner. But he couldn't very well second-guess a man he'd never met before, now could he? And besides, Jaina had made a point of telling him that she and Skip had been buddies since childhood.

Well, he didn't like her buddy. Not one bit. He didn't like the way Skip looked at Jaina and he certainly didn't like Skip thinking she might even marry him.

Would Jaina say yes to Skip? he wondered as his heart hammered. Why was it so quiet in there?

"So anyway," Skip continued as if in response to Connor's thought, "I decided that I have what you need—and you're not so bad-lookin' yourself—and since we have so much in common, we could make a go of this marriage thing."

Connor was clenching his jaw so tightly that his teeth ached. As Skip's question reverberated in his head, his fists ached for the same reason. As did every other muscle in his body.

He thought the long, silent pause might kill him. "Why doesn't she *answer?*" he whispered through his teeth, then offered up a quick and fervent prayer. *Please, God, let her say no.*

If he took half a step to the right, he discovered, he could see their reflections in the door's square, chicken-wired windowpane. He watched Jaina clasp her hands beneath her chin. "Oh, Skip," she said, sounding incredulous.

After a moment, he saw Skip put his hands on Jaina's shoulders. "So when do you want to do it?"

Jaina turned her head, and Connor could have sworn she had seen *his* reflection in the window, for it seemed that she was looking directly into his eyes. It was an eerie, uneasy feeling that set his heart to pounding again. He held his breath.

After another agonizingly long moment, she turned back to Skip. "Well, the paperwork has to be filed first...."

"Paperwork? For the justice of the peace, you mean?"

"To have you committed. You must be crazy if you think I'd marry you!"

Way to go, Jaina! Connor silently rooted.

"Well, seemed like a good idea in the middle of the night," Skip mumbled.

Connor had been up all night, too, imagining the rest of his life with Jaina. But did she consider *him* nothing more than a buddy, as well? Not that he had a problem with that—friendship was one of the most important components of a successful marriage, he believed—but he wanted more, much more, than just being her friend....

His secretary read three, four romance novels a week, and a year or so ago, Connor had picked one up. He'd selected a page at random, thinking he was in for a good chuckle, at least when he reached the parts where the passionate clichés began. But he hadn't so much as cracked a smile as he began to read.

Does she realize what she's *doing?* he wondered. Did she understand that her friendly greeting had done more than invite him inside? Was she aware that, as she plumped sofa cushions and poured hot tea to warm him, make him feel cozy and comfortable, *she had succeeded?* Or had it simply been an accident of fate, some curious coincidence, that her glittering eyes and lovely smile told him he'd always be welcome, wanted, accepted here, *despite* his unhappy past?

Connor had turned the page, uncomfortable with the fact that he had identified so closely with the story's hero. Perhaps a different passage would inspire the hearty laugh he'd expected.

It was more, so much more than his lips pressed to
hers. It seemed they'd become one living, breathing
being, united in heart and mind and soul by a thing as
innocent as a kiss. She knew, as she stood in the protective circle of his embrace, that near him was where
she wanted to spend the rest of her days. Because she
also knew, as his hard-pounding heart thrummed
against her, that he was a man capable of living and
loving to the fullest…to the end.

He wanted to make Jaina feel like that, wanted to be the
one who put stars in her eyes, caused her heart to beat hard
and fast, and made her ache with yearning when he was
out of sight.

"Let me know when you come to your senses," Skip
said, heading for the door. "But then, I won't hold my
breath…all things considered."

*And if Jaina will marry me, I'll be shouting from the
rooftops,* Connor thought.

"But you haven't had your French toast," Rita pointed
out.

"I guess I'm not hungry after all," Skip replied in a
disappointed tone. "Thanks anyway, Rita."

Connor recognized the defeated tone in Skip's voice and
even felt a bit of sympathy for the guy. Missing out on
marrying Jaina was truly a loss. But rather than offer his
condolences, Connor knew he'd better beat it.

He took one more longing look at Jaina's reflection in
the window of the diner's back door. Even the wavy glass
couldn't mar her sweet beauty. Quietly, he walked the
block and a half to the parking lot where he'd left his car.
In an hour or so, he'd return, broach the subject of marriage
again.

And again and again, until she said, "Yes."

Besides she'd been the first one to bring up the subject,

he reminded himself. She'd claimed it had been a joke, that she'd been teasing. But what was that lesson he'd learned in Psych 101? "There's a bit of truth in every joke."

He knew full well it might be a mistake to hang all his hopes on one lesson, learned so long ago. Revving the engine, he steered the sports car onto Route 40. As he merged into traffic, Connor considered all the pluses of his plan: Liam would have two parents, Jaina would have the baby *and* the house she'd always dreamed of, and he'd have the family he'd always wanted.

Jaina had been reading food orders for so long, it was second nature to her now. She hustled back and forth in the kitchen, helping Eliot fill platters and plates.

But her mind was not on her work.

She couldn't remember a time when she felt more confused. And there wasn't a soul she could discuss the dilemma with, now that Granny Chandelle was gone.

She had questioned herself intensively about this matter of falling so quickly in love with Connor Buchanan. Granny had always said, "Give a new love at least four seasons, so you can test its durability." Oh, to have the luxury of twelve leisurely months to define her feelings for Liam's uncle. Did she feel this way *because* he was related to the baby? Or were her feelings more personal than that?

She'd left his office that first day thinking he was a nice enough guy; he'd certainly been considerate when she'd nearly blacked out. Still, he'd seemed indifferent to Liam's needs, disinterested in how his own my-way-or-no-way mind-set might affect Kirstie. Nice, yes, but opinionated and stubborn, too.

Since then, she'd drastically altered her opinion. Now Jaina saw him as an unbiased, flexible, caring man. If his warm, devoted behavior with Liam didn't make him father material, she didn't know what did. And surely the fact that he refused to prosecute the woman who'd been harassing him was more proof what kind of man he was.

Certainly he could afford to live on some exclusive Nob Hill, in an impressive, contemporary style of house, with wide expanses of glass and filled with costly, one-of-a-kind furnishings. Instead, he'd purchased a dilapidated Victorian on the outskirts of town and refurbished it with his own two hands.

When he'd given her what he called The Grand Tour of the house, Connor explained how he'd sanded and refinished every window and door frame, every ceiling molding, every chair rail and panel of wainscoting. He showed her the wide-planked pine floors he'd preserved along with the original wood dowels that held them in place. She'd done enough to her apartment to know it had been painstaking, time-consuming work. She had loved every backbreaking, fingernail-chipping moment of it; he seemed to have enjoyed it, too.

His pride and joy, he'd admitted, was the small sunporch, added when he'd finished with the inside, so that after a harrowing day at the office, he could sit and stare into the woods along the banks of the Patapsco River.

Connor wasn't at all stuffy and pretentious, as she'd expected him to be. He'd worn sneakers and well-worn jeans to the Fourth of July parade...and a T-shirt that read "My golf score would be great...if I was bowling." And when she'd learned that he taught law part-time at the University of Baltimore, she'd remarked, "A professor...I'm impressed."

"Don't be," he'd cautioned, a sly grin on his face. "The hours are terrible and the money stinks."

"Then why do you do it?"

His smile had softened and he'd said, "Doesn't happen as often as I'd like, but once in a while, I get a student who loves the law as much as I do." He'd shrugged. "Those are the ones who'll help me dispel the idea that lawyers are like vultures, feeding off the misery of others.''

She'd smiled at that. ''You don't strike me as the type who pays much mind to the opinions of others.''

His blue eyes had widened and his brows had lifted, giving him an innocent, little-boy look. ''Of course I care,'' he'd said. ''At least…I care what *some* people think of me.''

His intense scrutiny had unnerved her, so she'd focused on the plaques and certificates he'd hung in a dark hallway. ''What are these?''

Normally, he was proud of his efforts, but somehow Jaina taking notice rattled him. She always rattled him.

Even in the dim light, she could tell her question had flustered him. He'd stammered and stuttered like a teenager on his first date, and if the light had been better, she was sure she'd have seen him blush like a schoolboy. ''Oh, those,'' he'd said. ''I've been working with the city's Stamp Out Illiteracy project for years.''

Jaina pictured the baseball player who'd started the program; Connor resembled the sports hero even more than the star's younger brother who played for the same team. Tall and well built, Connor's thick-muscled shoulders and biceps were those of an athlete. She wondered what sports he might have played in high school and college. Quarterback? He was certainly big enough, smart enough. Goalie on a soccer team? He had the strength and agility.

She wondered what his favorite subjects had been. Math and science, maybe. He was such a quick thinker. She could easily see him as president of the student council, standing at the podium introducing festivities at an assembly. Surely *he* hadn't been the type whose shyness kept him from volunteering.

Or had it?

She didn't like admitting it—given the fact that she had actually wanted to say ''Yes!'' when he'd brought up the subject of marriage—but Jaina knew very little about Connor Buchanan. What kind of people had raised him? Had he ever been married, and if so, had it ended because he'd been widowed…or divorced? Was he a churchgoer? Could he try to be?

What Jaina did know about him, she liked.

He craved order in his life. What more proof of that did she need than the way he'd organized his kitchen cabinets: mugs on one shelf, tumblers on another; pots and pans stacked neatly, each with its own lid upside down inside it; spices and canned goods, like toy soldiers standing at attention, had been arranged in neat, alphabetical rows.

He was not a bully, as evidenced by the way he'd reacted to the Chili Pot flood. Finding Liam in the sudsy water had upset him, and he'd said so in a firm yet calm voice.

He'd treated her so gently that day in his office. Held Liam with such tenderness. Spoke to her parents with respect, despite the fact that Rita resented him and made no secret of it.

And that kiss in his kitchen…

She'd been dreaming about it off and on for nearly a week now. The way he'd wrapped her in his arms had made her feel treasured, had awakened emotions she hadn't known possible.

One of the many things that stood out in her mind was the discussion they'd had about her limp. They'd barely gotten the blanket spread on the ground when he'd asked, "Do you mind if I ask you a personal question?"

"How can I answer that until I've heard the question?" she'd teased.

"You have a point," he'd agreed. "Let me preface it, then, by saying if it makes you in the least uncomfortable, feel free to tell me to buzz off, take a flying leap."

What could be so important, so serious, she'd wondered, that Connor had felt it necessary to apologize *before* he'd asked the question? "I might be forced to say mind your own business,'' she'd told him. ''But buzz off? Take a flying leap? I'm afraid that just isn't my style.''

Smiling, he'd gently deposited Liam in the center of the blanket, then sat down beside him. ''Does your leg hurt very much?''

Only then did she understand. He wanted to know if she limped because each step was painful for her, or if the accident had caused so much bone and tissue damage that she couldn't walk any other way.

''The doctors were forced to remove a part of my thigh bone,'' she explained matter-of-factly. ''It shortened my leg by nearly an inch.'' She paused to read his face. Satisfied he didn't feel sorry for her, Jaina continued. ''Sometimes it bothers me a bit, but no more, I imagine, than anyone else if they've been on their feet too long.''

''Good. I'd hate to think that accident had left you with pain to bear, too.''

Too? she wondered.

''I mean,'' he quickly inserted, ''you had so much else to contend with because of that…''

His gentle expression hardened, and hot fury blazed in his eyes. Jaina believed he must have read her face, seen the stunned reaction to his anger there, because he shook his head.

''Sorry,'' he said. ''Do you get a lot of dimwits asking questions about it, or am I the first?''

''Children ask me about it all the time. It's refreshing, really, how open and honest they are. I wish grown-ups would ask how it happened,'' she admitted. ''It'd be so much easier to take than their pitying stares.''

''So I take it you don't think I'm *not* a dimwit,'' he said, chuckling. ''I'm a *childlike* dimwit.''

There's nothing dim about you, Connor Buchanan, she wanted to say. *Not your eyes, or your smile, or your charming wit.*

''Truth is,'' he said, ''it's the only proof I have that

you're human. Though I still think you're way too perfect for the likes of me.'' He smiled, then said in a halting voice, ''So what's it going to be, Jaina? Are you going to marry me or not?''

''You're joking again, right?''

''I'm completely serious,'' he assured her. ''But don't worry. You needn't answer right now. Give it some thought. I think you'll see it's the best solution for everyone.''

She hadn't known what to say in response to that, and so she'd asked him to please pass her a soda from the plastic cooler they'd brought along.

For the rest of the day—and night—Jaina could think of little else. Connor had called his proposal a solution, but how could it be?

He knew everything there was to know about her, from the accident that left her scarred and, in all likelihood, barren, to the charges that had landed her in jail. He knew every detail, good *and* bad...

Considering all that, could he possibly want to marry her?

Besides, he didn't need Jaina on his side to adopt Liam. In fact, having her there might hurt his case. So why would he ask her to become his wife? The question rumbled in her head until her heart was reverberating with it, too.

Could it be that he loves you?

Instinctively, she tried to dismiss the idea as ridiculous. Silly. Too outrageous for further consideration. Just as immediately, it was back, bigger and more powerful than ever. She smiled slightly, considering the possibility that a man like Connor Buchanan—handsome, intelligent, successful, highly respected in the community and comfortably off financially—would have more than a passing interest in a woman who only had down-to-earth parents and an assortment of friends many would consider less than socially acceptable.

Not that she was ashamed of them. Jaina would have held any of them up for comparison against the so-called high-and-mighty muckety-mucks of the social scene. They had made some mistakes, but they'd learned from them and were God-fearing Christians, good to the bone. Still, he was obviously not interested in her because of her family background.

Or was he?

He as much as said he admired her work ethic. And he *did* say he liked the way she took care of Liam. She grinned, thinking, *He sure doesn't have any complaints about the way you kiss.* But then, it wasn't really fair to take credit for that since her behavior was nothing more than a reaction to *him*.

Until Liam came into her life, bringing with him his handsome relative, Jaina had resigned herself to living the rest of her life alone. Even if Connor did not love—would *never* truly love her—surely a marriage founded on mutual respect, affection and their love for Liam beat the prospect of life alone, hands down? Besides, being perfectly honest with herself, Jaina knew now that if Connor took Liam from her she would miss *both* of them.

Chapter Nine

When Pearl informed Connor that Judge Thompson's secretary had lost his petition for adoption he slammed down the phone. He could have Pearl run off another copy, but it was too late to get Judge Thompson's signature now. The old fellow and his wife would be leaving for Europe this afternoon to celebrate their fiftieth anniversary.

Fifty years with the same woman. Connor found it hard to believe any man could put up with a woman that long if they were all like Thompson's secretary. And they surely all *seemed* to be.

Well, that wasn't entirely true. There was Jaina....

His own parents had stayed together until their deaths, but he doubted they'd been happy in their nearly thirty-year marriage. Quite the contrary. They tolerated each other, and it was obvious to anyone with eyes and ears. Why couldn't they have been more like the Thompsons? Even a cynic like Connor could see that those two old people loved each other like crazy, and after half a century together yet!

Would he be a cynic still if he had a woman like Jaina

at his side? If he had someone like her encouraging him, supporting his decisions, being a true helpmeet?

Connor blinked and forced himself to focus on the matter at hand. He glanced at his watch. It wasn't even eleven yet. He'd done the elderly gent a wagonload of favors; surely the man wouldn't object if Connor dropped by to get the required signature. He had to at least give it a try.

He depressed the intercom button on his phone. "Pearl…you saved my adoption petition on disk, didn't you?"

"Course I did."

"Change it to today's date, will you? And print out another copy."

"Don't worry, boss," she replied breezily. "I'll get right on it."

She had the document ready for his approval in less than five minutes. And five minutes after that, Connor was in his car, headed for the judge's house.

John Thompson lived in an old, established community on the outskirts of town. Elegant and stately, his house was emblematic of his lifestyle, complete with wrought-iron gates, manicured lawns, ornate flower beds. Connor parked in the circular redbrick driveway and headed for the front entrance.

"Well, if it isn't Connor Buchanan."

A quick look around told Connor the source of the deep baritone had originated from the rose garden. "Judge Thompson," he said, smiling and extending his hand. "All set for your trip?"

"I should hope so," the older man said, stuffing his pruning shears into a back jeans pocket. In a conspiratorial whisper, he added, "Millicent has had this thing planned for a decade!" Pumping Connor's arm vigorously, he said, "Good to see you, son. What brings you here?"

Connor held up the manila envelope that bore his petition

for adoption. "I need your signature on this. I wouldn't bother you at home...especially not today...but..."

The judge ran a hand through his thick white hair. "C'mon, let's step inside, get out of this heat," he suggested.

As he followed Thompson into the house, Connor had to admit that the elderly fellow amazed him. Pushing eighty, the judge walked ramrod straight and quick as a man of forty. In every courtroom in the tristate area, he'd earned a reputation for having a mind sharper than a new-honed blade, and it didn't appear to be growing any duller with age. Connor had heard it said that what a man becomes in his old age is determined by the wife he'd chosen when he was young. If there was any truth to the old adage, Judge Thompson had chosen well.

"Now then," Thompson said once they'd settled in the library, "what can I get you? A glass of lemonade? Some iced tea?"

"Nothing, thanks." He slid the petition from the envelope. "I know you're busy, getting ready for the—"

"Nonsense," the judge interrupted, smiling. "There's nothing to do but call a taxi to take us to the airport." He held a forefinger in the air. "You're forgetting...I'm married to a woman who believes organization and planning are next to Godliness!" He clapped his hands together once. "Well, son," he said, settling into a buttery black leather recliner, "what can I do for you?"

"This petition for adoption we discussed last week..."

Thompson's brow furrowed. "It isn't like you, Buchanan, to say you're going to get right on something and then procrastinate. Especially something as important as—"

"You don't have to tell me. Your Mrs. Miller has already raked me over the coals for my shoddy work."

He held up a hand as if to silence Connor. "*My* Mrs.

Miller? She doesn't get upset over... Wait. Let me guess. Dorothy misplaced it, didn't she?''

Connor averted his gaze.

And the judge sighed. ''She means well, but I'm afraid Dorothy isn't the crackerjack secretary yours is.'' He relieved Connor of the envelope. ''So tell me, how'd you get such a gem, if you don't mind my asking?''

''Just lucky, I guess.''

''Please, please, take a load off,'' Thompson insisted, pointing at a matching recliner. Settling gold-framed half glasses on his patrician nose, he began perusing the document. ''You're still determined to go ahead with these proceedings, I see.''

''Yessir, I am.'' Connor's brows drew together slightly. ''You don't agree?''

''I wouldn't say that. But I've done a bit of digging myself,'' he said as he thumbed through the papers. ''This Chandelle woman who has your great-nephew... She's got quite a history, doesn't she?''

Connor swallowed. ''Well, that's the way it appears at first glance, but...''

Thompson peered over his spectacles to say, ''If the D.A. had brought a case like hers before my bench, I'd have laughed him out of the courtroom. It's as obvious as the nose on my face that the man was stockpiling guilty pleas to secure his own job.'' Thompson shook his head. ''I hate to see injustice done. You'd think after all these years, I'd be inured to it, wouldn't you?''

Thompson had earned a reputation for being a straight shooter. It wasn't easy being forthright and honest in a world of loopholes and nepotism; if Connor could retire with a record like the judge's, he'd consider himself fortunate.

Thompson sat taller in his chair, aiming his clear blue gaze directly at Connor. ''Are you a God-fearing man, Buchanan?''

The question rocked him. "Why, yes, I am. Why do you ask?"

"Most natural question in the world," the other man observed, "considering what you're proposing to do."

Connor leaned forward and rested his elbows on his knees. Smiling slightly, he said, "You're talking to a thickheaded Irishman, Judge. It might seem the most natural question in the world to you, but I don't have a clue what you're talking about."

"Thickheaded, my foot!" Thompson's gruff snort was quickly swallowed up by the carpeting and draperies in the well-appointed room. "I saw your bar exam scores. You were top of the class in every school you attended. Don't get me wrong. I find your humility charming. It's like my old grampa used to say, 'Woe to those who are wise in their own eyes and shrewd in their own sight.'"

"I prefer Proverbs myself," Connor said. "'Knowledge is a precious jewel.'"

Thompson nodded. "*Hundreds* of lawyers have stood in front of my bench over the years, and in my opinion, only a handful of 'em will ever amount to anything worthwhile. You know why?"

Connor shook his head.

"'Cause most of 'em are in it for the money. They don't love the *law*, they love what it'll *do* for 'em." He waved the paperwork under Connor's nose. "You believe in something far more powerful than the almighty dollar. I spotted that right off. It's just one of the reasons I've always liked you, Buchanan."

Chuckling, Connor said good-naturedly, "Coulda fooled me. Sometimes I thought if you'd been allowed to keep a loaded gun up there on that bench, you'd have used it...on *me!*"

The judge laughed. "I admit I was hard on you. But I was testing your mettle." One snow-white brow rose high on his wrinkled forehead. "You passed with flying colors, son. Those others…'' His face contorted as if he'd inhaled an unpleasant odor. "You're in a league of your own.''

The compliment might not have affected him had it come from someone he respected less. But coming from Judge Thompson, it was high praise indeed. Connor felt the heat of a blush creeping into his cheeks.

"If you're a God-fearing man, why are you going about this the hard way?''

"The hard…?''

"Why not just put it in God's capable hands. See what He wants you to do with it?''

Connor shrugged. "I'm ashamed to say I never gave it a thought.''

"You're probably wondering what any of that has to do with your petition here, aren't you?''

"Well, frankly, yes.''

"As I said, after you spoke to me about your great-nephew, I took it upon myself to do some checking on this young lady. Millicent and I have taken a few meals in her diner since then, I'll have you know. Fine woman, that Miss Chandelle. Hard worker, bright, good-natured…'' He winked mischievously. "And mighty easy on a man's eyes, wouldn't you say?''

"I'd be a liar if I denied it.''

"And a fool to boot!'' The old man's laughter bounced off every wall in the room. Suddenly, the judge was all business. "Now give it to me straight, son,'' he said, giving the petition a shake. "What's this really all about?''

"I want to adopt the boy,'' Connor said.

"That's nonsense!''

Connor swallowed. He wished now he'd taken the judge up on his offer of a soft drink because his throat was as dry as sand. "I beg your pardon?''

"Don't beg *my* pardon. Beg that lovely young woman's! She's doing a Grade A job taking care of that youngster. I've seen it with my own eyes.''

"But…but he's *my* nephew, my blood kin."

"No one's disputing that. I'm just remembering how well she handled it when her diner turned into a three-ring circus. Water everywhere…people falling on their posteriors… She'd make a magnificent mother if—"

"You were there?"

"You seem surprised." He slapped his knee. "Well, here's something else that'll surprise you even more. I was in The Judge's Bench recently, so I've seen the two of you together more than once. You're in love with that pretty little gal. Not that I blame you.…"

Were his feelings for Jaina that obvious? Connor wondered.

"I'm sure you've heard the old saying, 'You can't have your cake and eat it, too.'"

Connor nodded.

"Marry that girl and you *can*. You'll have her and the boy, as well!"

"So you aren't going to sign the petition?"

"Course I am. You want to be the boy's father legally, don't you?"

Another nod.

"Then you'll need all the *i*'s dotted, all the *t*'s crossed." He strode to his desk, withdrew a gold pen from a side drawer and scrawled his name on the last page of the document. "Done! Now it only needs to be filed with the county records office, and providing there's no one who objects," he said, winking again, "you'll officially be a family man."

Thompson walked around to the front of the desk and handed the pages back to Connor. "Course, if you ask me, you're not really a family man until you have a wife to go with that youngster."

Connor slid the petition back into its envelope. "I don't know how to thank—"

"How old are you, son?" the older man asked, still towering over Connor.

He cocked a brow. What could his age possibly have to do with anything? "I'll be thirty-five in a few weeks."

The judge harrumphed. "Land's sake," he said, shaking his head, "I was married with four kids by that time. What in the world are you waiting for?" Thompson laid a fatherly hand on Connor's shoulder as the two men walked side by side into the sunny foyer. "They say free advice is worth what it costs you, but I'm going to give you some anyway."

Connor grinned. "I'd be honored to take it."

"The right woman only comes along once in a man's lifetime. If you let her get away, you'll regret it for the rest of your days." The judge opened the door. "Millicent and I will be back in early September. Give me a call. You can fill me in on the details."

Connor wished him a safe flight and a pleasant trip, then held up the envelope. "I don't know how to thank you."

Thompson gave one last wink. "By inviting me to the wedding so I can dance with the bride," he said, and closed the door.

As he drove away from the impressive estate, Connor couldn't get Thompson's words out of his mind. The judge had been right; life was fraught with regrets. Why add another to the already too-long list?

As soon as the adoption papers were filed, he'd visit Jaina, tell her exactly how he felt. Hopefully, she'd agree with him and say yes when he popped the question.

Jaina hadn't been in when he stopped by, so Connor asked Rita's permission to take Liam for a drive in the country. Had it been up to her alone, the answer would have been a terse no. Thankfully, Ray had been there, too.

Connor decided to stop off at the office first, to file his copies of the paperwork…and to show Liam off to Pearl.

He heard the music even before the elevator doors opened. Standing in the waiting room, he teased, "You're not going deaf on me, are you?"

"Course not," she called from somewhere in his office.

"Then why is the radio turned up so loud?"

"Can't hear it when I'm in here. Besides, that song the DJ is playing is one of my all-time favorites. Has been for years."

Until that moment, Connor had only been half listening to it. Something about it sounded strikingly familiar. "Nice," he admitted, nodding as he sat on the couch across from Pearl's desk, "real nice."

Liam bounced up and down on his knee. "Mmumm-mmumm," he said excitedly, pointing to the stereo. "Mmumm-mmumm?"

He looked into the boy's eyes. O'Dell had told him she'd had one hit record. Could this be it, and had Liam recognized her voice?

"In your eyes, love," the singer crooned, "I see my future. When you smile, my whole world is at peace. When that old world starts closin' in around me…wrap your lovin' arms 'round me…"

It was Jaina all right. Either that, or there were two women in America who had deep, sultry voices. If he remembered correctly, she'd written the song herself.

"Kiss me soft, love, and let me hear you sigh. Only in your arms, love, do I feel free…so wrap your lovin' arms 'round me…"

Had she written it for that no-account Bill Isaacs? A surge of jealousy sizzled through him. Connor hoped not because, someday, he wanted her to sing it for *him*.

"I will love you until the day I die. I'll never leave you, never make you cry. I've just one dream for all eternity…that you'll wrap your lovin' arms 'round me…that you'll wrap your lovin' arms 'round me…"

Pearl bustled into the room, dusting the palms of her

hands together. With a flick of her wrist, she turned off the stereo.

"No...don't," Connor said.

"The song was over anyway." She walked closer, then bent over slightly and rested her hands on her knees. "Well, what have we here?" she cooed to Liam. "I haven't seen you for such a long time, little fella. Lookin' good. Real good." Gently, Pearl touched the tip of his nose. "Do you have any idea the effect you've had on your Uncle Connor?"

One finger in his mouth, Liam peered up at her through long lashes and grinned flirtatiously.

"You've turned a grumpy old meanie into a young, happy man, that's what."

For the second time that day, a secretary had referred to him as mean. He couldn't have been that bad...could he? "Liam and I are going to take a ride in the country," he announced. "Soon as I stop by the house and change into jeans, I'm going over to Marriotsville Road to check out those horses for sale."

Pearl straightened up and crossed her arms in front of her. "You have the perfect place for them. All those rolling acres...that big red barn... It'll look like a picture postcard with a couple of beautiful horses grazing in the corral."

The only reason he'd considered the idea at all was because Jaina had told him in the parking lot after their lunch that she loved to ride. But he couldn't very well admit that to Pearl. If he did, her romantic matchmaking side would never let him hear the end of it. Connor was contemplating what he *would* say when the ringing phone rescued him.

"Mr. Buchanan's office. May I help you?" Pearl nodded, held one hand over the mouthpiece. "It's Mr. O'Dell," she whispered. And making a silly face at Liam, she added, "You want me to get a number? Tell him you'll call him back?"

The baby giggled at her, and Connor kissed his cheek.

"Nah, I'll take it. O'Dell is usually to the point." He stood and handed Liam to her. "You don't mind, do you?"

Beaming, Pearl cuddled the baby to her ample bosom. "Mind? I should say not!" She pulled open a desk drawer as Connor headed for his office. "Look what your old Auntie Pearl has for you," she cooed, handing him a tea biscuit.

"Not too much junk food now," he said, grinning.

She never took her eyes from the baby as she waved his comment away.

He picked up his phone. "Hey, O'Dell," Connor said. "What's up?"

"Good news, bad news."

Connor sighed deeply. "Okay, let me have it."

"Good news first this time. I found your niece."

"Kirstie? Where?"

"Small hospital outside of Chicago."

"Have you seen her?"

"Yeah…that's the bad news."

"Not good, huh?"

"'Fraid not. You want to see her, better get here fast."

Connor felt his heart sinking as he jotted down the address and phone number of the hospital. "I'll be on the next flight to O'Hare. Can you meet me?"

"Sure thing. Just let me know when and where. And Connor?"

"Yeah?"

The man hesitated. "Never mind. Just hurry up, all right?"

They hung up simultaneously. "Pearl," Connor said, stuffing the message slip into the breast pocket of his suit, "I need to be on the next plane to Chicago."

She stopped bouncing the baby on her knee. "But…but you have appointments up to here, both in the office and in court, and—"

"Make my apologies and reschedule what you can."

"O'Dell found your niece?" she asked, standing.

Connor nodded. "She doesn't have long." She handed Liam back to his uncle and riffled through her Rolodex. While she was dialing the airline, he said, "Reserve two seats."

"Two?"

"One for me, one for my boy here."

Smiling, she nodded understandingly.

"There's a plane leaving BWI in an hour," she said a few minutes later. "You might want to stop by your house and—"

"No time for that," he said, hoisting Liam up. "I'll stop at the store for some necessities. Whatever else we need I'll buy when we get there." Then, "Will you—"

"I'll call O'Dell, give him the flight number and arrival time. I'll call Jaina, too."

Connor gave Pearl a small peck on the cheek. "Thanks."

She pressed her fingertips to the spot he'd kissed. "For what?"

"For being a gem."

He left her there, blushing and looking puzzled, and headed straight for the airport.

"What do you mean, he came and took him away?" Jaina's heart beat double time as she slumped onto the padded seat of a booth.

"I mean," Rita said, "he said he was going to take him for a drive in the country. He promised to have him back by six."

Jaina glanced at the antique grandfather clock in the corner of the diner. Any minute now, it would strike eight. "Maybe they got hung up in traffic. You know how crazy that beltway can be on a Friday night."

"Nonsense," Rita said. "He's taken him away, and I don't think he'll be back."

"Have you called his house?"

"No."

Jaina hurried to the phone behind the counter and dialed Connor's home number. The answering machine picked up, and she left a brief message.

"He can be a real workaholic. Maybe he stopped by his office," she said, thinking aloud, "to pick something up, or drop something off, or—" Again, a machine intercepted her call. She hung up quietly and, leaning both elbows on the counter, hid her face in her hands. "I hope there hasn't been an accident." Horrible as the thought was, it seemed almost preferable to the alternative.

"He isn't home and he isn't in his office and there hasn't been an accident. I think you should call the police," Rita said, "because that no-good lawyer has run off with Liam!"

"Mother," Ray said, "calm down now. You know that it isn't good for you to get so excited."

"Well, pardon me all the way to town and back," Rita fumed, "for having a normal human reaction to this fiasco."

"Mom," Jaina said softly, "Dad's right. I can't believe Connor would...that he'd just *leave* without a word. I'm sure there's a reasonable explanation."

"You could be right, but I don't think so."

It wasn't like Rita to be so pessimistic. Jaina recalled the night Kirstie had left Liam in their care, when her mother had accused *her* of being cynical. *Think positively,* she told herself. *Anything else is unacceptable, intolerable.* Since her accident, it had been *Jaina's* nature to be distrustful. How many times had Rita called her a gloomy Gus, a doubting Thomas? And how many times had she excused her own negative behavior by saying that people deserved her cynicism?

Too many to count.

But Liam had changed all that.

Liam...and his uncle....

She refused to believe Connor had simply waltzed in and taken the boy away with a promise to return if he had no intention of doing so. There was a reasonable explanation for his sudden disappearance. There *had* to be.

Connor *couldn't* have done anything as despicably thoughtless as stealing Liam.

Because if he could, it meant she'd let herself fall in love with the wrong man...again.

Connor had never been so well looked after during a flight in his life. He knew without a doubt he had Liam to thank for the nonstop service. Even before the plane got off the ground in Baltimore, the baby had won the hearts of all the flight attendants. Upon their arrival in Chicago, one pressed a colorful sticker of gold wings to his shirt, while another propped a tiny cap bearing the airline's insignia onto his head.

As promised, O'Dell was waiting for him at the gate and drove him to the hospital. He didn't waste a moment explaining the situation to the nurse on duty, who insisted on taking care of Liam while Connor spoke with Kirstie's doctor.

Dr. Ginnan quickly updated Connor on her condition, explaining the type of cancer that was draining the life away from her.

"How long does she have?"

"Couple of days, a week at the outside."

"Is she in pain?"

"Well, we have her on a painkiller IV. She can dose herself any time she feels the need."

"That doesn't answer my question, Doc."

The physician sat back, folded his hands atop his abdomen. "Kirstie seems determined to tough this thing out." He removed his eyeglasses and placed them on the desk. "May I ask you a question, Mr. Buchanan?"

Connor nodded.

"She told us she had no family, made it clear she didn't want anyone notified of her condition. How did you find out she was with us?"

"She left her son with…" Connor did *not* want Dr. Ginnan getting the impression that his niece was a flighty girl, too immature to be a good mother. He had two heartrending notes to prove the contrary. "Kirstie left Liam with a friend who contacted me, and…" He shrugged. "I didn't want her spending her last days alone, so I hired a detective to find her."

The doctor pursed his lips and nodded thoughtfully. "I see," he said. He shoved back his chair and stood. "I'll let you see her now. Perhaps you'll be able to convince her to take advantage of the medications. There's really no sense in her suffering."

Connor stood. "Will we—her son and I—have unlimited access to her room?"

"Naturally. Have you seen her?"

"No. Not yet."

"Then let me warn you. She's very weak and pale, and she's lost a lot of weight."

On the way, Ginnan stopped at the nurses' station so that Connor could retrieve Liam, then led the way down a long, polished corridor.

It was quiet inside, so hushed that it reminded Connor of an empty church. After the warnings from O'Dell and the doctor, Connor had expected his niece to be attached to numerous monitors and feeding tubes. Instead, there was one plastic bag hanging from a tall metal stand beside her bed.

"Kirstie," the doctor said softly, laying a hand on her shoulder, "there's someone here to see you."

She saw Liam first, and her eyes instantly filled with unshed tears. Her pale cheeks flushed with sudden color, and smiling, she held out trembling arms. Connor gently deposited the baby beside her.

"Mmumm-mmumm." He seemed to sense that he must be gentle, and snuggled quietly up to her.

"Oh, sweetie, I can't believe you're here. Let Mommy look at you...." She kissed his cheeks, his forehead, his chin. "You're beautiful! I was right, Jaina is taking good care of you, isn't she?"

Jaina. Oh, how Connor suddenly wished she were here, her remarkably strong, peaceful presence bolstering him.

Only then did Kirstie seem aware that she and Liam were not alone in the room. "Uncle Connor?"

The doctor gave him a polite little nod of his head and quietly stepped out of the room.

"How did you know who I was?"

"I'd know you anywhere. Mom described you to me ten thousand times." She emitted a weak laugh. "I have to admit you're even more handsome than she said."

Connor scooted the bedside chair nearer and sat beside her.

"How did you find me?"

"I hired a private detective."

"That was *you?* I thought...I thought it was Jaina."

"I know. She showed me the letters."

"You and Jaina...you've met?"

Connor explained how, the day after Kirstie had disappeared, Jaina had come to his office. "I'm so sorry you overheard that argument. I wish you had stuck around, told me to my face what a mean old grouch I am."

Another feeble laugh.

"If you had," he continued, "I would have kept you with me, seen to it you had only the best care."

"They've been taking good care of me here."

"I see you have a morphine drip," he said, nodding toward the bag. "Do you use it often?"

"So Dr. Ginnan put you to work, too, did he?"

"I'm afraid I don't—"

"He wants you to talk me into using the morphine, right?"

She seemed far too perceptive for one so young, Connor thought.

Kirstie wrinkled her nose. "I don't like the way it makes me feel, all groggy and thickheaded. I want to be aware that I'm alive, right up to the last minute." She hugged Liam a little tighter. "Especially now."

"But, honey," he urged, his fingers gently caressing her forearm, "if you're in pain..."

"I'm fine." She met his eyes to add, "I'm sorry for acting like a spoiled brat that day...running away from your office like a big scaredy-cat. I should have known you weren't as mean as you sounded."

Connor couldn't help but chuckle at that. "You know, this is the third time today that women have told me I'm nasty, mean, grouchy, grumpy."

"Pity you're so tall..."

Still smiling, he rumpled his brow.

"...because if we could find a theater where they're doing *Snow White,* you could play the part of all seven dwarfs!"

Laughing, he shook his head. "My, but you're a lot like your mother."

"That's the nicest thing you could have said to me. She was a wonderful woman."

He wanted to talk about Susan. Wanted to ask the questions that had been stewing in his brain since the day she'd left home. But these were Kirstie's last hours.

"She always felt bad about the way she left. But she was afraid that if she contacted you, your parents would make your life miserable."

"That's what I figured. Sometimes," he said, "I wish she'd been more selfish."

"Why?"

"If she wasn't always worrying about me, maybe she'd

have gotten in touch. It would have been worth a little aggravation from the folks just to know she was all right.''

''She'd never have done that. Mom said if you ever found out where she was, you'd come to her. She couldn't let you do that.''

The conversation was wearing the poor girl out. Her whispery, raspy voice proved it. ''Shhh, sweetie,'' he said gently. ''Why not take a little nap and—''

''I have one, maybe two days left on this earth. Please don't ask me to sleep away my last hours.''

He swallowed, biting back the tears that stung his eyes.

She laid a cool hand on his. ''Mom said if you had come to Chicago, you wouldn't have gone on to college, or law school, or—''

''She knew about that?'' he asked, incredulous. ''How?''

Kirstie gave him a knowing grin. ''She kept tabs on you for years. Remember Miss Bonita?''

A soft smile creased Connor's face. ''The old lady who lived next door? If it hadn't been for her, your mother and I might have gone stark raving mad.''

''She sent us articles and…and things.''

He remembered the way the old woman had insinuated herself into so many family functions, pretending to be interested in his parents' religious activities. She'd attended his high school and college graduations. Had baked him chocolate chip cookies when he passed the bar exam. Quilted him a blanket when he got his first apartment.

''She never forgave them, you know.''

''Our folks?''

Kirstie nodded. ''She blamed them for your divorce. Said if they'd been good Christian parents like they pretended to be, they never would have let you marry that gold digger who broke your heart.''

Connor snickered a bit at that. ''Gold digger. I never thought of Miriam in quite that way before.'' He was having a hard time dealing with the fact that Susan had known so much about his life, yet he'd known next to nothing about hers.

He felt uncertain how to respond to this girl-woman. He'd come here to comfort her, not the other way around.

"Are you curious about how she died?"

Curious? Why, he was nearly *exploding* with the need to know. But he dared not admit it because Kirstie's worn-out body needed rest.

"She earned her living modeling. For catalog companies, for local store brochures. She even made a few commercials. Mom felt it was important to stay trim, especially as she got older, to stay ahead of the competition, you know? So her doctor prescribed a drug. She took it every day...." Her voice trailed off as she stared at some unseen spot across the room. "She did a lot of damage to her heart..."

Connor laid a finger over her lips. Certainly she didn't need to say it any more than he didn't need to hear it. The image of his dear Susan, wasting away, nearly broke his heart.

Kirstie mustered enough strength to push his hand away. "She died when I was twelve."

Ever so gently, he lifted her hand, pressed it to his lips. "If you knew where to find me, Kirstie, why didn't you call? I would have—"

"All I knew about you was what I'd heard...I thought you'd be too busy and too important to have time for me. And, I was afraid." Kirstie gave him an unsteady, mischievous grin. "What a little chicken, huh?"

He kissed her hand again, then tenderly brushed the bangs from her forehead. "Kirstie, you're the bravest girl I've ever known."

Liam sat up just then, met Connor's eyes. "Mmumm-mmumm," he said, patting his mother's other hand. He reached for Connor. "Dih?"

Kirstie began to cry, softly at first, then harder, until the sobs racked her puny little body. "What's wrong, sweetie? Are you in pain? You want me to call the doctor?"

She waved his concern away. "No," she sniffed, pulling herself together. "It's not that. It's just…I'm so happy.…"

Connor leaned down, hugged her and Liam both. "Well, you sure have a funny way of showing it," he said, winking and tweaking her nose. He pulled a tissue from the box on her nightstand and blotted her tears. When her breathing returned to normal, he said, "Now, really, what was that all about?"

Kirstie exhaled an exhausted sigh. "I never thought I'd see him again," she admitted, lovingly stroking Liam's cheek. And meeting Connor's eyes, she added, "And I *never* thought I'd meet *you*." Another raspy breath rustled from her. "I have a family," she said, lower lip quivering as she grinned. "A *family!*"

It was a slow night in the diner. Rita and Ray were working in the kitchen, and the rest of the crew, sensing her need to be alone, were flitting about pretending to be busy. She'd just concluded a short prayer of thanks for her good friends when the bell over the front door tinkled.

Her mother had been certain Connor had stolen Liam, that he was off making the adoption legal. But Jaina refused to believe it. He'd been straightforward and honest with her to this point, had asked her to marry him, so they could raise Liam together. "He wouldn't do anything so underhanded," she'd said in his defense. She'd believed Connor would never knowingly hurt her. She trusted him. Yet, she'd been a poor judge of character before, putting her trust in the hands of a man who was undeserving of it.

While Jaina mulled over her worries about Liam and Connor, and tried to avoid checking the clock, a woman of perhaps sixty hustled inside. She looked vaguely familiar. Not until she plopped her suitcase-size handbag on the

counter did Jaina recognize the wide, friendly smile.
"You're Connor Buchanan's secretary, aren't you?"

"Name's Pearl, and I have a message from Mr. B."

"I've been trying to get in touch with him for *hours!*
Where has he *been?* Is he all right? Is Liam okay?"

"And I've been trying to get in touch with *you,* to tell
you he's left for Chicago. Your line was busy for the lon-
gest time here, so I decided to stop by on my way home,
but the traffic was awful, and then my car overheated," the
older woman rattled on. She stepped up behind the counter
and helped herself to a cup of coffee. "You want some?"

Jaina nodded.

"Straight, or cream and sugar?"

"Just black, thanks."

Pearl poured a second cup, handed it to Jaina. She came
around to the front again and straddled a stool. "Sit down,
honey. Take a load off." Unceremoniously, she dumped
three sugar packets and two cream containers into her cup.
"He was just planning a little drive in the country," Pearl
said, her spoon clanking against the mug as she stirred.
"He came into the office to get another set of adoption
papers."

"Adoption papers?" Jaina's heart beat hard with fear
and dread.

"Yeah. The original petition apparently went missing
and was never filed at the courthouse. Anyway," she continued, seemingly oblivious to Jaina's distress, "he was
about to leave when Buddy O'Dell called."

"Who?" Was he another lawyer? Someone who'd help
Connor take Liam away?

"Private detective...the one who found Kirstie."

"Who found..." So *that's* why he left the way he did.
She *knew* there was a good reason! Her thoughts turned
immediately to Kirstie. "She's dying, isn't she?"

Sipping her coffee, Pearl nodded.

"And Connor went to Chicago to be with her...to let

her see Liam for the last time.'' She glanced at her watch. ''He's probably with her by now.''

She loved him more at that moment than she'd ever loved anyone in her life. He *hadn't* lied to her. She *hadn't* been wrong about him.

The grandfather clock struck the hour. Nine o'clock. The past three hours had felt like a lifetime. But Liam was safe. *Thank you*, she silently prayed. She pictured him, fast asleep by now. ''What about the baby's food, and diapers, and—''

''Mr. B. said he'd buy whatever they needed when they got to Chicago. Don't worry, the little guy's in good hands.''

Pearl was right, of course. Connor loved Liam at least as much as she did. Of *course* he'd take care of—

''He loves you, you know.''

Jaina pictured his chubby little face, his dimpled little hands—

''He needs you, too. I've known him for years, and I tell you, I've never seen him so happy.''

Known him...for years? But he's only seven months...

Jaina realized suddenly that Pearl was talking about *Connor*, not Liam.

Pearl rattled on, ''I've seen him with plenty of women. Not a one of 'em made him happy. He didn't smile, least not with his eyes. And when he laughed, it was that fake thing folks do to be sociable, you know? Work, work, work...for a handsome young man, he just plain wasn't enjoying his life very much. But since he met *you*...'' Pearl winked, grinning. ''Since you came along, Mr. B. is a different man.''

''That doesn't mean—''

''Honey, I'm going to be sixty-five on my next birthday, and I know love when I see it. And you can deny it if you want to, but I know that you love him, too.''

Jaina stared at her hands. ''I won't deny it,'' she said

softly, "because I can't." She met Pearl's eyes. The woman believed what she'd said. A warm glow flowed through her as the shadows lifted from her heart. Exhaling a sigh of contentment, she reveled in the peace and happiness Pearl's words had given her.

Then a disturbing, agonizing thought smothered the pleasant feelings. What if Pearl was mistaken? What if the changes she'd seen in her boss had been caused by *Liam*, and not her?

That was it. That *had* to be it.

The idea raised a panic inside her like she'd never known. A chill black silence engulfed her as a pulsing knot formed in her stomach. To be jealous of Liam was unthinkable, unspeakable. What kind of horrible person was she?

She looked hastily away from Pearl, uncomfortable with the thoughts churning in her head, embarrassed that she'd professed her love for Connor to this virtual stranger. An oddly primitive warning whispered in her head as she considered the disquieting fact: She'd fallen in love with a man who would never love her in return.

She chewed her lower lip and pulled composure around her like a cloak, determined to sheathe her innermost emotions. Jaina stifled a bitter laugh. *Isn't it a little late to hide your feelings, now that you've confessed your best-guarded secret?*

His image floated through her mind, his name lingered on her lips—*Connor, Connor, Connor*—as she recalled every minute detail of his face, his touch, his voice…

One nagging thought refused to be stilled: Connor loved Liam. Loved Kirstie, too. If he could care so much—and he did care, deeply; she could see it in his eyes—for those two destitute children he'd known for such a short time, was it really too much to hope that Pearl might be right? Was it unreasonable to believe he *might* love her…if not today, then someday?

Jaina smiled, remembering a verse from Psalms: *My times are in Thy hand...*

Several chattering ladies entered the diner as Pearl rose to leave. "Get some rest," she said, chucking Jaina's chin. "He's gonna need to lean on you when he gets back. Gonna need you like he's never needed anyone before."

Chapter Ten

"Uncle Connor?"

Connor hadn't intended to doze off when the nurse took Liam for a walk, but...

He was beside her in a heartbeat. "What is it, sweetie? You okay? You need the doctor, or—"

She took his hand. "You have a birthday coming up. We should do something special to celebrate."

Chuckling affectionately, he patted her hand. "I'm too old to celebrate birthdays."

"Thirty-five isn't so old. What would make you say such a thing?"

"I've lived alone so long, I feel ancient sometimes, that's all."

"Liam is going to be good for you, then." An almost indiscernible sigh escaped her lungs. "Amazing, isn't it?"

"What's amazing?"

"The way God brings people together, exactly when and where they need each other most? I mean, if I hadn't over-heard that argument in your office, I'd never have left Liam with Jaina, and then you two wouldn't have met." She managed a grin. "*She'll* be good for you, too."

Picturing Jaina, Connor smiled.

"I'm so happy Liam is going to grow up in a house with a mommy and a daddy who love each other. It gives me a lot of peace, knowing that."

He couldn't very well burst her bubble, now could he? In place of a response, Connor got her brush out of the nightstand drawer and began pulling it gently through her thinning blond hair.

"Feels nice," she sighed, closing her eyes. "Just the way Mom used to do it...." And then she was asleep.

She slept in fits and starts, he'd discovered; a moment here, five more there. He'd brush her hair all day long if he thought it would encourage some much needed peaceful sleep. As she dozed, Connor recalled the conversation they'd had in the middle of the night.

"Tell me about the girl of your dreams," she'd said.

"I don't have a—"

"Oh, yes, you do," she'd said, feebly shaking a finger at him. "We all have dreams."

He didn't know why, but the comment had made him think of Jaina's house. *His* house...

He'd leaned back, with Kirstie still holding tight to his hand. "Okay...here goes. For starters, my dream girl will have a lot of patience and a really big heart. She'll have to, to put up with the likes of me," he'd said, winking playfully. "Plus, she'll want a lot of kids to fill up the big old house we live in. And in order to keep us all happy and healthy, she'll be as organized as a marine drill sergeant."

"Blonde, redhead, or brunette?"

Oddly, though every woman he'd ever dated had been a blonde, the girl of his dreams had dark hair. Chestnut-colored, to be exact.

"Sort of auburn."

"What color are her eyes?"

That had struck him as strange, too, because the women

in his past—including the one he'd made the mistake of marrying—had had blue eyes.

"Brown."

"Is she tall?"

"Actually, she's rather short."

"Petite," she'd corrected teasingly. "Short girls like 'petite' better."

"Is there no escaping political correctness?" he'd asked, chuckling.

"Is she pretty, or sort of average-looking?"

"She's a livin' doll, with the voice of a songbird and—"

"She sounds just like Jaina."

Kirstie had been right, and the proud expression on her ashen face told Connor she'd known it.

"When are you planning to tell her?"

"Tell her what?"

"That you love her, of course!" She'd given his hand a small squeeze. "Men. You can be so exasperating sometimes! You can't put it off, you know. While you're waiting to share your big news, what if she goes and falls in love with someone else? Wouldn't that just *devastate* you?"

"That would be awful," he'd admitted, pretending he hadn't seen the teasing glint in her eyes. She was playing the old reverse psychology game, and he'd known it. But the thought of Jaina, in love with another man—even in his imagination—had been agonizing.

Suddenly, Kirstie awoke and gave his hand a hard squeeze, interrupting his reverie. "Uncle Connor...it's time."

"Time for what?"

"For me to go to Jesus."

He wanted to shout "Kirstie, no! Don't leave, not yet. Not when I've finally found family." But her sallow complexion, her faltering voice, the pain that lined her brow, told him he *had* to let her go.

"Would you find Liam for me? So I can..."

He patted her hand and kissed her cheek because he knew why she wanted to see Liam right now, and he didn't want to hear her tell him why. "Sure. Course I will. You just lie still, okay? I'll be right back."

He hesitated in the doorway.

"Don't worry," she said, "I'll hang on till you get back." And with a quavering smile, she added, "But... don't be too long...."

In the hallway, once her door hissed shut, Connor pressed his forehead to the wall. Tears filled his eyes. It was so unfair and unjust that she should be fading away like this. His fist pounded the cold tiles, once, twice. It was so cruel and—

"Mr. Buchanan?"

He scrubbed a palm over his face, turning toward the familiar voice. "Dr. Ginnan."

"Is everything all right with Kirstie?"

"Yeah. No. Well, she, uh..." He swallowed, praying for the self-control to get through this—for Kirstie, for Liam. Standing taller, he ran both hands through his hair, held them there a moment, then cleared his throat. "Kirstie sent me to find her son so she could..."

The doctor clamped a hand on Connor's shoulder. "So she could say goodbye?" he finished.

Connor nodded.

"Don't be ashamed of your feelings, Mr. Buchanan. Kirstie is a lovely, loving young woman. The disgrace would be if you *didn't* feel this way about being so close to losing her." He gave the shoulder a squeeze. "There's a chapel down the hall if you'd like to visit it."

Connor stared at the highly polished linoleum beneath his feet, thumb and forefinger rasping over his day's growth of whiskers as he tried to steady his quivering jaw. "Maybe later," he said slowly, quietly, "after..." And pocketing his hand, he headed down the hall.

Ginnan was with her when Connor returned, Liam in his

arms. She reminded him of the beautiful little angel his mother took out only at Christmastime, made of fragile, translucent china. Kirstie smiled when she saw Liam, held out her arms. "Hello, sweet boy." The words rasped from her like steel wool.

Connor tucked Liam in beside her, and he laid his little head on her shoulder. "Mmumm-mmumm," he whimpered, a thumb in his mouth.

"You're going to be just fine, baby, 'cause you'll have a mommy and a daddy who will always love you very much."

A daddy *and* a mommy? Well, if the idea gave her comfort, who was he to burst her bubble? Connor perched lightly on the edge of her bed and rested a hand on her knee.

Kirstie hugged Liam, kissed his baby lips. And eyes squeezed tight, she held him close for a long, long moment. Then, abruptly, she said, "Take him away. Take him now." Turning from him, she choked out, "I don't want him remembering…what's about to happen…for the rest of his life…."

Dr. Ginnan put a gentle hand on her shoulder. "You're quite a piece of work, Kirstie Buchanan," he said past a trembling smile. "I'm proud to know you." He picked Liam up and walked quickly, deliberately, from the room. To Connor, he added, "If you need me, I'll be right around the corner."

He nodded, and when Kirstie crooked her finger to summon him closer, he stood, placed a palm on either side of her head and leaned closer to her small, pale face. "What is it, sweetie?" he asked. "What can I get you? Do you want anything? Name it, and it's yours."

"Anything?"

"Anything."

Her heavy-lidded eyes opened wider, gleaming with

fierce intensity. "Marry Jaina," she said in a sure, strong voice. "That's what I want. That's *all* I want."

His heart thundered. Connor would have moved heaven and earth to grant her last wish. But *this?* He couldn't do—

She gripped his wrists with a strength that belied her condition. "Oh, Uncle Connor…it hurts…hurts so bad."

"I know, sweetie," he said, although he didn't know. How could he, when he'd never suffered like this? "Just let go, sweetie. I'll be with you all the way."

She groaned. "I can't…I won't go. Not until you promise…."

Connor could see that she was in excruciating agony. Pain shimmered in her eyes like diamonds and dotted her brow and upper lip with perspiration. He couldn't stand to see her this way. *Give* me *her pain, Lord,* he prayed. *Let* me *take on this confounded disease instead of*—

"I want to go, want to go so badly. But I can't. Liam needs you. He needs you *both.*"

He didn't think he could stand to watch her torment a moment longer. Much as he detested dishonesty, he would have told her anything she wanted to hear right then to calm her, to comfort her, to ease her mind. And it wasn't really a lie, he reflected, since he had already proposed to Jaina. The problem might be getting her to accept. "All right, Kirstie."

She squeezed his wrists tighter still, lifting her head from the pillow. "You mean it? You'll marry Jaina? You'll *both* be there for Liam?"

His pounding heart thudded against his rib cage, reverberated in his ears. "Yes."

Her eyes never left his as she dropped back onto the pillow, spent. "Promise?"

She was not teasing now, as she had been when she suggested Jaina might fall in love with someone else. She was racked with misery from the pain. He wished she hadn't been so all-fired stubborn about taking the painkiller. It would have eased her suffering and—

"Promise?" Kirstie's burning gaze bore deeply into him, reading him, assessing him. If he lied now, she'd know it.

Later, he could deal with the consequences, with the details. Right now, this child deserved to be set free from her anguish. "I promise, sweetie. I promise."

The moment the words were out of his mouth, she closed her eyes and exhaled a long, relieved sigh. The furrows disappeared from her youthful brow as though the gripping, deadly pain had been vanquished by the utterance of those two simple words. "Thank you," she murmured. "Oh... thank you...."

Her grip on his wrists loosened, her jaw slackened. It was happening right before his very eyes, and Connor was powerless to prevent it. What had he ever done in his miserable, self-absorbed life, he wondered, to earn him the privilege of being the one to spend these last moments with this dear, sweet girl?

He was still leaning there, one hand on either side of her head, staring into her face. He hadn't noticed before—the light hurt her eyes, and so the staff kept the lights low—but she had freckles, dozens of them, sprinkled across the bridge of her upturned nose. *Freckles,* he said to himself, *like a little girl.*

And that's exactly what she was.

She was an eighteen-year-old *girl,* he fumed inwardly. This shouldn't have been happening...not to a *child!* Jaw clenched, he held his breath, helpless frustration prompting him to grip her pillowcase tight in his fists. He wanted to warm her, protect her, *save* her. But he couldn't, and he knew it.

And so Connor did the next best thing.

"Oh, Kirstie," he groaned, lifting her into his arms. Holding her gently, tenderly, he kissed her temples, her cheeks and chin, and that adorable freckled nose. "I love you, sweet girl. I love you...."

Her lashes fluttered, and she met his eyes. Laying a cool, dry palm against his cheek, she smiled sweetly. "I love you, too, Uncle Connor." A weak little giggle popped from her dry, graying lips. "You'll think I'm as silly as silly can be."

"Shhh," he said, biting back a sob as he rocked her. He smoothed the hair back from her forehead. "I won't think you're silly. Honest."

She tilted her head back, looked long and deep into his eyes, then smiled serenely. "It was truly a pleasure, you know, meeting you."

And just as the world darkens gradually at sunset, the light in her bright eyes dimmed by slow degrees until there was nothing, not a spark or a glimmer of life left in them at all.

He remembered bits and snatches of a verse from First Corinthians. "And lo, I will tell you a mystery: In the twinkling of an eye, the trumpet will sound, and the dead will be raised imperishable, and we shall be changed."

She was with her sweet Jesus now, free of all her pain and worry.

With a trembling hand, Connor closed her long-lashed eyelids, then buried his face in the crook of her neck. He didn't know how long he held her, rocked her, wept into her hair—ten minutes? thirty?—he only knew that he felt like bellowing at the top of his lungs. *Someone should have held her this way while she was alive!* But his embrace wasn't warming or consoling or comforting her, wasn't doing her any good now.

And so Connor eased her back against the pillow, lovingly arranged her shimmering hair around her face, tucked the covers up under her chin. When he stood to kiss her forehead, one shining tear landed on her cheek. It slid down, disappeared, quickly absorbed by the crisp white pillowcase. The way it was swallowed up by the cotton reminded him how it felt to stand alone, barefoot on a beach at low tide, watching the soft sands drink up gently ebbing waves.

"The pleasure was all mine," he whispered. "All mine."

Kirstie hadn't been gone an hour when he called Jaina. "Liam and I will be coming in on the one o'clock flight."

"I'll pick you up," she'd said.

"I'm bringing Kirstie home. I want her buried in Baltimore, to be near her family."

"Of course you do. Don't give it another thought. I'll take care of whatever needs to be done."

And she had.

The wake, the funeral service, the cemetery plot, even the marker...she'd thought of everything.

The other mourners—Pearl, Ray, Rita, the Chili Pot staff—had taken Liam back to the diner, leaving Connor and Jaina alone in the graveyard.

He slipped an arm around her waist. "I like what you had them put on her marker." He read softly, "'Kirstie Ann Buchanan. She was loved, and she will be missed.'"

Jaina leaned her head on his shoulder. "I'm glad you were with her, and I'm glad you brought her home."

"I want to thank you, kiddo. I don't know how I could've gotten through this without you."

"You'd have managed it like you manage everything else...with quiet efficiency."

He inclined his head and winced. "If this had been business as usual, maybe. But I would have cracked if I'd had to make all the arrangements after...after..."

She turned to face him. "You've had a couple of pretty rough days, haven't you?" she sympathized, absently smoothing the black lapels of his suit coat, straightening his tie, rearranging the silk hankie in his pocket.

Someday, he'd tell her all about it.

Someday…but not today. "There at the end, Kirstie asked me to make her a promise."

Jaina's brows rose. "Oh? What kind of promise?"

He rested his hands on her shoulders. Such delicate shoulders, he thought, yet so strong and capable. *And it's a good thing, because…* "It seemed so important to her. I don't know if I'll be able to live with myself if I go back on my word."

"I can't imagine why you'd have to."

Connor's mustache tilted in a sad, half smile. "You might feel differently when I tell you *what* I promised."

She shrugged, cuffing the sleeves of her maroon blazer. "Why?"

"Because it involves you."

"Me?" Jaina undid the top button of her white silk blouse.

"Kirstie thought the world of you…"

Jaina sighed. She glanced at Kirstie's coffin. "I thought a lot of her, too."

"…thought *so* much of you, in fact, that she made me promise to marry you."

"Stop teasing, Connor," Jaina said, shaking a maternal finger under his nose. "We're in a cemetery, after all."

He tilted his head slightly, waiting for her to realize it wasn't a joke. He watched her dark eyes widen, her mouth drop open, heard her quick intake of air.

"But…but *why?*"

"Because, as she put it, Liam needs us both."

She seemed to hesitate for a moment. "And you agreed?"

He nodded. "Didn't have any choice." He hesitated. "I asked you once. You didn't say 'yes,' but you didn't say 'no,'" he reminded her.

Jaina sighed. "Well, we've been batting the idea around for a while…"

"So…you promise to marry me, then?"

When Jaina met his eyes and nodded, Connor's heart thudded with relief. Smiling, he said, "You could do worse, you know."

She gave him a puzzled look. "What are you going on about?"

He shrugged a shoulder. "I mean, you could be marrying somebody else…someone like *Skip*."

All eight fingertips covered her mouth. "Skip is a dear, but I don't think there was ever a real chance of that happening, even for Liam."

Connor chuckled softly. "Glad to hear it," he said. After a long, silent moment, Connor added, "I'll understand if you don't want to go through with it. It was *my* promise after all, not yours."

She clasped her hands at her waist, chewing her lower lip. "The thing is…I think she's right," she said quietly, staring at the coffin. "Liam does need us both." She stiffened her back and, looking up at him through thick, dark lashes, said, "Maybe you were right when you said you should get the adoption papers finalized first. That way, my background won't hurt your chances."

"Nonsense. Judge Thompson has already put his John Hancock on the petition. Liam is as good as mine…ours," he quickly corrected.

She bit a corner of her upper lip. "Well, if you're sure…"

"We can't let Kirstie down, now can we?"

He didn't know how to define the expression that flitted across her face just then. Disappointment? Hurt? Regret?

"No. I suppose we can't."

He took her hand in his and led her toward his car. "The sooner the better, I say. What do you think?"

"Why put off till tomorrow what you can do today?" she answered, reciting the age-old adage.

"How's August 5 sound to you?"

"Sounds fine."

He unlocked the passenger-side door of his car. "Good," he said as she slid into the bucket seat. "Then it's all settled."

There was a spring in his step as he walked around to his side of the sports car. As he unlocked his door, he gave one last glance at the graveyard. Sunlight, bouncing from one of the brass handles on Kirstie's casket, flashed like a beacon—on, off, on, off…

Was it a signal? he wondered. Some sort of sign? God's blessing on the deal he and Jaina had just struck?

A robin began to trill in a nearby tree, and a soft, warm breeze rustled the leaves. The sky seemed bluer, the clouds whiter as Connor remembered the way the pastor had concluded the burial service.

"'The righteous are taken from calamity,'" he'd quoted Isaiah, "'and he enters into peace, he rests in his bed who walks in uprightness.' Kirstie walked in uprightness on the earth," the pastor had said, "and she will walk with God her Father all the days of eternity."

It seemed to Connor that it had all happened so fast. One minute, they were shopping for wedding bands. Then they were booking the church. And now, here he was, at the front of her church, waiting for her.

Jaina seemed to float rather than walk toward him down the long, carpeted aisle, a vision in white. The satiny sheen of her gown reflected the sunlight, muted by the rainbow of stained glass. He blinked and rubbed his eyes, hoping she was real and not a figment of his imagination.

Oh, she was real all right. More real than any woman he'd known. And soon, she would be his *wife*.

The wedding procession finally ended, and Ray left her there alone beside him. Connor took a deep, shuddering breath as the pastor read from the Good Book and led the congregation in a prayer, then said a blessing on the couple who stood at the altar of God.

But he barely heard any of it.

He'd heard women described as dazzling, pretty, even handsome, on their wedding day. But the only word Connor could come up with to describe her had been worn thin by overuse. Still, it was the only word that would do: beautiful.

He didn't recall feeling this way when he'd married Miriam. Didn't remember his heart beating this hard and fast, his palms sweating, or—

"Connor Liam Buchanan..." The pastor's voice penetrated his fog. "Do you take this woman, Jaina Clarisse Chandelle, to be your lawfully wedded wife?"

He glanced at her, smiled slightly and raised a brow, then mouthed "Clarisse?" Behind the gauzy veil, he saw her eyes crinkle in a mischievous grin. She pressed her lips together to stanch a giggle before sending him a comical "Behave yourself!" expression.

"I do," Connor said.

"And do you, Jaina Clarisse Chandelle, take this man, Connor Liam Buchanan, to be your lawfully wedded husband?"

He saw her long, dark lashes flutter, saw her bite her lower lip, heard her whisper, "I do."

She had hesitated for at most a fraction of a second, but that infinitesimal space of time was long enough to cut him to the quick. Miriam had done the same thing, he recalled.

"I now pronounce you man and wife. You may kiss the bride."

Connor lifted the filmy white fabric and laid it gently atop her head. She seemed so small, so vulnerable, standing there blinking up at him. Setting aside his own dashed hopes, male instinct made him want to wrap her in a protective embrace and shield her from all harm, from all pain, for a lifetime. All right, so she didn't love him now. But maybe someday, he prayed. Someday...

Gently, he pressed his palms to her cheeks and let his thumbs tilt her face up to receive his kiss. He'd intended a light brush of the lips, nothing more. But the moment his mouth met hers, Connor's spirit soared, and the gloom that had enveloped him since Kirstie's death lifted. *Once I was lost, but now I'm found,* flitted through his head, *and Jaina will lead me home.*

"Atta boy, Connor!" a male voice called out from the back of the church as the congregation applauded, shattering the moment. He ended the kiss and stood back, hands still cupping her lovely face. Slowly, her eyes fluttered open and met his. For a moment, he thought he saw love, real love, sparkling there among the green and gold flecks in her brown eyes, and his heart lurched.

She'd only agreed to this charade of a marriage because he'd told her about the promise he'd made to Kirstie on her deathbed. He remembered the day he'd slipped the engagement ring onto Jaina's finger, when she'd insisted he make a promise to *her.* He was never to tell anyone why they'd decided to get married. She claimed it was because she didn't want people thinking he'd married her out of pity. But he knew better.

His jaw tensed and his brow furrowed with determination. He'd have to harden his heart to her.

Either that, or learn to live with a breaking one....

She thought about it as they walked down the aisle arm in arm, smiling for the cameras, and as they stood on the steps of the church, accepting the congratulations and good wishes of friends and neighbors. It was on her mind as they sat side by side at the reception, eating their first meal as man and wife, and as they bade their guests good-night. But try as she might, Jaina didn't think she'd ever forget the cold, detached expression he'd aimed at her immediately after their kiss at the altar.

Ever since she was a little girl, she'd stuttered when nervous or tense. Jaina had learned that taking a deep breath and repeating the last thing a person said could prevent it. She certainly hadn't wanted to do a Porky Pig impersonation on her wedding day. *Do you take this man...?* she'd repeated mentally before saying in a sure, clear voice, "I do."

And then he'd given her that *look.*

You little fool, she scolded herself. *How can you believe he's really in love with you? Those longing looks, those sweet words...they're part of an act...a very well-orchestrated plan that's helping him fulfill Kirstie's dying wish.*

Well, she'd said yes, after all. And because she'd gotten swept up in the moment, in the hurly-burly rush of wedding plans, there hadn't seemed to be time to change her mind.

She was married now.

To a man who didn't love her.

And you have no one to blame but yourself.

Well, at least one good thing had come of the wedding. She was guaranteed a lifetime with Liam.

Jaina had made Connor swear that he'd never tell another living soul that their phony courtship, their so-called engagement, the marriage itself, had taken place for no reason other than to bring peace of mind to his dying niece. And she had to give him credit; Connor had done a dandy job of making it look good—for her parents, for her employees, for *everyone....*

He'd been the perfect gentleman...opening doors, pulling out chairs, offering her his arm as they moved around town. It was *because* he was a gentleman that she could trust that no one would ever discover the humiliating truth—that he wouldn't have married her if not for that promise to Kirstie. All that talk on the Fourth of July was, well, that's all it had been...talk. The proof? That *look.*

It was going to be next to impossible, she believed, pretending she didn't love him.

* * *

Jaina squared her shoulders and told herself that if she could so quickly fall *in* love with Connor, she could fall *out* of love just as easily...provided she put her mind to it. They'd been married exactly twenty-four hours, and already she'd had it up to here with his cool, detached demeanor.

To keep up appearances, he'd booked a room at a quaint inn in Pennsylvania. No one knew them there; no need for pretense in this charming little town. So why had he brought her breakfast in bed? Why was he standing there in the doorway with that gaudy silver tray in his hands, smiling like an innocent, wide-eyed boy who'd just picked his best girl a fistful of posies?

Connor put the tray on the table near the patio doors and selected one red rose from the three in the crystal bud vase. Bowing low, smiling, he held it out to her. "For my beautiful bride."

Her insides trembled. Jaina prayed it wasn't visible. "Thank you." Their fingers touched as she accepted his gift, sending a burst of fiery currents straight to her already pounding heart. Instinctively, she held the flower near her cheek. "It's lovely," she admitted, closing her eyes to inhale the delicate aroma of its velvety petals.

"Not nearly as lovely as you."

She opened her eyes and met his. Something burned in those icy blue orbs. *Fire and ice,* she warned herself. *He'll burn with his passion...or he'll freeze you out.* There would be no in-between, she believed.

"We should eat before it gets cold..."

His brows drew together as if she'd hurt his feelings. She certainly hadn't intended *that.*

"...since you went to so much trouble to bring the food up here and all, I mean."

He sat at the table, and Jaina poured coffee into the two snow-white china cups on the tray and steeled herself to his hard expression. *You'll be a kind and dutiful wife,* she told herself, *but you will* stop *loving him. You will stop, no matter how difficult it is!*

No…that was too much to ask. The most she could hope for was to be able to hide her heart away. Only with Liam could she ever wear it on her sleeve.

He lifted his fork, then speared a slice of bacon. He couldn't seem to meet her eyes, which reminded her again of that young boy, this time caught red-handed with his fingers in the cookie jar. For the life of her, Jaina didn't understand why her ''let's eat'' comment should have hurt him since he so obviously didn't love her. But he did appear to be pouting.…

She glanced up at Connor, who continued to eat in somber silence. She had discovered, during their brief courtship, that as well as losing his beloved sister, Susan, he'd buried his grandparents and parents, lost a child and divorced the wife whose betrayal had caused its miscarriage. And now he'd been forced to marry a woman he didn't love—would likely never love—because his bigheartedness wouldn't allow him to refuse his niece's last request. *Oh, Lord,* Jaina prayed, *make me a good wife for him. He's suffered enough!*

Without even thinking about it, she impulsively reached across the table and placed her hand atop his. ''This is a nice beginning to our…to our partnership,'' she said, choosing her words carefully.

His expression softened slightly.

Surely Connor had dreams. As time went by, she would coax him into sharing them with her. Then she'd stand beside him, through good times and bad—just as she had promised at the altar—and help him turn his dreams into realities. Because they were married now, for better or for worse, and she had never done anything halfway. *Why start now?* Jaina asked herself.

Would he notice the little things she'd do to make his

life more comfortable? And if he did, would he treat them as gifts or as duties? She smiled to herself, for while there was much about Connor that Jaina didn't understand, she believed she knew the answer to that question. He was, among other things, a good and decent man with a warm and giving heart. He would never take her caring and devotion for granted, not even if their marriage lasted as long as his friend, Judge Thompson's.

Jaina had no desire to burden him with the feeling that he must protect her from her own silly schoolgirlish wishes. And surely that's what a man like him would do...a man who'd go to such lengths to grant a dying girl her final wish.

"You were right," she said.

His left brow rose. "Really. About what?"

"I could have done worse." She smiled affectionately. "Much worse."

They'd been married all of two weeks when Connor had come home from work and announced they'd been invited to a posh charity ball. Black tie, tux, evening gown...the works. "I don't particularly want to go to this shindig," he'd said distractedly, putting the tickets in the sideboard drawer, "but I don't have much choice. Everybody who's anybody is going to be there."

"Maybe you ought to go alone."

"What?"

"I don't want to embarrass you."

He tore off his tie. "Embarrass me? What are you talking about?"

He watched her puttering around in the kitchen, drying blue-stemmed goblets with a terry tea towel, stirring the spaghetti sauce that was bubbling on the back burner. He'd always loved this house—especially the kitchen—but never more than now, with his beautiful bride in it. She'd insisted on handing the reins of The Chili Pot over to Ray, claiming he'd been the one who'd run the place all along anyway. So every day, when he came in from the office, she had a kettle of soup bubbling, a pot of stew simmering, or a roast in the oven. He'd never weighed more than 185 pounds, and in the weeks since they'd been married, the scale soared all the way up to 190.

"Well, you know…someone might remember about me and…"

"And *what?*"

She faced him, aiming that dark-eyed gaze his way, and set his heart to thumping like a parade drum.

"And…they might make life difficult for you."

The only one making life difficult for me is you, he told her silently, *standing there and looking at me with those eyes of yours, when I can't touch you.…*

"People have plenty of dirt to dish up these days. They've got Hollywood and New York and London. And if they're really bored, they've got Washington, D.C., to gossip about. They don't need to dredge up stuff from your past."

Connor wished he knew what she was thinking because those closed-off expressions that flitted across her face from time to time drove him *nuts*.

"And then there's the matter of my limp. You don't want to be seen—"

"Hold it. Hold it right there," Connor had interrupted. "Your limp is barely noticeable…except to you." He tossed his tie on the antique buffet she'd found at a shop on Main Street. "If you don't want to go, just say so. I'm not about to force you to do something you don't want to do." And the proof of *that,* Connor fumed, could be found at the top of the stairs…in two separate bedrooms.

She stopped putting dishes away. "I never said…I didn't

say…of course I want to go. I was only trying to give you an out…in case you wanted one.''

The way she was standing there, blinking those sad brown eyes at him, made him want to hug her. Kiss the daylights out of her. Take her upstairs and…. ''Jaina, sweetie,'' he said, softening his tone, ''if I didn't want to bring you, why would I have brought the tickets home?''

She'd sighed heavily. ''I guess that would have been the thing to do. Or not do, rather. If you didn't want to bring me, I mean.''

He had fumbled around in his briefcase, not knowing what else to say.

And here it was, two weeks later, and he was standing in the master bathroom, this time fumbling with his bow tie.

Almighty God, he prayed.

It wasn't much of a prayer. Wasn't a prayer at all, really. Still, the power of those two simple words seemed enough to distract him from the feelings that simmered inside him. Feelings that, if he allowed himself, might one day make him forget that he'd promised to give Jaina the time and space she'd said she needed.

''Are you almost ready?'' she called from the hallway.

''I don't think it would violate any rules if you came in,'' he said dryly. ''I mean, you make up the bed every day, put my laundry away. We haven't needed a chaperon…so far.''

''You're usually not here when I do those things.''

And then she stepped into the room, a glass of water in one hand, a black beaded purse in the other. ''Jaina!'' he gasped. ''You're…you're *beautiful.*''

She blushed like a schoolgirl at his compliment, and that only made her all the more beautiful to him. Her black gown accented her ivory complexion. Accented her feminine figure, too. The satiny material clung to her shoulders and arms and tiny waist before skimming over her hips and ending above matching shoes. As she moved, it shimmered with the silvery glow of reflected light, reminding him of what the pastor had said to him on their wedding day: "You married the prettiest girl in Maryland, Connor. She'll be a beacon in your life."

"You look pretty good yourself," she said, her voice cracking slightly.

He wanted to crush her against him. Wanted to welcome her into the room with a warm kiss. Wanted…

Get a grip, pal.…

For weeks, he'd put on a show for her parents, for the men and women who worked at The Chili Pot, for Pearl, telling himself that the marriage—though nothing but a matter of convenience—must always appear as real and genuine as the diamond she wore on her left hand. He owed her that much—to protect her from the gossipmongers— didn't he?

He watched, his breath caught in his throat, as she raised the glass to her parted lips and drank.

She put the glass and the purse on his dresser. "Come here," she said, pulling him closer by tugging the ends of his tie. "Let me do that for you."

He stood there, arms hanging limply at his sides, and watched her tilt her head, studied her adorable little frown as she concentrated on the task. She smelled heavenly, looked lovely, and—

"There! That's got it," she said, smiling finally as her fingertips tapped the tips of the bow. Jaina turned him around to face the dresser. "See?"

He met her eyes in the mirror. "Perfect. Thanks."

She grabbed the glass and the purse, her pretty dress swishing softly as she moved toward the door. "I'll wait for you downstairs," she said. "There's no real hurry. We have about fifteen minutes before it's time to leave."

"Right. No hurry," he echoed. "I'll be down in a bit." When she was gone, he slumped onto the edge of his bed, held his head in his hands, then extended his arms and stared at his palms. "How are you gonna spend a lifetime under the same roof with a woman like *that*...and keep your mitts to yourself?"

Connor thought he heard music, then went to stand at the top of the stairs. Yes, definitely music, he realized. A tune he'd heard before...

He took the stairs two at a time, stopping in the foyer when he spotted her. She was in the living room, sitting at the piano, singing. "She has the voice of a songbird," Ray had told him just the day before yesterday. As if Connor didn't know it by then. He'd caught her humming as she dusted, as she fed Liam. Once, he'd come home for lunch and heard her singing Liam into his afternoon nap. She could croon every word from here on out and he'd never tire of the sound.

If he'd never met her, he might never have discovered the difference between a boy's love for a girl and the love a man feels for his woman. He might have gone right on believing that what he'd once felt for Miriam had been *it*.

But he had met Jaina, and now that he knew how deep and all-encompassing love could be, he wanted more than to share this house with her. Wanted more than to sleep across the hall from her. For weeks now, he'd kept his word, never crossing that boundary line. The dilemma...how to tell Jaina he wanted to forget their agreement.

He looked at her, innocent and pure and so alive! He was a man, full-grown and with a man's needs and desires. The solution to his problem scared the daylights out of him. He'd have to admit he loved her. Somehow, tonight, he was going to let her know how he really felt…how he'd felt almost from the first moment they met.

Almighty God, he began to pray. If the Good Lord felt any mercy, any compassion for him at all, He'd see to it that Jaina felt the same way.

"Connor, how long have you been standing there?"

He shrugged. "A while," he said, grinning.

She stood, smiling, and smoothed the skirt of her dress. "We'd better get Liam, head over to Mom and Dad's, or we'll be late. I hate to make an entrance." Jaina draped a deep maroon satin shawl over her shoulders. "I've already packed his diaper bag and his toys," she said, bending to lift him from the playpen, "so if you'll…"

She pressed a palm to the baby's forehead.

He read the look of alarm that widened her dark, glittering eyes. "What? What's wrong?"

"He's burning up with fever, Connor."

They stood hand in hand under the glaring emergency-room lights, watching their boy sleep. She had saved his life, and if he didn't already love her like crazy, *that* certainly would have clinched it.

The resident on duty hadn't seemed overly concerned when they brought the red-cheeked baby into the hospital. "It's the start of the flu season," he'd said offhandedly. "No big deal. Just give him baby acetaminophen and see that he gets plenty of liquids."

Jaina wasn't having any of that! Hands on her black-satined hips, she stood on tiptoe and said into the young doctor's face, "My father nearly died of something like this a few years ago, so I know what I'm talking about. Liam has the same symptoms. This is *not* the flu. It's meningitis, and if you don't do something soon, it could—"

"Mrs. Buchanan," he said soothingly, trying to calm

her, "I've seen dozens of kids the past couple of days with the very same symptoms your son has. Trust me, this is a simple case of the flu."

She rattled off a list of medications and treatments the hospital should begin to administer immediately. When he protested, Jaina planted both feet on the floor and, though she couldn't have been more than five years older than him, wagged a maternal digit under his nose.

She'd been cutting articles out of newspapers and magazines since the day Liam had come into her life. The shoe box she kept clippings in to start with had soon overflowed with ideas and tidbits about baby care and child rearing, and Jaina had had to move her collection to a larger box. If she believed Liam had meningitis, Connor thought, then the boy had meningitis!

Connor stepped up and, crossing both arms defiantly over his chest, threatened to use the doctor's stethoscope in a way he'd never believed possible. The commotion alerted the resident's superior, who examined Liam herself and ordered a battery of tests that, in the end, proved Jaina correct.

If they had listened to that resident, Liam might be seriously ill right now, instead of sleeping contentedly as they awaited his release forms. Connor's relief was so great and so heartfelt, it nearly drove him to tears. Jaina might be stubborn and opinionated, but she was kindhearted, loving and bound and determined to do the right thing.

Almighty God, help me, please, he prayed.

A moment of silence passed before she cut him a sidelong glance. "What did you say?" she whispered.

Well, you said *you were going to tell her how you felt, and that you would do it tonight.* He turned her to face him, then drew her near. "I said, 'I love you.'"

Wide-eyed and breathless, Jaina licked her lips, swallowed, blinked.

He tucked a wayward curl behind her ear. "Well...?"

"Well what?" she asked, the beginnings of a smile tugging at the corners of her mouth.

He made a "come on" rolling gesture with his right hand. "This is where you're supposed to reciprocate."

Tilting her head, Jaina studied his face for a long, silent moment. Then she wrapped her arms around his chest and snuggled close. "Reciprocate." She sighed. "Such a romantic word!"

Connor grinned, then kissed the top of her head.

"I love you, too," Jaina said. She took a step back and looked deep into his eyes. "I think I've loved you from the moment we met."

He remembered the conversation he'd had with Kirstie about the girl of his dreams. "I can top that," he said tenderly.

"Oh, yeah?"

"Yeah. I've loved you all my life."

She nodded as though she understood. And then she said, "We made quite a team tonight, didn't we?"

Laughing, he shook his head. "I'll say. That resident won't forget *us* any time soon."

"I imagine we were quite a sight...you in your tuxedo and me in my evening gown...threatening to do bodily harm if our son wasn't given the proper care."

"Our son," he echoed. "I like the sound of that."

"Kirstie was right," Jaina said. "Together, we'll be good for Liam."

"Together... I like the sound of that, too."

"So do I." She snuggled close again. "When we get home, I'd like to do some rearranging."

He'd lived with her long enough to know that she could

pick some odd times to move furniture, knickknacks, pictures… "Couldn't it wait until tomorrow, sweetie? Because I'm—"

"No," she said, bracketing his face with her hands, "it can't wait."

He took a deep breath. She had just saved Liam's life. How could he refuse her anything? "Okay," he agreed, smiling. "Soon as I change out of my tux. What do you want to move?"

"Me."

"You?"

"What's the matter…you don't want a roommate?"

A roommate?

She drew his face near, then kissed him, hard and full on the lips.

Epilogue

Six years later

"Mommy, Susan is in my room again."

Jaina trudged up the stairs and stood in Liam's doorway, one fist on her hip. "Susan…"

The four-year-old stuck out her tongue at her brother. "He called me a geek!"

"Liam, what have I told you about calling your sister names?"

The seven-year-old hung his head. "That it isn't nice?"

"No, it isn't." To Susan, she said, "And neither is sticking out your tongue." The little girl looked at the floor, too. Their mother knelt on the floor and held out her arms. Both children flew into them. "Now, what do you say we go down into the kitchen and whip up a batch of chocolate chip cookies? If we're very, very quiet," she added in a whisper, "maybe we can finish before your little sister wakes up."

Liam rolled his big blue eyes. "Not a chance. Kirstie will smell the dough and she'll—"

"Don't pick on her, Liam," Susan said. "She's just a baby."

"Not *baby*. My teacher said when you're two, you're a toddler."

The brown-eyed girl looked to Jaina for confirmation, and when her mother nodded and pointed at herself, she said, "Oh, I get it. A *baby* lives in *here*." Grinning, she patted Jaina's well-rounded tummy.

"Right you are, Suzie-Q," Connor said from the doorway. "Did I hear something about chocolate chip cookies?"

"Daddy!" the children chorused, snuggling into his outstretched arms.

"Can I measure the flour, Mommy?" Susan asked, clapping her hands.

"And can I break the eggs?" Liam wanted to know.

Connor helped Jaina to her feet. "I'll tell you what," she suggested, giving her husband a sideways hug. "If you go outside and play quietly while Mommy and Daddy talk, the two of you can do *all* the work all by yourselves!"

They scrambled from the room and thundered down the stairs, squealing with glee, reminding her what a happy six years this had been. The children had both learned to ride the horses Connor bought from a farmer on Marriottsville Road, she'd sold The Chili Pot to Eliot, and her parents had retired to Florida. Skip had married a co-worker and now had two children. The Buchanan peace was nearly constant.

She had even returned to singing, at weddings and funerals and in the church choir.

Once they were alone, Connor pulled her into a bear hug. "C'mere, you," he growled lovingly, "it's been a long, hard day and I need a kiss."

"But...it's not even lunchtime yet."

He grinned. "So whatcha gonna do...sue me?"

She took his hand, led him into their room and closed

the door. "Maybe we can settle this out of court," she suggested.

Connor took off his tie and smiled as Jaina picked up her guitar. He sprawled across the neatly made bed and tucked his hands under his head.

He could be patient because experience had taught him that when her song ended, the *real* music would begin....

* * * * *

Coming in May 2004

MOTHER BY DESIGN

by three *USA TODAY*
bestselling authors

SUSAN MALLERY

CHRISTINE RIMMER

LAURIE PAIGE

Three best friends take fate into their own hands when they decide
to become mothers. But their friendships are strained when dark
secrets come to the surface. Can they heal their relationships—
and even find love—before their due dates?

LOGAN'S LEGACY

**Because birthright has its privileges
and family ties run deep.**

Available at your favorite retail outlet.

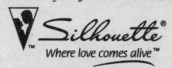

Where love comes alive™

Forrester Square

LEGACIES . LIES . LOVE .

The mystery and excitement continues in May 2004 with…

COME FLY WITH ME
by
JILL SHALVIS

Longing for a child of her own, single day-care owner Katherine Kinard decides to visit a sperm bank. But fate intervenes en route when she meets Alaskan pilot Nick Spencer. He quickly offers marriage and a ready-made family… but what about love?

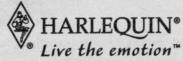

HARLEQUIN®
Live the emotion™

**Visit the Forrester Square web site
at www.forrestersquare.com**

FSQCFWM

Coming in May 2004 to Silhouette Books

When Jake Ingram is taken captive by the Coalition, a sexy undercover agent is sent to brainwash him. Though he finds her hard to resist, can he trust this mysterious beauty?

Five extraordinary siblings.

One dangerous past.

Unlimited potential.

Look for more titles in this exhilarating new series, available only from Silhouette Books.

June 2003 ENEMY MIND by Maggie Shayne
July 2003 PYRAMID OF LIES by Anne Marie Winston
August 2003 THE PLAYER by Evelyn Vaughn
September 2003 THE BLUEWATER AFFAIR by Cindy Gerard
October 2003 HER BEAUTIFUL ASSASSIN by Virginia Kantra
November 2003 A VERDICT OF LOVE by Jenna Mills
December 2003 THE BILLIONAIRE DRIFTER by Beverly Bird
January 2004 FEVER by Linda Winstead Jones
February 2004 BLIND ATTRACTION by Myrna Mackenzie
March 2004 THE PARKER PROJECT by Joan Elliott Pickart
April 2004 THE INSIDER by Ingrid Weaver
May 2004 CHECK MATE by Beverly Barton

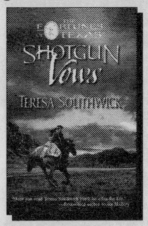